Fractured Families

Books by Charlotte Hinger

The Lottie Albright Mysteries
Deadly Descent
Lethal Lineage
Hidden Heritage
Fractured Families

Fractured Families

A Lottie Albright Mystery

Charlotte Hinger

Poisoned Pen Press

Library of Congress Catalog Card Number: 2016952023

ISBN: 9781464205613   Hardcover
      9781464205637   Trade Paperback

Poisoned Pen Press
6962 E. First Ave., Ste. 103
Scottsdale, AZ 85251
www.poisonedpenpress.com
info@poisonedpenpress.com

Printed in the United States of America

For my darling grandchildren:
Leah, Dana, Audrey, John, Abigail, and Katelyn

For those who exalt themselves will be humbled,
and those who humble themselves will be exalted.
—Matthew 23:12 (NIV)

Chapter One

I blinked my icy lashes but it didn't ease the brittleness of my contacts. I eyed the darkening sky and my anxiety grew with every ominous cloud bunching in the west.

"We should be getting back."

"Okay. Just a few more pictures."

I groaned. I was in the strangest place in all of Kansas—The Garden of Eden. It gave me the creeps under the best of circumstances. Today, the approaching storm added to the sheer looniness of this creation, which is officially one of the Eight Wonders of Kansas. My husband's visiting aunt, Dorothy Mercer, wanted to see all of these tourist attractions.

I usually liked this woman. But not today. She had airily dismissed my earlier concerns about the weather. "My name might be Dorothy, but I've too much heft to be blown away in a little breeze," she'd said.

I faked a smile although I am totally weary of Oz jokes.

It was a good two-and-a-half hours back home from Lucas to Gateway City and weather changes in a heartbeat in Western Kansas. I wished we had postponed this trip.

I wasn't sure why we were here. Keith's Aunt Dorothy is a mystery writer and she refuses to give the slightest hint about any of her plots in advance. This ill-advised outing might be related to a forthcoming manuscript, or the whim of her overdeveloped curiosity. Or the damned Fiene perverse streak. Who knew? She lives in New York and her books regularly came in at eleventh or twelfth on the *New York Times* best-sellers list. Fourth, on a couple of occasions.

The wind increased. Snow began coating the sculptures, obliterating details. "Five more minutes, then we are leaving. That's final." My teeth chattered as I spoke.

She turned and looked at me with the disbelieving glance of a woman who was not used to being ordered around. Taller than I, even without her long black Chesterfield coat, she looked like a solid block of ice ready for the sculptor's scalpel. She used a near-black walking stick heavily carved with a murder of crows. But her stride was sturdy and confident so I suspected the cane was along for whacking something or someone, not for steadying her gait.

A plain woman with a severe mannish haircut, Dorothy is a walking encyclopedia of historical and cultural information. She retains every bit of information she comes across and reveals very little about herself. We are all under a microscope. She likes me better than most of the Fiene inlaws because I have a PhD in history and am struggling to create a regional crime center. Which makes me a mighty interesting specimen indeed.

I held my ground. She grunted. I took it as consent.

"Okay. Let me focus on *Reaching Woman.*" As soon as she lifted her Nikon, snow blocked the lens. She gave up and pulled a pen out of her purse and dictated her observations. A clever little device. Bluetoothed to a computer, her speech was subsequently transcribed into type.

"There are good postcards of *Reaching Woman*, Dorothy. We've got to get on the road." A light snow was one thing. No problem. But a light snow could turn into a lethal blizzard.

"Okay. But I want to glance at the mausoleum, then, before we leave. I insist. Just a quick peek. I'm obviously going to have to come back this spring if I want to take my own photos. Damn. You know how much my fans appreciate my research. When I say I've visited a place, they can count on that being the truth."

The Garden of Eden takes up a city block. It was created by Samuel Dinsmoor, a Civil War soldier and radical populist.

One hundred and thirteen bags of cement were used to create the joined sculptures that border the inner edge of the sidewalk and soar above the gloomy winter-stunned cedar trees. The figures illustrated Dinsmoor's view of politics and damned the doctors, bankers, lawyers, and preachers he held responsible for America's economic woes. His style was unique, yet reminiscent of ancient Mayan finds.

A glassed-in coffin of Dinsmoor himself lying in a state of perfect preservation topped off the exhibitions. He had studied mummification and left explicit instructions for the handling of his remains.

"You can't take pictures inside the coffin gazebo," I warned. "They keep it dark. And don't trip over the concrete jug at the foot of his coffin. Dinsmoor said if he has to go below on Resurrection morn, he will grab it and fill it with water on the road down. If he gets to go up, he has a concrete angel outside the door to take him there."

She shot me a look.

"God's truth. Read his little autobiography if you don't believe me. And if you leave him a dollar he promised to wink at you."

She scowled. "Dead men aren't funny, Lottie. The things I could tell you."

I shut up. Oh, the things I could tell *her*.

I didn't go in with her. I had been here several times before and knew what she would find. The old man lying inside a glass-lidded concrete coffin. A macabre double-exposed life-sized photo of Dinsmoor viewing his own body completed the bizarre exhibition.

Dorothy came rushing out a few minutes later.

"Lottie, there's a body in there."

"Of course. That's what this place is about. Concrete bodies."

"No, a real one."

Blood hardened in my icy veins at her announcement.

Icicles were now forming and hanging from all the bizarre shapes and bodies surrounding this block.

"Stay here." I brushed past her and darted inside.

Crumpled behind Dinsmoor's life-sized portrait was the body of a young man wearing a backwards seed cap. His denim jacket hung open to show a green plaid pearl-buttoned Western shirt. A patch of blood stained the right chest of the jacket.

Not much blood. Just a bullet's worth.

His lashes were long and delicate. His mouth was a sweet rosebud parted to expose white, white teeth. His cheeks were fuzzed with the light beard of early manhood. Scarcely out of high school, I guessed. Starting his life.

The top two buttons of his shirt were open and I could see the white t-shirt underneath printed with the bright green 4-H logo. In each corner of the four-leafed clover were white H's.

Somebody's son. I didn't know him. My husband probably would have if he had come with us today. Keith is a veterinarian and a lot of 4-H kids raise livestock. My throat tightened. This man-child had no doubt earnestly recited his dedication to the four H's every month:

"I pledge my head to clearer thinking,
My heart to greater loyalty,
My hands to larger service,
and my health to better living,
for my club, my community, my country, and my world."

The 4-H logo was plastered all over Carlton County; on fair booths, on parade floats, on posters around town, on bumper stickers. Signs on corner posts of family farms proudly proclaimed, "a 4-H family lives here." The 4-H t-shirt told me he was rural. The fact he was wearing it beyond high school said he didn't mind being thought of as square. I didn't want to concoct a stereotype right off the bat, but the clothes! The t-shirt, the Western shirt, the denim jacket. His identity was as obvious as a gang tattoo.

I winked back tears. 4-H members wanted to be good citizens. Good people. "To make the best better," was the national motto.

My thoughts were irrational. All murders are wrong. Everyone matters. But it was especially offensive to me that someone would have killed this young man in the prime of his life who had wanted to make the best better.

I went back outside. I glanced at Dorothy. She didn't belong here. Not now. But there was nothing I could do about that. Even though I'm setting up a regional crime center, I'm still the undersheriff of Carlton County. As an officer of the law it was my duty to deal with this murder right here and now.

There was a hell of a gap between my training and the pseudo accuracy of a mystery writer. But it could have been worse. I had read all of her books and knew she would respect the importance of staying out of a crime-scene investigation.

She intuited my concerns. "I'll keep out of your way."

Her voice quivered with indecent excitement.

"Observe. That's all. Come with me to the car while I phone Frank Dimon. He's the KBI agent assigned to this region."

"Won't Sam be in charge?"

"No. It's not in Carlton County's territory." Dorothy and Sam Abbott, the sheriff of Carlton County, had hit it off quite well. He appreciated her nuts-and-bolts questions and preened when she was around. She, in turn, admired Sam. She liked law-enforcement people capable of a few heroics when the occasion called for it. Sam's the man for that. He looks like he stepped out of an old Western movie. He has a white droopy mustache, white hair that skims his shirt collar, a military bearing, and a distinguished Roman nose. He's my husband's best friend. They are both long on logic.

Dorothy strode beside me, slipped into the passenger seat, and kept quiet while I used my cell phone to call Frank Dimon at the KBI in Topeka. I gave Dimon the bare facts. "So we need a team here right now."

"Actually, the sheriff's department in Russell County is very effective. You need to notify John Winthrop immediately."

"Sheriff Winthrop. I've met him. It's his third term, I think."

"Right. Their force is larger than most. Six deputies. They have a lot of activity because of Wilson Lake."

"I'll do that right away. But I called you first because the ball is in your court. You need to sort this out. There's a sign out front. "This property has been placed in the National Register of Historic Places by the United States Department of the Interior."

Dead silence. Dimon never wasted words. He reminded me of Hotch on *Criminal Minds*. Then, "All right I'll make the phone calls to see if this is FBI or KBI, or whoever. Seems like you brought trouble with you. For now, get the Russell County Sheriff's Office involved immediately."

"Okay. But I'm sure they won't have a good team of criminalists. This will be mostly a courtesy call. Don't be surprised if he tosses this right back in your lap."

"That's what I'm here for. You can't be the one to officially call me in. It has to start with Sheriff Winthrop since it's his county. But it might be your first regional case, so stay there."

When I called Winthrop he decided in seconds to turn it over to the KBI. "We'll be there right away to secure the scene and to supply manpower, of course. But we'll leave the forensics to the big boys. We don't have the expertise."

Smart man, Winthrop. I knew him from the regional planning meetings to develop an intra-county law-enforcement center with shared resources. I am the coordinator for this half-birthed enterprise.

"Thought you were going to fix all that for us, Lottie. So we don't have to go begging to Topeka when we need help with forensics."

"We're not that far along on the regional facility, John. In fact, there's a huge fight right now over which counties in Northwest Kansas are included. But I'll tell you all about this later." I explained the complication of the Garden of Eden being a historic place and its connection to the Department of Interior. "So that's why I called Dimon in the first place. Not that it isn't a knee-jerk reaction by now."

He guffawed. "I can understand why. Hope you didn't bring trouble with you."

I winced. The same words Dimon had used. "Crime isn't contagious. By the way, Keith's aunt, Dorothy Mercer, is with me in the car. The reason we were here in the first place was because she wanted to see the Eight Wonders of Kansas and this was first on her list."

"*The* Dorothy Mercer?"

"The same."

"Wow. I've read all of her books. Hope she's taking notes. It never hurts to have someone else's impressions."

Dorothy heard. She was indeed taking notes. And clearly tickled pink to participate in a murder investigation from the beginning.

"I'll be there in a flash."

I hung up and we waited for the team from Russell County. "You'll like Winthrop," I said. "He and Sam are good friends." I started the car and turned up the heat, then eyed the gas gauge. I didn't dare leave the car running for long. Shit. I couldn't leave Dorothy sitting in this cold car. I had to take her with me.

"What a crime scene," Her eyes darted all around.

"I'm going to call Sam in, after all, because for now the regional center is based in his office and Dimon wants to cover all of the jurisdictional possibilities."

Even though I am Sam's undersheriff, until the end of last summer I worked full-time at the historical society. Now I take oral histories and help edit difficult stories for the county history books. However, as soon as it's up and running, I will move on from being Sam's official sidekick to being the full-time director of the Northwest Kansas Regional Crime Center. I'm looking forward to it, despite loving every minute of my association with Sam.

Carlton County is the Kansas Bureau of Investigation's worst nightmare—underfunded and manned by part-time deputies. We lead Western Kansas in murders, per capita. A regional center will change our approach to forensics and the need for the KBI to send a team from Topeka.

My husband, who is also our deputy, Keith Fiene, is officially sort of retired from law enforcement and officially sort of retired from his veterinarian practice. But he is still a reserve deputy and can be called on in a crisis situation. And, as for his retired vet status, the new Doctor of Veterinary Medicine, a recent graduate from Kansas State University, doesn't like to work with large animals and he calls Keith for every little whipstitch.

In the past, my twin sister, Josie, a clinical psychologist, had consulted for our county. After several scary episodes, I doubt if she will step into that role again.

I grabbed my notebook. "I'm going back, Dorothy. I've called everyone I need to call." There was a solar blanket in my emergency crate. And a hand-warmer. Maybe she would be warm enough without keeping the car running. "Why don't you wait here? No point in you being out in this."

She looked at me hard, made a sound somewhere between a scoff and a grunt and opened her door.

We trudged back to the mausoleum. I was freezing. Light snow was now light sleet. I glanced at Dorothy. How many layers of clothing did she have under her coat? She masked every expression. If she was weary or miserable, who would know?

We peered at the body. "He was murdered yesterday," Dorothy concluded.

I stared at her. "Beg your pardon?" It was a rather stark assumption without having done any forensics. The man was wearing jeans, so she couldn't tell anything about blood pool. Or much else.

She gave me a quick amused glance, sensing my doubt that she could know such things. "Nothing as dramatic as forensic work, my dear. In fact, I'm surprised you didn't notice it yourself. The Hill City paper is sticking out of his back pocket. Yesterday is the date."

I was too embarrassed to speak.

Chapter Two

The Russell County Sheriff's car approached without lights and sirens. He pulled up silently and parked in front of the house. I waved him over.

"The victim is inside the mausoleum, John. And this is Keith's aunt, Dorothy Mercer."

He swept off his hat. "I'm a great admirer of yours, Ma'am. I've read every single book." He stuck out his hand tentatively, as though he felt unworthy of initiating contact with this woman.

"A faithful follower of a series is the greatest compliment any author can receive." She stepped forward and used a two-handed clasp. "Truly. I'm very grateful."

Oh, brother. I loathe phony sincerity.

"I'm sorry you had to be here for such a grisly event."

"Please. You certainly don't owe me any apologies. This is not under your control."

"Of course, we are interested in any comments and observations you might care to make."

Unbelievable. Winthrop asked for her observations first. Not mine. But Dorothy had told me once that people expect mystery writers to be experts in every single field of investigation. She certainly knew a great deal more about forensic protocol than the average person. I was still embarrassed by the swiftness of her newspaper observation while I lamented the loss of a 4-H'er.

"I've shared my first observation with Lottie. He was killed yesterday. The *Hill City Times* is sticking out of his back pocket.

Yesterday's dateline. Plus, there's a drop or two of blood on the corner of it."

I hadn't noticed that either.

I cleared my throat to bring the star-struck sheriff's attention back to the investigation. "When I called this in to Dimon, and told him that this place was on the National Register, he said jurisdiction might get a little funny. We haven't heard back yet."

"We'll do whatever he says. No egos in the way out here. We pretty well know our limits. I must say I'm looking forward to your setting up the regional center. It's ridiculous to have to wait for someone to come out from Topeka whenever something comes up. I'll do everything I can to be included in the regional territory."

Oh, boy. This was happening more and more. The territory should be only the nine counties in the three tiers that make up Northwest Kansas. Now sheriffs in counties bordering the nine were lobbying to be included. It would be a larger area. Require a bigger staff. More transportation vehicles. More money.

My phone rang. Dimon. "A team is en route. You're in luck. We have permission from the Department of the Interior to conduct this investigation on a state basis, and we've all agreed—since you are the new regional director, even though you don't have a building and office yet—that you are the ideal chief investigator."

"Can I put together my own team?"

He hesitated, knowing who I would pick first, and Dimon didn't like Sheriff Abbot. "Yes." His voice was tight.

"Fine. I assume I'm to keep you posted?"

"Yes."

"And I can do this any way I want to?"

"Yes."

"With adequate special funds to hire any men or women I need?"

"Yes."

"Fine. I'll e-mail a list of personnel as soon as possible."

Sure of my place now, I turned to Winthrop. "That was Agent Dimon. They are putting this under regional jurisdiction and I will be in charge of the investigation."

"Even though you haven't put the regional center together yet? That's strange," John said.

"Yes. Well, it's true we don't have a building and a formal structure but we're working on it. Dimon just gave me the authority to put together a team and tap law enforcement personnel from each county."

Even as I spoke, I realized that this approach could be dynamite. I had fought the regional concept tooth and toenail in the beginning, but Dimon was right. We would be higher, faster, and stronger.

"Of course I want you to be involved with this one. After all, this is your county. You're familiar with every crook and cranny. I can't think of anyone better qualified to assist."

"I hope you are going to include Ms. Mercer, here."

Dorothy stood imperiously, and waited quietly. *Why not? What could it hurt?* She could serve as a consultant. Same as my sister, Josie. "Of course. Would you consider that, Dorothy?"

"I would be honored."

"Thank you. Now, let's all stand right here where we are. I doubt if anyone has been here since yesterday for any tour, so the ground will be untrammeled. The place doesn't give tours this time of year except by appointment. There will be a record of the last time anyone was here."

"Officially here," Dorothy said. "Murderers don't sign registers."

"Yes," I suddenly felt witless. "John, I've already called Sam in since the regional center is temporarily at his office. I want him to be here when the forensic team arrives."

"Isn't he a lot closer than the crew in Topeka?"

"Not by much."

"Damn this snow. It's going to make everything a lot harder." Winthrop rubbed his gloves together. "We'll be as stiff as that dead body if we keep standing out here."

"Let's start. Do what we can with what we have on hand here now, before it gets any darker. Dorothy, I didn't bring crime scene stuff with me. I have a camera in the car, but it's no real prize. The one I usually use for investigations is back at the office. Would you please start taking pictures and making notes?"

"Glad to. My own camera is a full sixteen pixels. No need to use yours."

"Awesome. And John? What do you have with you?"

"Quite a lot. A decent basic forensics kit. Crime-scene tape. Plenty of evidence-collection bags."

"Good. Let's get started while there's still some light. I'll leave analyzing the body up to the state men. But skip the crime scene tape for now. It will attract attention. We don't want a bunch of town-people tromping over and destroying evidence."

"This will be an absolute bitch," John said. "The snow will cover up all the good stuff by the time we get our act together."

"Can't be helped. But thank God that Dorothy has a decent camera. The first thing I'm going to do is a little test. I think the ground is freezing up faster than the snow is falling. That can work in our favor."

"Footprints will be perfectly preserved. Lucky break." Dorothy looked at me with respect. If she had had the same idea ahead of me, she was tactful enough not to mention it.

"Yes. I want us to all stand here toward the extreme north edge of the yard." We walked over to stand just short of the ditch. "John, you first. Dorothy, take a full-size picture of John, then I want him to step away and you photograph his footprints."

She shot from all angles. My "professional" camera was definitely inferior to her Nikon. Another item we needed to acquire for the regional center.

When John was done I moved into place and she completed the process again. "Now you, Dorothy. And I'll take the pictures."

When we finished, I walked over and brushed the snow away. Just as I suspected, the sheriff had not left any footprints on bare ground as it was already frozen underneath.

"Good! Now we'll create a grid and work it while it's still daylight. As far as I can tell there's not a single thing out of place or any trash lying around. If there is—we'll will find it on top of this white, white snow and bag it for evidence."

"Ah. And if there isn't," Dorothy said, "after the full forensic team gets here, they can brush away the snow and we will know that what remains was brought in yesterday or earlier."

"Exactly. But it won't be any earlier than yesterday. This isn't the first time I've been here. Part of my historical work is learning some of the standards for preserving sites. The groundskeeper goes over everything every single evening picking up trash and checking for vandalism. The standards for maintaining property listed on the National Register are very, very high. No one wants to lose that status. You can be sure the place is gone over daily with a fine-toothed comb."

"Not everyone would know that. Good thinking, Lottie. Anything the murderer dropped will likely be frozen into the top of the ground."

"Exactly."

"Burning daylight, ladies." John whirled around and went back to his vehicle. He came back with a forensics kit and a number of little plastic flags that could be used with a marker. "Son of a bitch. Doesn't seem right that that kid has to just lay there without someone trying to do the right thing by him."

"We *are* doing the right thing, John. Trust me. I've been involved in enough investigations by now to know the right thing to do is to involve the very best forensics people in the very beginning. This case is going to attract a lot of attention. Because of where it's happened, if nothing else. Believe me, Frank Dimon would skin us alive if everything isn't done perfectly."

"A freezing cold day is better than hot," Dorothy said. "No bugs will slow decomposition."

Decomposition. I swallowed. The image of the 4-H imprinted cloverleaves flashed across my eyes. We sounded so dispassionate we might as well have been discussing a dead sheep trapped in a bog.

"I'm glad that Dimon put this under regional responsibility. Joel Comstock, the district coroner, is top notch. We won't have to worry about some botched autopsy performed by a doctor who hates to do them in the first place." At least Kansas' county coroners were real physicians. Not just an elected official.

Winthrop nodded and looked at the darkening sky. "We'd best get started."

"It shouldn't take long. We're looking at white snow. But you're right. We should move quickly before the sleet gets worse."

"Goddamn maniac. Crazy son of a bitch."

I knew John meant Dinsmoor and not the murderer.

My dread increased. The times I had been here before were in broad daylight. Shadows deepened. The hairs on the back of my neck prickled. There were all sorts of places for a murderer to hide. There was a body in the mausoleum. Why not another one on the grounds?

We needed to stay together. Especially since there was someone along who wasn't familiar with police techniques. Even though she seemed to be well versed in forensics, Dorothy wasn't armed. Or at least I didn't think so. I am. Always now. With over seventy-five thousand Kansans owning conceal-and-carry permits, I figure I'd better join the crowd. It's amazing. Young, old, little old ladies, macho types, cowards, fools—hard telling who—are packing. And not all of them are bright. I have learned a lot by now and I didn't want any of us isolated in this haunted nightmare of a tourist attraction, even though presumably whoever did this was long gone. Presumably.

"We're going to go as a group."

"Not split up? That would be smarter, as fast as it's snowing."

"No, John it isn't. There's just the three of us. We need all our eyes focused on what is right before us and Dorothy needs to photograph every single formation front and back. We'll compare them to the guidebook later to save daylight. You carry a flashlight and code the grid as we go along."

And we need to stay together for safety's sake.

I tried to suppress the image of someone jumping out from behind the sculptures of Adam and Eve, who guarded the entrance. It was one of the few formations at ground level. I shuddered at the thought of the concrete snake around Eve's neck coming alive and handing me the apple.

We were barely three-fourths of the way around the block, with Dorothy's camera flashing, recording at manic speed, when Sam's Suburban pulled up. He turned on his spotlight and aimed it up at the ground where we were searching. Then we turned our attention to the bases of sculptures and around the fence.

Thank God we didn't find anything out of place—as far as I could see, that is. I wouldn't know for sure until the next day when we compared the photos with the guidebook's pictures and the KBI went around the whole block again.

Sam didn't waste time asking for information while we were working. His questions came immediately afterward.

"What the hell is going on here?"

"Murder. In the mausoleum. Before you make a single move, Dorothy has to take a picture of your footprints. Then you can go look."

"Good thinking, Lottie."

When he was done, he walked to the mausoleum, flashlight in hand.

"They don't allow outside light in there. It accelerates the deterioration of artifacts."

"They do now," Sam grunted. "Murder always trumps historical preservation."

He walked to the doorway and peered inside at the young body propped against the wall. Abruptly, Sam came back out. His lips were pressed tightly together. His cheeks sagged. He pulled out a red bandana handkerchief from his back pocket and gave his nose a mighty honk.

"Do you know him?"

"Hell, yes. Everyone does. Brent Suter. He was captain of the football team three years ago at Carlton County High. An honor student. Just missed being salutatorian. He's set to graduate from the community college at Beloit. It's taken him longer than most because he's been driving back and forth helping his parents on the farm. He had to take a light schedule. Last I heard he was going to K-State this fall."

"Do you know his parents?"

"God, yes. Salt of the earth. Help their neighbors when they can. Never cause any trouble. Ernie is an elder in the Presbyterian Church and his mom works at the Extension office, part-time. I'm surprised you haven't met her. Patricia Suter?"

"Suter. Patricia Suter. Oh, sure. I know who she is. She fills in for Priscilla Ramsey when Priscilla has to go to seminars. Sure. Brown hair, dark brown eyes? Medium height? Neat? Looks like she could be a model for an LL Bean catalog?"

"That's her."

"She's been at the Extension office several times when I picked up bulletins for Keith. Very friendly. Very efficient."

"The Suters are pretty good-sized farmers. A family corporation with a few scattered relations living in other states. The family was selected as the Farm Bureau Family of the Year in 2008? 2009? Something like that. Model citizens. I think they were community leaders for their 4-H club.

"Why on Earth would their son be here? In this godforsaken place?"

"No idea. And you'd better not let the people around here hear you refer to the Garden of Eden as godforsaken."

"Oh, you know what I mean."

"Yeah, but they won't. The population of this town is barely two hundred, and they won't take kindly to anything that might discourage tourists from coming to The Garden of Eden. In fact attracting tourists is why old man Dinsmoor built it in the first place. He deliberately made it as eccentric as he could to make him some money after the Civil War. Not that his religious and political ideas weren't for real. They were. But he was one hell of a showman."

Two more cars approached, escorting an ambulance. A very special ambulance.

"Will you inform the family, Sam? Since you know them?"

"I'd rather you did it."

"Since they live in Carlton County, I think they would like the high sheriff to do it."

He flushed. "You're right. But God I hate to."

I hated it too. My dread of telling families increased with every death. I risked a glance at Dorothy standing there impassively. If she asked to be included in the death visit I would be beside myself. But she didn't.

The district coroner rode in the ambulance. He would direct the removal of Suter's body after he completed his preliminary examination. As Sam predicted, the forensics team ignored the NO CAMERAS sign inside the mausoleum and began clicking away. I told the agent in charge about our pictures and the grid photographs. He seemed impressed.

"You've done a lot of our work for us, looks like."

"As much as we could before dark."

"All you needed to. We'll hole up at a motel in Hays and be out here again at daybreak. Unless you want to be included, you can go on home and we'll let you know at once what we find."

"Someone from the regional team needs to be here tomorrow morning. I think that should be Sheriff Winthrop. He knows this area better than anyone." *Regional team.* The phrase had a nice sound to it.

"Right."

"But I won't be back until I hear from you. I'm going to poke around in Carlton County. Brent Suter's from there. And Sam Abbott can't think of any reason why that kid would be here."

"Exactly."

Then we hushed as Dr. Comstock came out of the mausoleum. He beckoned to the ambulance driver who started to back up to the building. I stopped him immediately and rushed over to the vehicle. "Don't even think about it. Stop right there. We're going to go over every square inch of this land again after the team brushes away the snow."

"Sorry, Lottie. Wasn't thinking."

Sorry wasn't the half of it. It would be disastrous to leave ruts on these grounds. Heads would roll. Frozen or not, the ground wouldn't withstand the weight of an ambulance.

The men went over to the mausoleum carrying a body bag and a stretcher. In a short time we watched the ambulance pull away.

"Nothing more to do here. John, I want you out here the first thing in the morning when the team from Topeka shows up to see if they can find any more forensics. Then call me after they leave and tell me what happened. Sam and I and Dorothy," I said with a quick glance at Keith's aunt, "the Carlton County crew, or our crew so far at least, will start working the case from our end. Right now, I'm going to concentrate on getting leads about who would want to kill this fine young man and why."

Winthrop shook hands with Sam before he walked to his car. Both men were too dejected to speak.

"Guess we're done here." Sam said. "I'll go on. It's a long trip back. The roads are shit. You two be extra careful driving."

"We will."

We started toward the car, then stopped abruptly.

"Goddamn. Goddamn the mother-fucking son of a bitch all to hell."

I turned and stared at Sam. He shone his flashlight at his guidebook, then looked up at the towering sculptures again.

I looked where his light was shining. "My God."

I closed my eyes against the night that had now gotten darker.

Chapter Three

Up. Sam had always preached that up was a direction too. Always look up. *"Reaching Woman,"* I said. *"Reaching Woman.* Her arms are full."

"What's wrong?" Dorothy asked. I was familiar with the place. She wasn't.

"Whatever she is holding, it doesn't belong there."

"It looks like she's holding a baby."

"Yes."

"Jesus Christ." I couldn't see Sam's face. His voice was barely above a whisper. I turned and looked at Dorothy, now as frozen in place as one of the statues. My mind raced. This was officially my investigation. Dimon had said so. But there was no precedent for this and I was certain Sam didn't know how to proceed either. The moves were up to me. The first one was obvious.

I dug my cell phone out of my pocket and got ahold of the forensics team heading to Hays. "You need to turn around and come back. We've found something. Your job here isn't done yet."

We all stared up and I was aware that the three of us had jumped to a conclusion, but whatever was there had been deliberately placed.

"Well, one thing is certain," I kept my voice brisk. "We can no longer keep these grounds pristine. There's only one way I know of for a team to get up there by using the equipment that is likely to be in this town. The city crew that repairs lines and puts up Christmas lights will have a boom lift. John Winthrop will know who to call. It'll tear up these grounds, but it can't be helped. We need to do this right now."

Apparently John had only been a couple of miles up the road because he was back in ten minutes and the state forensics team was close behind. The boom lift arrived in short order. Lights went on in several houses across the street. Sam was right. There was no way to keep any of this secret.

But the wind still howled and snow still blew. It would be easy for people to think this was merely a crew out to fix a downed line. That was common enough. The forensics team in one vehicle, Dorothy and me in another, plus Sam. Just three parked cars. Perhaps we would have a little time before people realized there was something wrong. It would not be unusual for John Winthrop to be out and about this time of night.

We were all inside the border of sculptures surrounding the block. The boom lift had to stay outside on the street. There was no truck-sized entry into this square—into this death-spattered nightmare.

The boom lift maneuvered into place. The senior man on the forensics team, Joe Nelson, climbed into the bucket. I had gotten acquainted with him when he proved that some old Spanish maps were legitimate. The man operating the equipment took him straight up and then rotated Joe toward *Reaching Woman*. He had a powerful digital camera capable of bursts of five rapid flashes with one exposure. An extension arm with a remote-control lever allowed multiple angles. He took more pictures than I had ever seen anyone take of a crime scene.

If it *was* a crime scene.

Then he removed his warm lined protective gloves. His hands were now covered with the thin latex ones that were no protection from the numbing blowing sleet. He rapidly brushed away the accumulation of snow on *Reaching Woman*'s outer forearm and took more pictures. He took a whisk broom out of his duffel and took more pictures of all exposed areas before they could be covered with ice again.

Then he carefully removed the bundle from *Reaching Woman*'s arms.

"Bring me down," he hollered.

The boom lift operator lowered the bucket. He stepped out and we all gathered around. Joe held out a flannel-wrapped bundle. My stomach lurched. I pulled off my down gloves leaving only cold latex ones. I fumbled for the blanket. My hands trembled and it wasn't from the cold.

The silence was eerie. I glanced at the solemn faces with eyes peeking out from balaclavas, heavy scarves, and hooded coats. Then I drew a deep breath, almost welcoming the sharp pain from the cold air. I pulled back the flannel.

"Oh, God." Dorothy gave a cry and turned her face away.

It was a baby. Perfect. Frozen. Its tiny mouth pursed into a pink rosebud. My breath froze.

I'm good at hiding my feelings because of my work with oral histories. It's important to not show any emotion other than empathy when people are spilling their guts out for the first time—when they are telling a shameful secret about their family that would be better left untold. My sister, Josie, can do this too. In fact, she is even better at maintaining the wooden mask. It's part of her training as a psychologist not to show judgment or shock and to keep her disgust for aberrant behavior off her face. But this time…this time my mask failed me.

The wind howled and we were slammed with more sleet. Red eyes, red cheeks were a natural response to the icy force. Perfectly natural.

But I did not dare cry. I widened my eyes and took three deep breaths. If I shed any tears, I could hear these men saying later "She bawled like a baby. Should have seen her. Goddamn woman has no business in this job."

But the baby. The baby. With thousands of couples yearning to hold this sweet thing in a rocking chair. Buy stuffed animals. Protect this child. Love it forever. How could anyone do this?

My breath started again. I could cry later. I needed to think.

We were all professionals here except Dorothy and the boom lift operators. I turned to the three men on the forensic team. "I want every single detail of this kept quiet until you men complete your work. Everything. Understand?" They all nodded. "I don't intend to keep all of this secret for very long, but I want everyone to keep their mouth shut until we know how this baby died."

I gave the boom lift operators a hard look. "Of course this applies to both of you. Topeka might need a couple of days to complete all of the tests. Do I have your word?"

They both nodded.

"Even after that there might be some restrictions on what you can discuss."

They glanced at one another.

"What?"

"Who is in charge here? You or Sheriff Winthrop? Don't mean no disrespect but we would like to know, in case you both tell us different things."

I stepped in front of John immediately. "I am. I'm the regional director. All due respect to John, here, and he will be my main backup on this case. John, do you want to say a few words?"

"I guess you all know Lottie is trying to get a regional crime center started out here. She's the main man and I'll take my orders from her. And if she's telling us all to shut up until the state boys do their job, then I'm going to shut up. And both of you will too or you'll answer to me."

Under different circumstances I would have pointed out that by "answering" to him, he was undermining my authority right off the bat.

Furious, Dorothy stepped forward to make that point. She needed to shut up too. I intervened fast.

"This is Dorothy Mercer," I said quickly. "You may have heard of her. She has a *New York Times* bestselling mystery series. She's Keith's aunt and also will serve as a consultant for the new regional center." I was winging a lot of this since her involvement hadn't been made official yet. "She will be helping me with criminal characterization. I'll welcome any insights she might have, because I'm sure we'll need all the expertise we can get."

Dorothy was a quick study. She took two steps backwards.

"Two days, that's all I'm asking you to keep quiet about the death of this baby. Then I'll issue a formal statement and have a press conference. We'll release details about the Suter boy as soon as we notify his parents.

I turned to the EMTs. "Go directly to the KBI lab. Don't turn on your light bar or siren until you're on I-70, then go as fast as you can."

I glanced at the boom lift operators and the forensic team who were standing to one side. "Sorry. We need to finish everything up here tonight. As fast as possible. I don't want anyone to look out the window tomorrow morning and see all of us prowling around."

Dorothy stood to one side, most of her face shielded by a wool scarf.

"Dorothy, there is no point in your staying out here in the cold. Why don't you go wait in the car while we finish up?"

She refused again. "No way, Lottie. Don't worry, I'm up to it."

"You sure?"

"Yes."

Sam had been eying the area beneath *Reaching Woman*. "First thing I want to know is how someone managed to get a baby up there."

• ● ● ● •

The trip home took twice as long as it should. The roads were slick and the sleet mixed with snow. Dorothy didn't talk much, and I didn't want to. I focused on my driving.

"I want to rent a place of my own," she said finally.

"There's no need for that, Dorothy. We have plenty of room and you can stay with us as long as you want to. You're more than welcome."

"It's not that I don't appreciate your hospitality, Lottie. But I value my privacy. I need it. I want to be able to come and go as I please. And I want to buy a used car."

"There's plenty around. But we have an extra car. An old Thunderbird that's in good shape. No need to go to that much trouble."

"It's no trouble. I plan on sticking around for a while. I'll get some old trade-in and sell it again when I'm ready to leave. If I decide to leave. This town is really quite pleasant. It's low energy compared to New York. "

"You're kidding. You might want to stay here?"

"Why not? Not for good. Just occasionally. A lot of writers have summer homes in isolated places."

"I don't think you'll like our summers much, but you've got the isolated part right."

"I'll just want a little cottage. Something with a front porch. A bungalow style. Just so there's a place for me to set up an office and a place to sleep. A galley kitchen, a front room. Maybe a detached garage so I won't have to scrape ice off my car."

Her list kept growing.

"I would like to be able to walk to the grocery store."

An OnStar call came through. I used my thumb to punch the button on my steering wheel. "Hello."

"You okay? Where are you? I was expecting you two back four hours ago."

"I wish! Dorothy and I are fine, but we ran into bad trouble at Lucas. I'll tell you about it when I get home."

"Another murder?"

"Was that just a guess or have you already heard something?"

"No. I haven't heard anything but I figured something serious came up to keep you gone this long."

"Talk to you when I get there." As far as I knew, OnStar was safe but I didn't want to take a chance on anyone overhearing. I certainly didn't want to talk about a dead baby, and it would be best if he heard about the Suter boy from me face-to-face.

Dorothy stared straight ahead. It was too dark to see her expression.

"Right now I need to pay attention to my driving."

"Okay. Be careful."

Chapter Four

Keith stared out the window and didn't, or couldn't, speak. Because they knew the family so well, just he and Sam had delivered the news to the parents after Dorothy and I got back to Carlton County. Dorothy went straight to her room, but I stayed up and waited for Keith to come back. It was useless to try to sleep.

A heavy accumulation of snow bent the branches of the cedar windbreak surrounding our farm. When we were first married, the trees had seemed like a blue-black prison fence through which I could not escape. That feeling was gone now. When I felt lonely and yearned for stability, the trees gave me a sense of security. But right now no outside element could whisk away last night's horror.

Keith had taken the Suter boy's death hard. The baby's death even harder. Last night when I asked him how it went when he returned from the Suters' his eyes flashed at the stupidity of the question. "Bad. End-of-the-world bad. Their son was everything to them." I fell silent.

This morning, he was as restless as a caged tiger. Beneath his flannel shirt his muscles bunched with barely contained rage as he gazed at the whiteness. He is a man of action and there is no more dangerous combination than rage and helplessness. He turned away from the window and paced.

I said nothing. Simply watched. There is a type of body strength that cannot be obtained through working out. It's acquired by physical labor starting in childhood on a farm. Calculated by wise fathers to not be so hard or dangerous as to break the boy, the relentless steady rigor builds men with bones of steel, stomachs as hard as a brick wall, and the shoulders and necks of linebackers. A lifetime of hoisting bales of hay, leaping from horses, branding cattle, corralling large animals that didn't want to be vaccinated had made Keith into one hell of a man. But his power was of no use now.

He returned to the window and scraped off a feathery line of frosty crystals at the bottom. He fingered the break in the caulking and retrieved his memo book from his shirt pocket and made a quick note. I didn't have to read it to know "repair caulking" would go on his to-do list immediately.

I sat curled in my leather chair sipping coffee. Thinking... thinking. Or as much as I could in between flashes of a perfect frozen baby.

The house phone rang. I answered it in the kitchen. It was Dimon.

"They pushed the autopsies right through. John Winthrop was there to observe because we wanted to include a member of the regional team and establish the authority of the new organization right off the bat."

"So soon? All the lab work too?"

"No, we will probably have to wait for all those to be included, but I wanted you to know right away that it was a bullet lodged in the Suter boy's heart. A close-range shot using hollow points. Someone who knew what he was doing. There's no doubt about the cause of death, but of course we have to run all the other tests too."

"A hollow point. My God, Frank." A lethal bullet. Made to explode inside a body. Made to kill instantly. "And the baby?"

He hesitated. "Bad news on that. The little girl died of exposure. Sorry to say she froze to death. Better news would be that she was dead before this monster put her there. Not that the bastard just let her freeze."

A little baby girl. I could cry freely now. In my own home with only my husband around to bear witness, the tears could flow. But I kept my voice steady.

"Okay. That will affect the investigation." I didn't want to talk to Frank Dimon anymore. Not for a while. "I'm going to hang up and tell Keith about the results of Brent Suter's autopsy. He's taking it pretty hard. He's been out to that place a number of times since that kid was just a toddler."

"Does he have ideas on all this?"

"No. He keeps asking the same things as all the rest of us. What was Brent doing out there? And why in God's name would anyone want to kill him?" Wanting to know Keith's opinion comes up a lot. His intelligence coupled with a strong dose of common sense carries a lot of weight. He has a reputation for being right. About a lot of things.

"His murder seems doubly puzzling to me now. A hollow point sounds professional."

There was a noise in the background. Dimon had a habit of thrumming his pencil on the desk when he was thinking. "Some days I just barely have the stomach for this job."

It was the first time I had heard him admit to any weakness.

I hung up the phone, went back into the living room and told Keith about the autopsy reports.

"A hollow point! Did the bastard use a rifle or a hand gun?"

"I'm sure it would have been a hand gun because of the position of the body. The killer couldn't have gotten the right angle with a rifle. The coffin takes up most of the width of the mausoleum. There's no room to go around it. Brent was a little to one side of the opening. Like a kid would scooch down in a closet."

"Trying to hide," Keith rammed his fists together. "Hunted down like an animal." Then he looked at my tear-stained face. He held out his arms and pulled me against his chest. He's a tall man and although I'm five-foot eight, my ear was against his beating heart. The steadiness should have been reassuring but it sounded like a war drum.

He didn't need to say what he was thinking. There have been many battles in our marriage. He had married a historian and then I added undersheriff to my résumé. Now, despite his silent disapproval, I had gone a step further and agreed to be in charge of law enforcement in nine counties. A heavyweight. At risk when he wanted to keep me safe. Safe, as in writing academic articles.

"You're up against an evil person," he murmured into my hair. "Evil, Lottie."

The phone rang again.

"Winthrop here. Has Dimon called?"

"Yes." I caught him up on the autopsy reports. There was a long silence when I reported that the baby had frozen to death. "What kind of bastard…?"

"I don't know."

"How are the Suters doing?"

"Sam and Keith went over last night to tell them about Brent. I didn't go because I don't know the father at all and am just barely acquainted with Patricia. We hoped good friends might soften the blow a little, but no such luck. Keith said Patricia was in shock and not fit to answer any questions and Brent's dad was in terrible shape. Sam went on home, but Keith hung around long enough to make sure they didn't need any medical treatment."

"That's good."

"But if we are going to get anywhere at all we need to get some information from them fast."

"Will Keith go with you?"

I glanced at my husband. Because he is a reserve deputy I can call on him whenever I need to. Today he could go in an official capacity. Last night he had been there out of friendship. "Yes. I want him along. Someone who knows the family might help."

"Help, as in comfort? Or help, as in with the investigation?"

"Both, I guess."

• • ● • •

A collie started barking at us the minute we pulled into the Suters' driveway. A short white picket fence surrounded the large yard enclosing the neat white two-storied house. Chicken wire was stapled to the pickets to keep out any rabbits that threatened their vegetable garden. An enclosed porch had been built at some time and the whole house was faced with white vinyl. The Suters had thrown in the towel and protected the place against the pervasive blowing dust and wind by the most practical methods possible. We're big on vinyl in Western Kansas.

In short, everything had been streamlined with function trumping style. This was a working farm, geared toward production. An award-winning family used to managing time and resources. A neat but not showy place.

Patricia was already at the screen door before we even went up the steps. The screened-in porch served as a mud room with wire hooks for hanging coats and outerwear. A rubber tray held work boots and a couple of pairs of old-fashioned galoshes with clamping buckles. There was a large chest freezer. Next to it was a cardboard box with a calico cat and five newborn kittens. A straggly geranium plant atop a shelf beneath inexpensive all-weather windows reached up to the weak filtered sun.

"Patricia, I'm so sorry." The words sounded mechanical. I gave her a gentle hug. Keith removed his hat and nodded to them both. "Ernie, Patricia. Again, my deepest sympathy."

We went into the combined kitchen/dining room/living room. At one time the house had been a bungalow style, then obviously additions were made when need or inspiration hit. A sectional dominated the living room and faced a medium-sized flat-screen TV. Next to it was a large recliner. Comfort furniture to ease the bones after a long day of physical labor. A patch of duct tape mended one of the vinyl arms. Ernest rose and walked over to join his wife.

"Keith. Lottie. Have a seat." A wiry man with thinning brown hair, Ernest Suter wore jeans and a faded-red plaid flannel shirt. He had on fleece-lined sheepskin slippers that I guessed had been a Christmas gift. I doubted he would have bought them on his own.

Beyond was a teenaged girl with long dark hair huddled in one corner of the sectional. She stayed there, her hands clasped between her knees as though she would take flight if she didn't take steps to prevent it. Her eyes were swollen with weeping. "Our daughter, Merilee." Ernie waved his hand in her direction.

She mumbled a weak hello, but stayed curled up in her little protective ball.

A loud cuckoo clock ticked on the wall. I soldiered on, but I wished I had brought a food offering. Something to break this dreadful silence. As agreed, I let Keith take the lead so I could observe.

"We need to ask you some questions, Ernie. I wish we were simply visiting as friends, but we need to get right on the investigation."

Ernie nodded and waved toward the kitchen table. "Okay to sit over there? It will give you a place to set your stuff."

Patricia offered coffee. I never turn it down.

"I'll lead right off. First, do either of you have any questions we can answer before we start asking ours?"

"Just one. Who in the hell would want to murder our son? Our boy?" Ernie's face was stark white. More disbelieving than angry. Anger would come later, but for now there was only grief.

Tears streamed down Patricia's face. She rose and fetched a box of tissues. "He was a wonderful person. You know him. Knew him, Keith."

"Yes, he was," my husband said gently. "As good as they come. We need to know what was going on in his life. Anything out of the ordinary?"

Patricia shook her head and reached for another tissue. "No. Everything was as usual. Brent had decided to major in Agriculture Economics at Kansas State. In the meantime, he was taking Agriculture Equipment Technology at Beloit so there would be something to fall back on during hard times. In the beginning he wanted to be an extension agent, but I don't know. The chances of getting a job in that field weren't good."

"And wouldn't pay worth a damn if he did," Ernie added. "But that's all right, I guess if that's what he wanted to do." He stared out the window.

"Would his credits at Beloit transfer? And why there?"

"It was cheaper, for one thing. And Beloit has a good program. No problem transferring when he switched to K-State."

"Nothing that kid couldn't fix, even without some instructor telling him how. Nothing. He was a natural around a farm. Born to it." Ernie's jaw tensed and he worked his hands like they needed warming.

"He was so smart," Patricia chimed in. "He could have been an engineer. Anything. But he wanted to farm and help people. That's all he ever wanted."

Keith and I looked at one another. It was time to move on with some touchier questions. I took over.

"Did he like school?"

"He did. But he was just naturally one of those kids that seems to like everything and everybody," Ernie said firmly.

"No one he didn't get along with? No one he had quarreled with?"

"None."

"No one at all? That's pretty unusual."

"If there was, he wouldn't mention it. It's not his way. He keeps…kept his focus on higher things."

"Okay," I said carefully, "maybe quarreled is too strong a word. Anyone at all he disagreed with?"

"He mentioned some kid he had pissed off because he wouldn't loan him his car. But he was just looking out for us. The car is no real prize and we carry minimal insurance and the drivers have to be listed on our policy. If something happened, someone could sue the socks off of us. No, make that *when* something happened. *When*, not if. The car was a pile of junk. But Brent knew how to baby it."

I cleared my throat. "Did either one of you have any kind of conflict with your son? Over girlfriends, for instance? Or friends in general?"

"Never."

"There was a girlfriend," Merilee said suddenly. "One girl. A very special girl."

"No conflict." Patricia spoke quickly before Merilee could say another word. "They were getting awful serious. We just pointed out to Brent that if he wasn't careful he would end up being a father before his time and marry someone he wasn't all that crazy about or not marrying but paying child support all of his life."

"But he was crazy about her. He wanted to marry her," Merilee added.

Annoyed, Ernie gave Merilee a warning look. "Now don't you go making a mountain out of a molehill, Sis. We just told him to wait, that's all."

"We would just as soon not talk about her. Bad memories there and it has nothing to do with what happened to Brent. Put it out of your mind."

Merilee's lips clamped shut again. I made a mental note to get her by herself.

Keith took over again. "Folks, I hate to ask you this, but it's something I have to do. Did Brent use drugs or was he involved in any of that sort of thing? Anything at all."

"No." Both the parents spoke as one.

"Gambling, or helping people gamble."

"No. What the hell, Keith? You know better than that."

"Yes, I do, but these are questions I have to ask."

While Keith was asking these questions I kept my eyes on Merilee. Her blank expression did not change. Not so much as a flicker. No outrage either at our probing questions.

"My boy was going to take over the farm someday. After he got his degree." Ernie blurted. Then he lost it and left the room.

Keith glanced at his watch. "Thank you so much for your time, Patricia. This is enough for today. We'll keep you posted. And I'm sure you know that there's going to be a lot more questions for you to answer. Depending on what comes up. Right now you've answered everything we need to start with."

"Merilee." She turned toward me when I said her name. "Please keep your eyes open at school. Especially pay attention to people who want to talk about Brent a lot. I can't imagine what anyone might know or have seen, but you never can tell. Tell us about anything that you think might help."

Patricia saw us to the door. Ernie was not in sight.

"Nothing we couldn't have learned through back issues of the paper," I said as we got into the car.

"Nothing unique volunteered and enough tension to start a war. Not visible. Just there." Keith turned the key and automatically checked for livestock before he backed.

"Yes. Merilee knows more than she told us. Her parents want to shut her up. Did you see them tense up when I was asking about girlfriends?"

● ● ● ● ●

Dorothy came to the back door to meet us.

"How did it go?"

"As to be expected. It was miserable. There's nothing I hate to do more than ask questions about someone who has just died. Unless it's delivering the news in the first place." I wanted to think. Not answer questions. But she was officially part of the team. Right now I couldn't remember why.

"I can just imagine. Did you learn anything new?"

"It's not what we learned this time so much as what we didn't learn. We both picked up on one thing. The daughter is hiding something. Not just something. A lot. We need to talk with her when her parents aren't around."

"While you were gone, I found a house in the newspaper I want to look at, and a car, too. If Keith has time to take me into town, I'll look them both over and I'll be out of your hair."

"You're not in our hair! I hope we haven't given you that impression."

"You've both been just wonderful. I'm not leaving over any lack of hospitality, believe me. In fact, I'm gaining a whole new understanding of why you two live out here. But for my part, I can't believe how little I know about small-town forensics. This is adding to my research. I should be paying you."

I laughed. "Stick with me, Babe, and you'll even get to learn how a regional center works."

"Plus, having me in town will give us a whole new vantage point. I plan to eat breakfast out every morning. There's a little café just down the street from the house I'm interested in. People talk over morning cups of coffee. You can't tell, I might run into someone who knows something."

"Let's go now," Keith said. "I'm ready wherever you are. You want to go too, Lottie? I'm going to drop by the office and talk to Sam. To see if he knows anything new. Or something old, for that matter. First of all, I want to know about passing down Suter's farm. That's a big deal out here. Who gets it now that the son is dead?"

"Sure. Knowing Sam, he probably started reading old files to see if they contained any information about someone who might have killed a baby. Maybe he's found something."

● ● ● ● ●

Dorothy sat in the back and we didn't talk much during the drive.

"Where do you want to start?" Keith asked. "The car or the house?"

"The car. I can pick out the house on my own. If the one in the paper is impossible, it might take more time than you want to spend looking today. But I know nothing about cars. I need your advice on it."

Keith swung into the Chevrolet dealership. Dorothy carried the ad into the shop. She was a formidable woman in her own right, but with Keith standing in back of his aunt, I doubted that anyone would try a bait and switch. She zeroed in on the used Taurus that had been featured in the paper and bought it right on the spot.

"I'll stay here and take care of the paperwork. You two go on." Dorothy turned toward the dealer. "You'll take a check, I presume."

He blinked hard. "You bet."

"Keith, Lottie, you can catch me up later if there's anything I need to know. If I don't find a house right away I'll rent a room. At least I'll have a car to drive around. It would be a waste of your time. Both of you."

The Queen of Brisk. Everything taken care of in short order.

Chapter Five

Two days later I insisted on manning the office so Sam could go home. He desperately needed sleep, although I was aware from past experiences that he wouldn't really rest until we found Brent Suter's killer. But since I was still officially the undersheriff of Carlton County, I wanted to pull my weight. Sam was supposed to appoint someone to take my place when I became the regional director but obviously it wasn't a priority for either of us right now.

Until our new building was erected, I was forced to use the old antiquated sheriff's office for the regional headquarters. Down the street and around the corner was the office of the Carlton County Historical Society, which had every current electronic device a body could wish for. I knew that because I had bought and paid for all of them. Previous to accidentally becoming an underpaid and underappreciated officer of the law, I had been the underpaid and underappreciated editor of the Carlton County history books.

I was still the official supervisor of the third volume of the Carlton County history books and not one word was to be published without my approval. But after a harrowing summer I had turned the day-to-day operations over to a staff of three: Margaret Atkinson, Jane Jordan, and Angie, Keith's youngest daughter. Margaret saw to it that there was a rigid pecking order with her at the top, of course.

I could go there at any time and use my very own state-of-the-art equipment but I tried to stay out of the courthouse because somehow they became a trio of blithering incompetents the moment I walked in the door. They seemed unable to trust their own judgments for decisions they usually handled just fine.

The agreement was that the staff would call me if anyone wanted to give an oral history, or if I was needed to give my approval before pages were finalized and sent to the printer. Sometimes they were simply stumped and needed advice.

Today, I was jittery tired and couldn't think of a single sensible action to take on solving the two bizarre murders. We had to wait until Topeka finished processing the forensic work before we could do a darned thing. Questions rotated through my mind. A dull circle of unanswered puzzles. Who would want to kill a baby? Why was it in *Reaching Woman's* arms? And Sam's question: how in the hell did it get there in the first place? The next questions all concerned the Suter kid.

I jumped when Jane Jordan came through the door carrying a book in her arms. Apologetic, nervous, she thrust it toward me. "Margaret thought we should throw this away. I think we should keep it. She agreed to let you decide."

"Good!"

"We hated to interrupt you."

"Nonsense. How are things going?"

"Fine. Just fine."

They probably were, and I suddenly missed the smell of glue pots and musty books.

"I have to get back now. Angie is laying out some pages and I'm looking up some information on early railroading for some caller from Texas. And Margaret is planning next week's projects." She moved toward the door. "Bye, bye."

"Goodbye. Say hello to everyone. Tell Margaret I said you all did the right thing. Let me decide this kind of stuff."

She left. She looked happy. Hell, they all looked happy every time I saw them. Why not? They all knew what they were doing and what the outcome was supposed to be. None of them had risen to their highest level of incompetence like me.

I was over my head in the worst kind of way with this double murder. A dead 4-H'er. A dead baby. A setting that breeds nightmares.

I carried the heavy three-ring binder to my desk. It would give me something to do while I waited to hear from Topeka.

The first page was illustrated by hand with a border of vines and diamond motifs.

My Commonplace Book
By
Franklin Slocum

A commonplace book! They were a nineteenth-century pastime. Commonplace books were not journals or diaries, although some contained such entries. They held a hodgepodge—poems and programs and words of wisdom, observations. Whatever. But a three-ring binder was obviously not nineteenth century. Who would keep such a thing, and why would they call it a commonplace book? It was such an odd thing to do.

The next page began with a sort of free verse written with a hand as beautiful as calligraphy. Fascinated, I was finally able to turn my attention to something other than murder.

I quickly realized this was not an ordinary commonplace book, either. It was filled with diary and journal entries.

There was a picture of a very young boy about six or seven, I guessed. Was this the book's owner? There was no way to tell, but whoever was writing was a quite a bit older. The same boy? Perhaps.

The third page introduced an entry that made the book different from a classic commonplace book. The name again.

Franklin Slocum
My Life Story

Once again the page was elaborately decorated in calligraphy. The next page began:

I was born but I shouldn't have been. My mother told
me so. I have been all wrong since the very beginning. My
feet do not work right. They are the first thing people notice
about me. My feet turn toward each other so I can't run.
Not really. I would look like a bear trying to run on two
legs except I'm not as big as the other boys. So bear is the
wrong word.

The other boys have a father. Biddy won't talk to me
about him at all. Her face gets red and she gets that look
on her face that I know means she hates him all over
again.

She comes into my room at night and stands by my bed
staring at me. On the worst nights she sits in a chair by
my bed and I can feel her looking at me. When I peek, her
hands are clasped so hard her knuckles are white. I know
she is trying hard not to kill me. I know she won't because
she is my mother and she knows it is wrong. I pretend to be
asleep, but when her head is lowered I look and her hands
work the corner of her apron over and over.

The entry ended abruptly. Then there was a carefully glued
fragment of a robin's egg and a clipping about the nesting habits
of robins from an old newspaper. The next page contained a
staff of music and the beginning of a song. This was typical of
commonplace books. Random. Disorganized.

His life, page two:

Biddy takes me with her when she cleans people's houses.
I can't talk right either so she tries to work when they are
gone and don't ask so many questions. They tell Biddy they
are so so sorry her child is retarded. They can't see how mad
that makes her, but I know. I always know. There's a place
on her neck that moves in and out.

My name is Franklin but everyone calls me Dummy
because I can only make funny noises, or Duck Boy because
my feet won't work right either.

She made me go to school and then everyone was mad. The teachers were mad because they had to put up with me. "It's the law," Biddy said triumphantly when she drug me to first grade. "Kansas law. Mainstreaming. Every child gets a chance at an education."

Some of the parents were mad too. They said their kids should not have to go to school with a retard. The kids said mean things to me at first, but I was lucky most of the time. I could not talk right, so I didn't talk at all. I wouldn't cry so they found other kids who were not retarded and more fun to torment. I sat like a lump. Was a lump. But when the teacher talked I paid attention. No one could stop me from paying attention.

I learned to read and figure. They didn't give me any tests and when I shambled off to the library and started hauling books back to read, they were mostly relieved that I never caused trouble. I don't know what they thought I was doing when I turned the pages. Liking the flutter, I guess.

Biddy gets some money for taking care of me so she picks me up in her car after school. It's important to her to have people think she's taking care of me. When we get home she lets me do anything I want to. I can go to the pond or stay out all night. She doesn't care. I can walk well enough to suit myself so that's what I do. I know she hopes I will die. But I don't want to.

My friends are all the animals. Once when I was around one of the churches I found a bulletin about the animals.

I turned to a separate page and there was the order of service for the Blessing of the Animals. In honor of St. Francis of Assisi.

A lovely prayer. Just lovely. It was a litany of all that animals had to teach us.

The phone rang, jarring me from the commonplace book to the real world. It was Sam.

"Need to give you a heads up. All hell is breaking loose. The *Salina Journal* just ran a story headlined 'The Ghost Baby Killer Strikes Again.'"

"One death and they have a label on the tip of their tongue?' I was furious. When we hung up I was going to call the editor and give him a piece of my mind.

"No. Apparently not. The most important word in that headline is 'again.'"

My heart sank. "Don't tell me this kind of thing has happened before."

"Well, it did. And I remember the other one now. I didn't pay enough attention at the time because the death wasn't in my county. There was a similar one involving a baby ten years ago."

"In the Garden of Eden?"

"No. At Hays. There was the body of a dead baby."

"Where?"

He cleared his throat. "The Elizabeth Polly Park."

"Elizabeth Polly? The Blue Light Lady?"

"Some call her that, yes."

"Oh, Sam. Where was the baby found?"

"In Elizabeth Polly's arms."

"Pete Felten's statue of Elizabeth Polly?" I tried to process what he had just told me. "Another female statue? But her arms are at her sides. She's clutching a bouquet of flowers in one hand. No place for her to hold anything."

"Doesn't matter. Stuffed between the bouquet and her right side was a dead baby."

"It was ten years ago? But my God, how can it not be the same person?"

"We need to talk. I'll be in the office tomorrow." He sounded weary. Worn down. "Do you want me to read the article to you?"

"No, I'll read it online. I'll go to the historical society and do some extra research before I head home. And you get some rest."

We hung up. I looked at my watch. It was after four o'clock. The historical society would close in another hour. I should be able to access old newspapers from this office but it would take a while before our computer system was in place.

I called the historical society to let the women know I was coming.

• • ● • •

"You all can leave early if you want," I said when I breezed in the door. "I need to work here for a while."

I headed for the server and Angie proudly showed me the latest pages all ready for the printer.

"I'll copy these right now so you can take them home with you tonight."

After they left I turned on the microfilm printer and inserted the *Hays Daily News* reel and forwarded to the date Sam had given me.

Baby found in Elizabeth Polly Park

The Ellis County Sheriff's office has called in the KBI to investigate the discovery of a dead newborn baby in the arms of Pete Felten's statue of Elizabeth Polly in the park named for her. The infant was judged to be less than a day old by the coroner and was swaddled in a blanket and wedged between the side of the statue and the bouquet of flowers she holds. The park has very few visitors in the winter months and the baby was likely placed there under the cover of darkness during the blizzard. It was discovered by some children who were playing hide and seek. There is no record of any woman giving birth within the last twenty-four hours at any of the area hospitals. Please call in any tips or information to Sergeant Lightner at 785-482-2213.

Elizabeth Polly gave aid to Fort Hays soldiers during the cholera epidemic of 1867. Fort Hays was closed in 1905 and the bodies moved to Leavenworth, but hers was

*left behind. Her spirit allegedly roams the
cemetery in a long blue dress searching for
the missing bodies of the soldiers. She is
said to carry a lamp and has a blue aura.
Hence, Polly is often referred to as the
Blue Light Lady.*

I scrolled to the next months' pages to see if there were any follow-up announcements. None. No progress whatsoever. I printed out the relevant pages, then rewound the film, placed it back in its folder and put it back in the file drawer. Any updates could probably be found through Google and police databases.

On the drive back to the farm, I kept thinking about these perfect little babies struggling to draw one more icy breath.

Kansas has Safe Haven laws. Babies can be left at fire departments, hospitals, and police stations without fear of prosecution. In a day and age when hospitals and fire departments have programs that let mothers drop newborns off at a hospital with no questions asked, why in God's name would anyone want to let a baby freeze to death?

In addition to that mystery was how a new mother could have the strength to leave an infant in Elizabeth Polly Park or the Garden of Eden? The answer was obvious—they couldn't. No woman who had just given birth would be physically able to put a baby in *Reaching Woman*'s arms. In fact, Sam was still puzzled as to how a man in his prime could manage it. Putting an infant in the arms of Elizabeth Polly's statue would be easy physically except that it happened in the dead of winter during a storm. What woman who had just given birth would be up to walking in a blizzard to leave her baby in a strange place?

Sam would be pleased that I finally could say one thing with absolutely certainty. We could rule out the mother in both situations.

Chapter Six

My cell vibrated. I glanced at Keith's text message:

Dorothy here. Fixing supper.

Great!! I pushed Send, knowing he would think I was referring to having a hot meal waiting. But I also meant "great" because I could tell them simultaneously about the baby in Elizabeth Polly Park.

I turned into the lane leading to our large three-story house. Where were the mothers? Were there any missing women reported at the time the babies were discovered? Women who were pregnant?

An even harder job would be discovering women who had given birth. There would be no records, no birth certificates since the births obviously had not taken place within hospitals. According to Gene Romney, the head EMT, the baby at the Garden of Eden had been alive less than ten hours before she froze to death. Ten hours. No hospital would have kicked a mother out that fast. As to the Elizabeth Polly baby, we would need to track down police records as I was certain no medical or birth information existed.

Secret pregnancies didn't really make sense. I know there are reports all the time of women who didn't know they were pregnant or ones who hid their condition from their boyfriends or family and later stuffed all evidence of the delivery—including the baby—in a trash barrel. But this was blatant murder. Not a furtive attempt at disposal. There was obviously a connection between these Ghost Baby incidents. It had to be the same killer.

Ghost Baby. I couldn't believe I had just used that term, even in my thoughts.

The job was making me crazy.

My next step was to assemble a team. I wanted my sister to step in right away. Her reputation was spectacular now. It was formidable enough to begin with. Then after two bizarre encounters here in Carlton County she decided to expand her degree in clinical psychology to an additional one in forensic psychology. Recently she became board certified. Never mind that she was family and her involvement would raise a few eyebrows. She was the best.

Twice before, I had gotten her into situations psychologists don't sign up for. Like near-rape, near-death, near-mutilations. She had escaped all three but "near" was too close. She always swore that it was her choice—she could have refused. But this time I wouldn't give her a choice. I wouldn't hesitate to persuade her by any means necessary.

As for the two other family members on the team, Keith was a solid gold addition even though it was inclusion by default because of his friendship with the Suter family. He wields enormous authority because of his integrity. People listen to him. Besides, when his relentless energy is focused he's like a bloodhound and he never gives up. That makes him a valuable asset in any investigation.

And then there was Dorothy. I had acquired her by popular acclamation. It wasn't any of my doing at all. But in a short time I'd learned her powers of observation were second to none. Either that or she was blessed with extraordinary visual memory. However, I was wary of her intense curiosity and her pleasure at being included on a crime team. There was an unseemly excitement present on her face. Too much enthusiasm for the hunt. For a large woman she was light on her feet and seemed to be shifting her weight from one foot to another like a prize fighter spoiling to get in the ring. But to her credit she had not interfered once, despite her near-miss involving the misogynist boom lift operator.

My assessment of Keith and Josie and Dorothy was detached and ruthless, but essential. I couldn't afford to mess with mediocrity. If any of the three had been screw-ups I would have ditched them in a heartbeat. My job was to find the Suter boy's murderer and whoever killed the precious newborn. Period. If members of my family were the best, they were best. I couldn't help that. My job was to find a killer by whatever means.

Dorothy's car was parked out front. The garage door opened and I steered my Tahoe inside, then walked into the kitchen. Keith was seated at the table.

"I'm celebrating," Dorothy said. She wore an apron and was busy stirring a family favorite, "Drop Noodle Soup," a combination of beef simmered in watered-down potato water gravy with little dumplings added.

"Cooking a meal for us isn't exactly celebrating."

"Cause enough. I found a great house to rent."

Ruefully I scolded myself for being affronted by Dorothy's interest in the case. I hoped she was renting the house because she wanted to and not because we had offended her in some way.

"On the bad news side Dimon called," Keith began. "There's been a new development."

"It's a game changer," Dorothy added.

"There was a note wrapped in the blanket." Keith's fingers tightened on his coffee cup. "Handwritten, Dimon said. 'See how the mighty have fallen.'"

"My God."

"Yes."

"There's a worse development. I'm going to call Dimon right now."

I glanced at their faces as I dialed the KBI's number and put the phone on speaker so they could hear every word. This was the A team and I needed all the help I could get. That meant giving them access to information. Dorothy was already sworn in as a consultant and Keith was a reserve deputy. There was no reason why they shouldn't hear.

If it was possible to hear someone suck in a deep breath, that was what I was hearing when Dimon listened to my report of the baby discovered ten years ago in the arms of the Blue Light Lady.

"Son of a bitch."

I waited.

"Well, the ball is in your court, Lottie. This is yours. You wanted to be in charge of a regional crime center. Figure out what to do next. Keep me updated down to the last detail. Let me know what resources you need, including people."

"Okay. I'm home now. After I get to the office tomorrow and look over the rest of the autopsy reports I can be more specific, but it the meantime here's what you can do a lot better than I can from here. Find out if there were similar murders."

"God, Lottie." He fell silent.

"I know," I said, "but you've just now learned about the Blue Light Lady. There was no reason for that thought to enter your mind right off the bat."

"Well, you've obviously beat me to the punch."

That concession surprised me. The regional center had been his idea to begin with but he wanted the staff firmly under the control of the KBI, not the warring collection of counties that formed the western third of the state. But I had out-maneuvered him.

"I'm not taking credit, Frank. This information came from Sam and unfortunately he read about it the *Salina Journal*. The headline couldn't have been worse. "Ghost Baby Killer Strikes Again."

"I'll get right on it. We've got to keep a step ahead of the press. The first thing we should do is call in the very best psychologist in the state. And I guess we both know who that it."

"My sister."

"Right. You make the call, Lottie."

"And I want Keith too."

"Naturally." He sounded weary, reluctant. Despite the seriousness of the situation I knew he was sick to death of the Fiene family. In fact he once accused us all of having something in our blood that caused "all these damned murders."

Wait until he heard about Aunt Dorothy.

"Do whatever you need to do, Goddamn it."

We hung up and I turned to Dorothy and Keith. "I didn't want to overload on family, but you are both now officially members of the task force investigating these murders because you are the best qualified. He even suggested I call in Josie."

"Dimon is backing you on everything? That's a new one." Keith got up and went to the stove to ladle a bowl of soup. "And he wants Josie on this too? He must have had a major change of heart."

"No, I don't think so. I think this is so important that he doesn't dare risk having any major screw-ups. At heart he's a good man. He…"

"He's a major control freak, Lottie."

"True. I'm not saying he isn't, but at heart he wants to protect and serve."

"He wants to protect his ass. And serve his own self interests."

I laughed, then explained to Dorothy the basis of Keith's antipathy toward Agent Frank Dimon. We sat down and Keith said grace. Dorothy glanced at us curiously as he made the sign of the cross and I didn't.

I was much too exhausted to go into our complicated religious histories. In fact, going over the details of the baby murders sounded like an easier topic.

"So, tomorrow I'll complete adding members to the regional team. Any ideas about where to start with a formal plan?" I knew that Keith's best ideas would come after he had time to think. Usually while he messed around with his guitar. "Dorothy? Any ideas?"

"Yes." Dorothy carefully placed her soup spoon on the saucer beneath her bowl. "I think you should make a list of all the female statues around Kansas. Ones that have arms. Then the next step…"

"Yes!" I couldn't keep the admiration out of my voice. "Yes, of course. That would shorten the search for similar incidents by weeks if we started with the statues themselves instead of beginning with pregnant women who had gone missing. This also would stop us from looking into all the incidents of abandoned babies. Which sadly enough would be in the thousands. Yes, female statues that have arms. If we can't find something—then, and only then—will we expand the search."

"Then try to find out if there were any other deaths at the same time. But somehow I don't think there will be." She rose and went back to the warming oven and put a fresh supply of buttermilk biscuits on a serving platter and waited until she was seated before she finished what she had been going to say. "I think the Suter boy's murder might be only accidentally connected to the Ghost Babies."

"Are you saying his murder isn't linked? I want to know what in the hell he was doing there." Bewildered, Keith looked up from the biscuit he was buttering. "His family is hiding something and I'm going to get to the bottom of it."

"I'm not saying there's no association between the deaths." Dorothy glanced at Keith's bowl. "You need more soup." She rose, picked up Keith's bowl and headed for the stove. He looked at me with a wry smile and shrugged like he was getting used to being bossed around by the women in the family.

Dorothy wore simple jeans with ease at the waist and a hand-knit gray cable pullover that came to the top of her hips. It was no nonsense attire that was in keeping with her very practical observations. She could fit in anywhere. And did. If people didn't know she was a best-selling novelist, she was invariably overlooked. In a restaurant, on a bus, standing on a corner. There was nothing that called attention to herself.

She placed the bowl in front of Keith. "I'm saying there's a different element in play. We've already found a similar case to the abandoned baby in the Garden of Eden. We have babies that died of exposure shortly after birth. In freezing weather. Placed in the arms of women that were statues. The Ghost Baby deaths are connected in several special ways and Brent's isn't directly linked to anything."

Keith nodded. "I see what you are getting at. Hard proof."

"Yes. We only have theories so far." We were silent and concentrated on the meal. "The statues are also well known," Keith added. "That's another connection."

"Only by Kansans," I argued. Ideas were flowing now. I stood and went after the notepad by the phone and brought it back to the table.

"Oh, they are known beyond Kansas," Dorothy said. "Not famous exactly, but a lot of artists know about Pete Felton's work. And the Garden of Eden certainly has a national presence. I agree that it might not be everyone's cup of tea." She reached for a biscuit. "Another thing, do those two statues look like they have something in common to you? I mean *Elizabeth Polly* and *Reaching Woman*?"

"Yes." Keith replied quickly like he had been thinking about it. "They both have a heavy look. The features are more suggested than spelled out. One made by Dinsmoor and one by Peter Felton. They are not romantic and don't have lot of detail."

"Exactly."

Dorothy rose, carried the bowls to the sink, and began clearing the rest of the table. "After I collect my things from your bedroom, I'll go on to my new place. I'm basically a morning person and need to get my rest. I'll stop in at the sheriff's office tomorrow to see what has developed. After I've finished my writing."

"No need to rush off," Keith said. "Have another cup of coffee. This little discussion is doing quite a bit of good."

"No more coffee for me tonight, but I agree that we should put our heads together."

"It's done more than a little bit of good. Thanks, Dorothy, for suggesting that we start locating female statues first. But while you are here and I've got the go ahead from Dimon, I want to talk about where I want you and Keith to focus."

My husband smiled at my injection of authority. He was used to taking orders from me, and Dorothy obviously wasn't.

"Keith, I want you to go back out to the family tomorrow. The reaction of the Suter family has bothered you from the very beginning."

"There's something off there."

"See if you can talk privately with the daughter. Don't wear your uniform shirt or your badge. I want them to think of you as their friend, not as an officer of law."

"I *am* their friend," he said sharply.

I sighed. "I know that, honey. You know what I mean. But this family is going to resist talking about things we need to know. They are too proud to air the family laundry in public. You stand the best chance of getting information."

"Dorothy, can you manage to hang out around town some more without seeming to be too obvious?"

"Sure. There's nothing more natural than a writer in a coffee shop. They'll all feel free to come over and talk to me. I'm like a magnet. I'll just tell the owner I'm having trouble with my Internet connection at my house. They have Wi-Fi in the coffee shop. For free. Students bring in laptops all the time."

"Instead of using the library's server?"

"Yes, and all kinds of people come to The Coffee Shop. People that never go to the library. It's gossip central." She glanced at her watch. "The Coffee Shop. Not the catchiest name in the world, by the way. Reminds me of a certain editor that used to rework my headlines."

"And they just come right up and talk to you?"

"Right. Because I'm a writer. Especially because I'm a novelist. And you won't believe the number of people who want to tell me their life history. Or their family's most intimate secrets."

"I hope you're not planning on getting any work done."

"No, but everything is grist for the mill. The only ones I really dread are the ones who want to give me their idea, have me do all the writing, and then split the money."

"How do you handle that?"

"They are the only ones that I don't encourage to hang around. I tell them I have an even better proposition. I'll give them an idea, they can do all the writing, and we'll split the money."

While she was upstairs I went into Keith's office and removed his Bible from his desk. When Dorothy came back down with her suitcase and her knitting bag I was waiting for her.

"We need to make this official. Consultants take the same oath as deputy sheriffs. At Sam's insistence."

She slowly set down her baggage and walked over to me. She repeated the words with a little quiver in her voice. When she vowed to uphold the Constitution of the United States, tears formed in her eyes.

Touched, Keith looked away.

"All done," I said cheerfully. "Nice and proper. You are now officially an officer of the law."

"Well." She stood there as though uncertain of her next move. "Well. So I am."

She retrieved her luggage again and we walked her to the door. I saw her off with a simple wave. There was nothing huggable about Dorothy Mercer. She drove around the circle in front of our house and her taillights disappeared down the lane.

Keith went to the music room, and began picking around on his favorite guitar. He played a variety of soft instrumental compositions. Nothing as revealing as a ballad. I smiled and paused in the doorway. "I'm going up to bed. Good night, honey."

He went on searching for a chord as though he hadn't heard me.

"Good night, honey," I said again.

At this he looked up and nodded. "Night. I'll be up pretty soon." His fingers found the pattern he had been searching for. "Aren't you going to call Josie?"

"Not tonight. I'm too tired. I'm going to wait until morning and then I want to be at the office."

As I walked toward the stairs I thought about Dorothy's tears during the oath. She'd been awestruck. Honored. Validated. Transformed into the real thing. Not just a writer about the real thing.

Then I mulled over her comments about The Coffee Shop. I wished she didn't see everyone as grist for the mill. It sounded morbid.

Chapter Seven

Keith was already out choring when I got up in the morning. Normally he depended on our hired hand, Zola Hodson, to have things started. But she was off visiting relations. She had begun as my housekeeper, then answered Keith's ad for a hired hand, which shocked the hell out of both of us.

Amused, she had presented us both with her credentials as an estate manager who had worked for wealthy film families in California. Through her grandfather who had managed estates in England, she became skilled at working with animals. She was the greatest gift our complicated household could possibly have received. But with her fabulous carriage, whippet-thin body, and sculptured hair she could easily step into a modeling job if our place burned to the ground.

When I got to the sheriff's office, I checked the desk for one of Sam's notes telling me what had happened the day before. Nothing much. Somebody's dog barked. Somebody's didn't. Animal Control was supposed to take care of both cases, but since the county commissioners had done away with that service the sheriff's office was expected to rise to the occasion: scold the errant owner in the first case and bury the dead dog in the second case. Sam had turned the phone over to Betty Central and took care of both dogs on his way home last night. I called Betty and got the phones transferred back.

I called Josie at exactly nine am. She would not be teaching at Kansas State today and, like me, was a morning person. Before she could answer, I hung up, switched to Skype and called her back. I wanted to see her face.

"Whasup, Dude?"

I smiled at her mock informality and replied with the obvious. "It's me." I knew she was trying to put me at ease because when I Skype, the conversation will involve police work.

"So I see."

"Have you been reading the papers? About the Ghost Baby?"

Her face froze. "Oh my God. Will this involve you, Lottie? When I read that article I was glad the death wasn't in Carlton County because the crime was so hideously deviant. I thought it was out of your jurisdiction."

"Guess again."

"Oh, no. Why?"

"The why is what I was hoping you would help with."

"No, I mean why would this be your responsibility?"

"Because I'm the brand new regional director, that's why. And, believe it or not, it's been turned over to the brand new Northwest Kansas Regional Crime Center. I'm calling because Frank Dimon wants to bring you in. Because you're the best at what we need right now."

I love Skype. She couldn't hide a single emotion.

"This is Frank's idea? You've got to be kidding."

"I'm not."

"Well, tell me what I need to know."

I went through the details of the Ghost Babies deaths, the connection with the female statues, the freezing weather. I could see Josie writing furiously.

"There was another death at the Garden of Eden." I told her about the Suter boy. "We were focused on that murder. Sam's the one who spotted the baby."

She didn't blink when I gave her the details. "Are the murders connected?"

"They have to be. But right now we don't know how. The Suters are longtime friends of Keith so he's the best one to question them. From a professional standpoint, what can you tell me about the kind of the person who might have done this?"

She looked up from her legal pad. "He's crazy."

"No kidding."

"Seriously, I'll have more for you this afternoon. This goes into some really unusual psychology. And I'm not a trained profiler. All you'll get is my educated opinion."

I cleared my throat. "That's not good enough, Josie. I'm formally calling you in. To be part of the task force."

Warring emotions and a deep sadness flitted across her face. "Lottie..." She stammered.

I was tempted to let her off the hook. She had a beautiful life as a teacher at Kansas State. She had a great practice and, through a nasty divorce from her first husband, more money than she would ever need. I had dragged her through hell twice before with other cases.

What I was asking wasn't fair, but finding this killer would make the reputation of the regional center and this approach would be a role model for police and sheriff's departments nationwide. I wanted to prove the worth of local and rural expertise. Privately owned and for-profit prisons were popping up all over and I didn't like them. Somehow Western Kansas was viewed as a logical solution to all kinds of social and environmental problems. All that space! And so few people! What a great place to dump nuclear waste. And store missiles. And conduct dangerous armament tests.

Like most of the citizens, I wanted all the bastards to stay the hell away from our prairies.

Besides, Josie had told me she loved her new role as a forensic psychologist.

But, oh, that rueful look on her face! I couldn't bear being the cause of it. Suddenly ashamed I said, "Josie, don't give it another thought." But I knew she wouldn't stop thinking about it. "I'll tell Dimon that you have too many obligations to take on another murder in Carlton County. Not murder, murders."

"No, I'm in. How can I not be? This will be the first time to apply all my expensive forensic training to a case this important. I hoped you would be spared this kind of problem. The other times have been logical. With a clear motive." She closed her eyes. "Problem. That's a stupid thing to say. This was a baby, not a problem. I apologize. Whoever did this is really dangerous. I'm trying to think of all the ramifications. And logical? Murder is never logical."

"I understand, but think it over before you decide for sure."

"I don't need to think. I'm in."

• • ● • •

After I hung up the phone, I read over the autopsy report of the Suter boy and the baby. There were no surprises. Gene Romney had already pointed out how very soon after birth the baby had died, and that Brent Suter had died of the gunshot wound to the chest. I already knew that. In both cases there were no traces of drugs in the preliminary toxicology report. They were forwarding samples anyway for further testing for substances that didn't show up in a routine screening. The only part of the report I couldn't bear to read about was the time it took for the baby to die of exposure. It doesn't take long for an infant to freeze to death.

I threw down the pages. Some of them fluttered off the desk. I picked them up and whacked the edges together. Dorothy would drop by sometime this morning and I wanted her to know I was handling all of this just fine. There was nothing to do in this damned office right now except think, and at the moment I couldn't stand that. In my mind there was an image of a tiny newborn pelted with ice and snow struggling to breathe in the arms of a cold, cold woman, reaching, reaching for something that would never be hers. A woman yearning for life but immortalized in cold concrete.

I picked up Franklin Slocum's commonplace book. It wasn't exactly cheerful reading but I hoped it would dispel the image of the baby.

*I learn mostly through the animals. It's fun to see if I
can do the same things they do. I've started a chart with
little boxes to check off when I think I'm good at doing
some of the same things.*

The chart followed:

◊ *Snakes—slither through grass*
◊ *Wood frog—live and hide anywhere even freeze
  and still live*
◊ *Possums—play like I'm dead*
◊ *Prairie dog—hide fast*
◊ *Fish—swim under water*
◊ *Squirrel—jump from branch to branch*
◊ *Owl—???*

*I read a book about Indians and how they can shape
shift and become an animal. I want to learn to do that.
First I must decide what I want to be. I think I want to
become a little wood frog because they make such a cool
sound and can hide anywhere.*

There was a three weeks gap between the dates. Usually he
wrote every day.

*They kicked me out of school for touching myself. I
didn't know it was wrong. It feels so good. The principal
said my behavior was inappropriate and disruptive for the
other children.*
*Biddy was so mad she took me to the doctor and asked
him to fix me. Then the doctor got really, really mad at
Biddy. He threatened to turn her in to social services and
have me taken away. He made her leave the room while
he talked to me. I know what to say to keep Biddy from
getting into trouble.*
*He told me that I would soon be starting puberty and
my body would be going through a lot of changes. I wanted
to ask him questions but I still can't talk right so I just*

nodded. *My face turned bright red. I could feel it. He gave
me a sack filled with a lot of pamphlets and brochures and
told me to read them.*

*When he let Biddy into the room again he had settled
down. He told her he knew how hard it must be, but his
voice was all fakey syrupy and I knew he was still mad.
Biddy made me sit in the backseat and wear my seatbelt on
the way home. She wants people to see her take care of me
and it's not all an act because she would not get her money
anymore if something happened to me.*

*I was afraid she would take the doctor's sack away from
me. She didn't seem to care what was in it but I knew
how fast that could change. When she was fast asleep I
crept outside and took it to the big cottonwood tree next to
the creek because Biddy changes her mind a lot and turns
mean. I have a plastic bag buried there where I keep all my
stuff. I learned to do this from all my little squirrel friends.*

*I'm free, free, free. They are not going to make me go to
school anymore. No more names. Just me and the animals.
I don't have to do anything. Biddy never pays the slightest
bit of attention to me anymore either. I don't have to take a
bath or wear clean clothes to keep the teacher from calling
social services. I can stay at the pond all day and all night
too if I want to. The State won't make the school teach me.
I'm so happy. I'm so happy.*

*I don't sleep in the house much anymore. I will when it
gets cold. But Biddy won't ever make me.*

*I'm studying the animals again. I like the owl the best
but I couldn't finish my chart because I don't know what
an owl does when it is worried. Snakes slither, beetles run
away, chicken sort of run around, possums play like they are
sleeping. Tomorrow I will go to the library and find out.*

There was a full month's gap in the entries. Then:

*I cry and cry. Even Biddy noticed that I've started sleep-
ing inside again and cry in my sleep or when I'm awake.*

But I don't know what to do. When I went to the library,
they wouldn't let me have any books. I wanted to get an
owl book. I found the book and went to check it out. Then,
the librarian told me I didn't have any rights anymore.
Because I am not in school. I was so ashamed. She said
that I only had been given a library card because I was
in school and now I wasn't. She said all the words really
loud like I couldn't hear since I couldn't talk. And like I
was stupid too. Like I couldn't understand all the books I
checked out before.

All the words that went through my mind were words I
heard at school.

Dumb bitch. Stupid cunt. But I couldn't say them.

My face was hot with blood. I left the book and shuffled
toward the door because I could not run. I could not run.
There are no animals that run on my chart because I can't
run. Now I can't go back to school because the State won't
make them teach me anymore. Everyone is glad but me.

Moved to tears, I stopped reading. The poor lonely child. My
mind raced as I imagined his life. He existed on a survival level.

I've decided to write my own books. Starting with this
one. No one can keep me from writing my own book. I'll
hide it in my trash bag so no one can steal it or tear it up.
Sometimes I find books that people have thrown away. And
other things. I found this binder down where people swim.
It was full of blank pages. I waited two days, but no one
came back for it.

I'm going to start a commonplace book. Benjamin
Franklin had a commonplace book. So did a lot of other
important people.

The phone rang and I set the book aside. I was expecting a
call from Keith or Josie, but it was Dorothy.

"Okay if I stop by?"

"Sure."

She was bundled up like she was getting ready for another blizzard when she came through the door. Surprisingly, she wasn't short of breath although her nose was bright red and her cheeks were burning from the cold air.

"Been at the coffee shop?"

"Yes, and that's what brings me here. More gossip."

"Not more babies, I hope."

"No. And nothing strange happening in Carlton County. But about three counties due east, there was a big to-do over some young girls who had disappeared."

"How many?"

"Three. Over a period of seven years."

"That's within a somewhat expected range. Not that anything like that is ever expected."

"That's what I think too, especially since they located one of them later. But after all this time, folks are sure aware of the two they didn't find. Especially the one last year, Joyce Latimer. They didn't say much about the first one, but they sure had an opinion about the Latimer girl because she was from around Hays.

"She was a senior in high school and had missed the bus. She lived out in the country and started walking home. It was May and a really nice day and her folks' farm was only a couple of miles west of the school. She had walked before. But she never made it home."

"They never found her?"

"Never. Not a trace. None of her books or clothes or anything. She simply disappeared." Dorothy's face was heavy, solemn. "That kind of thing is always tragic. She was an honor student. Everyone thought very highly of her. You can imagine what everyone thought happened."

"She sure doesn't sound like a runaway."

"But that's not what I came to tell you. Here's what everyone started talking about—the young boys that went missing in Northwest Kansas. And I'll guarantee you, that's a whole different situation."

"How young? How many?"

"Two. Both were around ten."

"No idea what had happened?"

"No. Not a clue. There were four years between the disappearances. They took place quite a while before something happened to this girl."

"In a small community two missing boys would be devastating. Everyone probably knew them."

"Yes, and nearly everyone was involved in the search. When the first boy just vanished it scared the hell out of everyone. Parents even started picking up their kids at school. After several months passed, everyone sort of settled down. Then four years later it happened again and the children might as well have been living in a city. No more days roaming pastures or creekbanks by themselves. Things changed for good with the second boy. None of the young boys are just turned loose for a day at a time. Families out here are so much more safety-conscious."

"That's true in general. And a good idea everywhere."

I have never been comfortable roaming pastures because of my aversion to snakes. I don't like them. Keith has tried to tell me that not all snakes are dangerous, but they scare me to death anyway.

"Well, I'm going home now." Dorothy slapped her hands on her knees then stood and walked to the door. She turned. "I haven't gotten a bit of real work done today and my books don't write themselves."

"Bye. And thanks."

After she left, I mulled over this bit of back history. Statistically, the disappearances were not significant but crime statistics didn't mean a thing to me. Someone's son, someone's daughter had gone missing. It wasn't a statistic; it was a tragedy. Families fractured forever.

For some reason, all kinds of people felt comfortable talking to Dorothy about everything under the sun. Perhaps it was because they assumed because she was a writer she was a very "sensitive" person who would understand them. Or that she wouldn't be shocked when they told her things about their family because she killed people on a regular basis. In a manner of speaking.

• ● ● ● •

Keith came into the office early in the afternoon.

"Anything?"

"I was right about the under currents. There's a lot going on in the Suter family. Nothing I would call sinister. Just stuff they would rather not talk about."

"That's normal anywhere and even more so out here where people don't approve of putting down their relations. Were you able to get the daughter isolated?'

"Yes, and I was expecting more resistance to that."

"They would have had time to coordinate any stories that they thought would look bad."

"Didn't have that kind of secrecy feel to it. In fact, I think they've decided to do everything they can to help us find out who murdered Brent. This is something else. Like they are holding back information they don't think would help us, simply because it's private."

"So you were able to talk to everyone separately?"

"Yes, and the daughter told me more about passing down the farm. The college majors the dad mentioned were farm-related. Ag Economics, Farm Mechanics, etcetera, but according to his sister, that's not what Brent had in mind at all. He wanted to major in sociology or psychology."

"No kidding?"

"I'm not."

I couldn't read the expression in Keith's eyes. He has this way of going opaque. He had inherited his father's homestead land. Had he regretted following in his footsteps? Did he wish he had made other choices? In a way he had by going to vet school. But the type of big animal practice that he specialized in was tied to agriculture. Not that far from the family's expectation. He did them both. Farmed and became a veterinarian. But were there secret dreams his family had never known about?

He was an extraordinary musician. Did he regret not going in that direction?

I studied his handsome face as he moved to the chair that was nearest my desk. There was no one around. Nothing to stop me from sitting on his lap. He would pull me to his broad chest and his kisses would make everything better. For a while at least. I could kiss the cleft in his chin, but that would lead to too much more. I blushed and he looked at me and his eyes widened as an amused smile stole across his face as though he could read my thoughts. No "as though" to it. He actually could.

I reached for a legal pad. "So did Merilee say anything else we should follow up on?"

His grin widened. He knew why I had changed the subject.

"Yes. She told me a little about the girlfriend that was upsetting his folks. And why they won't talk about her. She's not a problem anymore. Or not a current problem. It's a hell of a story."

The hairs on the back of my neck prickled.

Keith's expression darkened and he bent one knee and propped his foot across his thigh. "She was from Ellis County. And one hell of a basketball player. Intermural athletics are big out here. Straight A student. There is a lot of socializing after the games and she and Brent got acquainted. They started dating."

"Don't tell me she got pregnant."

"Nope. Worse than that."

My stomach flipped. I sensed what the next words would be.

"She disappeared."

"What was her name?"

"Joyce Latimer."

I nodded. I had been certain of it before I asked. "Dorothy just brought me some details about that. The county still hasn't gotten over it. There was an all-out manhunt. No stone left unturned."

"What do folks think happened?"

"They think she was abducted. Sold into white slavery. Or raped and murdered. Or whisked off to a life of prostitution. Or something just as dreadful."

"And what do the cops think?"

"I'll check all this out with Dimon, but from what Dorothy said the police seem to think she was a runaway, which is code for 'we're tired of looking. We aren't getting anywhere and this is going right to a cold case file.'"

"You know, in a way…"

"Yes, I know. It kind of makes sense and it wouldn't be the first time, but Keith, this girl was idolized. Just an ideal kid. Just like Brent. A fresh-faced All-American girl. A model 4-H'er."

"You're right. Just like Brent."

"I want to talk to Merilee myself. She might reveal even more to a woman. Sometimes that happens during interviews. People think women are more likely to understanding feelings."

"Even if they are meaner than snakes. I know that. Even if there isn't a word of truth to it."

"I'll set up an appointment. I have an idea about this."

"Bet it's the same one I have."

"I'm going to find out from Merilee if Brent ever really wanted the farm. If so, when did he change? What happened? His dad seemed confident about his major. And he was sure Brent would come back to the farm after he finished college. In fact, both of parents were pleased that his majors would complement his farm work. That's getting to be the norm out here. The son getting a college education and then coming back to run things. Lots of Ag Economics majors in charge of family corporations."

"Well, his sister sure didn't have the guts to tell them otherwise. She's keeping a lot back. But I couldn't tell if she was actually hiding something or simply didn't want to air her family laundry in public. No need to embarrass kin. Don't know when folks decided baring their souls on *Oprah* was the right thing to do."

I checked my watch. "Pushing dinner time. All the Suters will be at the house. I'll call right now."

Merilee Suter answered right away and I asked if I could come out around two o'clock. She agreed and then her mother took over the phone. "I'll be home too. If you want to talk to me. Ernie and I have put our heads together. We have a few ideas. I don't think they will help, but he says to let you decide."

"He's right. Sometimes the slightest thing can make a difference."

Keith was processing every word. I hung up. Sam's old Regulator clock began a long series of chimes. Annoyed, I waited it out. Usually I remembered to switch off the sound when I was going to be here by myself. I glanced at my husband. "I was going to tickle you into buying lunch, but looks like I've got other plans."

"That's okay. I'll ask my next best girl." He rose, smiled at my surprise, brushed the end of my nose with his palm and slapped his hat back on his head.

"Aunt Dorothy." He threw back his head and laughed as I waved him away.

Chapter Eight

If anything, Patricia Suter looked worse than she had earlier. She was polite enough. Even offered me coffee. She stayed in the same room with me and Merilee until I finally looked at her so pointedly that she said, "Well, I guess you want some time alone with my daughter."

"If you don't mind. And then I would like to talk to you."

"I've watched enough TV shows to know that splitting us up is customary," she said. "I don't know. This all just feels awkward. Like you are trying to trip us up." She reached for a tissue and dabbed at her cheeks. She rose to her feet, giving Merilee a worried glance, like she hated to trust her with me.

"We're not trying to trip you up. That's not what we are trying to do at all. The way this works is that people remember different things around different people. It's no mystery. If I'm around Keith's Aunt Dorothy I remember different things."

"Like I automatically start thinking of cooking when I'm around Ernie's mother. And how my house looks. I start worrying about my housekeeping. Seeing my place through her eyes. She keeps such a spotless house."

"Exactly. We react differently to different people. It will be your turn to be questioned next. I'll bet you have your own share of secrets."

"A few." She smiled and left the room.

Finally, I had the daughter to myself. "How are you doing, Merilee? I don't want to make this rougher on you than it has to be."

"This is as good a time as any, I guess. It's another snow day at school. The roads are still too slick for the bus. Too much drift." She looked out the window and her voice trailed off.

She looked cold. She had looked cold the first day we were out here and didn't look a bit warmer now even in a heavy turtleneck under a huge red plaid shirt-jacket that I suspected had belonged to Brent. Her dark brown hair was cut in a long shag. There was fresh blood on her cuticles. Her voice was tense and her mouth didn't open much. Like she had to force out the words.

I'm not much for shoving medicine down kids, but before I left, I intended to suggest to Patricia that this girl needed something to help her sleep.

"Merilee, I want to ask you some questions. I think something was bothering you when Keith and I were out here the other day. Something that you might have wanted to talk about if your folks weren't around."

Tears began to flow. I spied a box of tissues on the end table and got up and handed her the whole box.

Her voice was low. I had to strain to hear. "You saw how proud of Brent the folks are. *Were.* He's as good as people think he is. *Was* as good." She swallowed hard. "Never a better big brother. I swear."

"But there was something wrong, wasn't there?" Relentless prodding is part of police work. I was ashamed even if it is my duty.

"Yes. Wouldn't seem that wrong in anyone else's family. But it was the worst thing that could happen to my dad."

"Go on."

"Brent talked about taking over the farm ever since he was a little boy. There was nothing he liked better than riding the tractor with Dad or helping feed cattle. He was a Key Award winner, you know." She smiled at my blank look. "It's the highest honor given to a 4-H'er. Less than one percent ever get this honor. You should see his permanent record book. He started when he was seven years old."

At least I was familiar with the all-mighty permanent record book. Every seed planted, every cost incurred in a project, every moment spent mastering a skill. It was written there and the efforts evaluated at the end of a year. The range of projects offered were amazing. Everything from computer programming to clothing to astronomy to livestock. I knew a lot about the clubs from accompanying Keith when he judged model meetings at 4-H days.

There was no mistaking the pride on Merilee's face when she talked about her brother. I made a quick note. "And you? Were you into club work too? What were your projects? "

"Clothing and photography. One year I went to state with the suit I made."

"Did you continue with your club work?"

She smiled and shook her head. "I was done with all that by the time I reached high school."

"Did Brent go on to be a junior leader?"

"Oh, sure. He really believed in the program. And it is great, you know. I just quit because I didn't want to do it anymore."

"And your folks were okay with that?"

"Oh, sure. No pressure there. They knew Brent and I were two different persons. It's funny, though. In high school I could tell who had been in 4-H by the way they could stand criticism. We were sure as hell tougher. By then I had gotten enough white ribbons to face a firing squad."

My face must have shown what I thought. The first time I watched little kids' faces when they gave a speech that was not just perfect—and judges earnestly scribbling reasons for marking them down—I thought the whole process was barbaric.

She laughed, sensing that I was trying not to look judgmental. "It doesn't hurt, Mrs. Fiene. Honest! After a while we start thinking about how we can improve. Brent got his share of whites. No one is spared. And we also learn that some judges don't know jack shit. And that's part of life too."

I was losing control of this conversation. I wasn't here to talk about the merits of 4-H. "So what was the 'something wrong' we started talking about? What happened that would have 'just killed' your dad, Merilee?"

"You should have heard Brent and Dad at the supper table." Her voice softened. "They argued about seed varieties just like two grown men. Dad listened to Brent because my brother was smart and could hold his own. Dad respected him for it. He'd shake his head and tell Mom later, 'little shit sure can argue.'"

"What happened, Merilee?"

It was like pulling hen's teeth. She wanted to talk about anything else. She looked out the window at the swirls of snow. She gave me a wild, furtive look and her eyes wandered. She pulled the quilt around her and burrowed deeper.

I waited her out.

"Brent's girlfriend, Joyce Latimer, she disappeared. Just disappeared. They never found her. Never. Not even a trace."

"It was after that when Brent changed?"

"Yes. He hardly spoke to anyone at all for two months. Then when he did it was like he was going through the motions. Then at the beginning of last semester, he changed his major. He decided to go into sociology or psychology. He didn't want to be a farmer anymore."

"Did he tell you why?"

She nodded bleakly. "He wanted to find out what kind of a person would want to hurt Joyce."

"No thought of revenge? Hunting someone down?"

"No, Brent was gentle. I never heard him say he wanted to kill the bastard. I want to and I've heard plenty other people say that. But not Brent." Her quick defiant look daring me to judge her for the occasional weak profanity tossed my way said everything about her sincere industrious parents. Any rough talk she had picked up at school. "Brent told me he wanted to find out what made them tick."

"So, your dad had no heir."

"No, he didn't. Not with Brent gone. You might have noticed I'm not the ideal country gal. I'm not made for the life. I'm sick and tired of having every waking day depend on the weather and stuff my parents have no control over. I hate the wind and the dust and the work. And the heat! I want to be a flight attendant or a model or something."

"You'll graduate next spring. Do you plan to go on to college?"

"Yes. K-State. I'll think of something to major in after I get there." Her voice trailed off again.

But I was worried that she wouldn't have the strength to make to K-State. That she would end up taking "time off" from school. "There's something more, Merilee. Something that's worrying you. What is it?"

More tears. "I'm afraid the same thing will happen to me that happened to Joyce. Every time I leave the house or even if I'm standing in the yard, I hear sounds. I'm afraid the sounds aren't really there. I'm afraid that they are in my head. I see things. Like I've seen something out of the corner of my eye and I can't turn fast enough to see them. Or it. Flicks of cloth that are really my imagination."

My blood chilled like I had received a shot of anti-freeze in my veins. She had to have help. Right now. But mental health care was scarce as hen's teeth in this state. Kansas used to have one of the finest facilities in the world: The Menninger Clinic. It treated a number of celebrities: Judy Garland, Marilyn Monroe, Gene Tierney, Brett Favre. It was like a roll call of the rich and famous.

Now we were lucky to have a few storefront counselors scattered across Western Kansas. Their idea of mental health treatment was a cup of herbal tea. And, due to the extreme budget cuts by the most conservative state congress in the nation, the tea bag was used twice.

There was simply no place for someone with fixable problems like Merilee to go. I felt a passing flicker of guilt, but God help me, I said it anyway. "Merilee, I have a sister who is a psychologist. She's wonderful. I want you to talk to her. Please. I'll make an appointment as soon as I get back to the office. In the meantime, are you sleeping?"

This was *so* not fair to Josie. She had her own patients to worry about. I touched Merilee's arm and she flinched. Drew back like my hand held an electrical current.

"Sorry," she mumbled. "I'm jumpy."

"That's all right. It's natural under the circumstances. You've all had your slats kicked in."

"I miss him so much." She glanced at me like there was more she wanted to say but thought better of it.

Something wasn't right here. Something beyond the fact that Merilee was curled into a tiny ball. She was serious, self-contained, and mature. Oddly mature. Like she was a clear-thinking twenty-five-year-old instead of a seventeen-year-old. And when she talked about hearing voices and seeing visions, she was saying it dispassionately. Objectively, like she was putting herself under clinical observation. It meant something. Josie would know what.

"Before I go, Merilee, I have one more question. Do you know why Brent went to the Garden of Eden on Thursday night?"

The sound she made was somewhere between a sob and a wail. She began rocking in place, keening, her bloodless hands clamped between her knees, trying to say something, her breath just gasps without the strength to support words. I made her drink a sip from the bottle of water on the table beside her.

"I could have saved him." That's all she could manage until her voice evened out. When it did, I had to strain to hear. "I didn't want him to interrupt my TV program. I just kept watching TV. I didn't notice anything. Didn't ask any questions."

Her words choked off again. I made her drink more water and waited until she got her breath under control.

"There was a phone call. He answered it and then he left about ten minutes later. And I didn't pay one bit of attention." Tears began again.

"Were your parents home?"

"No. They were both in town. There was some kind of meeting at the community building."

"Did anyone know they would be gone?"

A weak smile. "Anyone who knows my folks knows that if there is any meeting about improving this community they will be there. This one was about raising money to buy playground equipment for our local kids' park. A merry-go-round. A slipper slide. That kind of thing."

"Did the call come on the house phone, instead of his cell?"

"Yes. The house phone. When he hung up he looked at me with this funny smile on his face. Like an eight-year-old who knows a secret that he's promised not to tell. Then he picked up his hat and left."

"Did he look scared? Happy?"

"Both. I noticed that much, but I didn't think about it until later."

"But he didn't come back."

Tears again. "No. I went to bed. So did the folks when they got home."

"When did you realize something was wrong?"

"About noon the next day. Brent never skips chores when he's home from school. I mean like never. It gives Dad a break and he likes to be around the animals again. Like I said, you can count on Brent. *Could* count on Brent. But he's in college now, and Dad said he had the right to raise hell and stay out all night if he wanted to without having to account for every second. So Dad picked up the slack. Fed the horses, watered the chickens."

"So your father wasn't upset?"

"Not then. Things changed around noon. We still hadn't heard from Brent. Then Mom found his cell. It was on the coffee table next to the TV remote. Brent had been watching the K-State game. He never leaves his cell."

Getting a cell number is difficult, but I wondered how the caller knew Brent would be the one to answer the house phone that evening. Did he know the parents would be at a meeting? If so, how? Were the family's habits familiar to the suspect?

"Does your house phone have caller ID?"

"Yes. I've already looked everything up. Reverse number info and all that. The call came from a number that I couldn't find anywhere."

"It was probably a burner phone." She looked at me blankly. "Available at Walmart and Target. Lots of other places. Burners are usually paid for with cash and the number is temporary. Not registered."

"I'll tell the folks about the phone call tonight." She trembled and curled up even tighter. "I'll take my lumps, no matter how much it hurts. It wasn't until you and Keith were here that I realized how important that call was. And started thinking about the look on his face."

Merilee stared out the window.

"You have no idea at all why he would want to go to the Garden of Eden in the middle of the night?"

Her voice rose. "I have no idea at all why anyone would want to go to that godforsaken place at any time of day."

With that, she fled from the room.

Patricia came to the doorway. "Is everyone okay in here?"

"As good as we can be. Merilee is upset. I think it would be best to postpone your interview about Brent because I have something else to tell you."

I swallowed, reluctant to heap more tragedy on this family. A dead son. A daughter afraid to go outdoors alone. And now more bad news that the family obviously wasn't aware of yet. Strange news. I had to tell the Suters about the baby right away. It would be all over town tomorrow.

When I finished, the blood drained from Patricia's face. I reached for her hand and patted it. "We don't know of any connection yet of the baby to Brent's death. If we find one, I'll let you know immediately."

"There isn't any connection. How could there be?"

I still hadn't had the kind of talk I wanted to have with Patricia. She was so shocked over the baby that it simply wasn't a good time to go into feelings and impressions. I told her that I thought Merilee needed some medical attention to help get her over this trauma. I usually know all the right words to say without causing undue alarm. But not this time.

"Merilee is very high-strung, right now," I said tentatively.

Patricia nodded. "I know. Even Ernie is getting worried about her and he usually thinks people should buck up and throw themselves into physical work. Merilee is more delicate. That doesn't work for her. But the child has become so stone-cold she could fit right into the scenery at the Garden of Eden. We'll make an appointment with Dr. Golbert right away. Was Merilee able to help?"

"Yes, but she wasn't able to help with what we would like to know the most. We still have no idea why Brent would go there. I would like to hear your thoughts on that but really think you've had enough for today. Tomorrow? Is that all right?"

She nodded. "The baby," she said, her eyes full of pain as she hugged her arms across her chest. "I just don't understand. How could anyone do that to a baby?"

Chapter Nine

I wasn't paying enough attention to my driving on the road back to town and hit a slick spot under the thick layer of powder snow. I took my foot off both the brake and the accelerator and steered into the skid. Keith trained me to do this maneuver because it goes against instinct to turn the wheels toward the direction the car is going. And to keep your foot off the brake. Thank God I hadn't been speeding.

Frightened by my carelessness, I gently turned the steering wheel back and forth, guiding my Tahoe between the ditches until it lost power and came to a stop broadside in the middle of the road. No oncoming traffic. But for a moment I was terrified by the "what-ifs." I covered my face with my hands and took a deep breath.

Ice-crusted tumbleweeds had blown against the fence. Diamonds sparkled across the fields when sudden gusts sent winking blasts of snow powder onto the nearest drifts.

Breathtaking. Magical. Normally it was one of my favorite landscapes, but today all I could think of was a tiny baby freezing to death. High up in the arms of *Reaching Woman*.

From then on I drove carefully back to the farm. Sam was on call and I wanted to talk to Frank Dimon before I went any further. Despite his cold-blooded approach to things that made my blood boil, there were times when Frank's ruthless logic got me back on track. He doted on procedure and had no use for my intuitive approach when it came to law enforcement. We should have made a great team. Instead, we fell to arguing most of the time.

I finally had something concrete to tell him. Brent had received a phone call. Probably delivered from a burner. His sister said he left about ten minutes later. She was positive he left because of that call. She had no idea what the call was about. Those were facts.

I wouldn't tell Dimon about Merilee Suter's state of mind because my impressions were based on intuition. Not evidence. No way to prove she was at her breaking point.

Keith was waiting for me but I could tell by the bleak expression on his face that he was stymied by the lack of progress. "Hi. Anything?"

"Maybe." I told him about my meeting with Merilee. "The mother doesn't have a clue, but I'll go back and talk with her tomorrow."

"Dimon called. He wants you to send him the names of all the people you want on the task force."

"Okay. He was next on my list."

I grabbed a cup of coffee and headed for the phone. One thing about catching Dimon up on an investigation, he doesn't waste time on pleasantries. He picked up after the first ring and barked his name into the phone without any "hello."

I told him about the visit to the Suters without any embellishments. "And that's basically all I have to tell you, Frank. Brent got a phone call and left immediately afterwards."

"Good work. It will give us a place to start. Give *you* a place to start."

"I'm going to have my first team meeting tomorrow. Did you find similar crimes involving a baby?"

"No, thank God. There are just those two. Both in Western Kansas. That was a great idea, by the way. Starting with the statues first instead of chasing our tails looking at all the abandoned baby lists."

"Thanks. But that wasn't my idea. Dorothy Mercer deserves the credit for that one."

" *The* Dorothy Mercer? The mystery writer?"

"The very same," I said dryly.

"What is she doing out there?"

"She's Keith's aunt." A cedar log suddenly crackled in the fireplace sending a spray of sparks toward the chimney. Eerily timely.

"You mean to tell me you have yet another Fiene relative dragged into yet another crime scene?"

"She's already on the task force. Sworn in."

"Look, Lottie. I'm sure she's a great addition, but we can't have this again. People are going to talk."

"Can't help what people say, Frank. She's really, really good."

"You all are. It's not that."

"Besides, it's a done deal."

I could hear his pencil thrumming on his desk. "There's someone else I want you to include on your team."

"I thought the members were all up to me."

"Yes. We had an agreement." He paused like he was searching for the right words. "To be honest…"

He nearly always was, but there's something about those words. Like the speaker's first choice would be to say nothing at all.

"Oh, hell. Might as well put all my cards on the table. I've received a call from one of our state representatives and he wants another psychologist included in this investigation. I owe this man a favor and he hinted he would go all out to see to it that our agency was well funded. For once. Lots of competition for money in this state right now. And I guess I don't have to tell you, funding for the regional center is a little wobbly too."

Ah, yes. The money angle. There's nothing like a little touch of blackmail. It works every time. "I can't see where it would hurt anything, Frank," I said pleasantly. "Josie is the best, but I guess two heads are better than one."

It wouldn't hurt to have Dimon indebted to me either.

His voice warmed immediately. "Thanks, Lottie. I appreciate it. This man has a stellar reputation."

"The state representative?"

"No, damn it, the psychologist. Dr. Evan Ferguson has actually been trained in profiling at Quantico. Moreover, he's a war hero. Plus, it will look better if you beef up the qualified expert side of consultants. It will look more professional than having another bunch of your relations poking around."

"Has he been vetted?" This doctor Ferguson's name had been sprung on me so quickly that the state representative must have had him waiting in the wings. Although it would look better not to have a task force loaded with Fienes, bringing in an additional psychologist would not necessarily help solve the crime. On the other hand, if I had been in Dimon's shoes, I might have done the same thing.

"Vetted? I'll say. It's not necessary for the KBI to duplicate the FBI's screening process. The Feds don't admit anyone to their ranks without subjecting them to intense scrutiny. You and Dr. Ferguson have probably crossed paths. He drives all over Kansas treating veterans with mental health issues. His specialty is Post-Traumatic Stress Disorder."

"Who is this representative?"

"Thomas Williams. He's struggling to get reelected and needs to raise a lot of cash."

"Who is pressuring Williams? You can bet your life someone wants him to win because he's promised to push through legislation that will mean big bucks for someone somewhere. Your psychiatrist is likely tacked onto the funding blackmail because someone's nephew or cousin wants to be in the limelight. Veteran-weary, maybe. Wants to build a private practice."

I tapped my nail against my front teeth. He thrummed his pencil. Neurotically rhythmic, both of us. But clearly he had sulled up.

"Nevertheless, we need all the help we can get," I said sweetly. "Can your Dr. Ferguson drive to Hays and meet with us at ten o'clock? I'll reserve a meeting room at the Holiday Inn. By fall, we should have our own place to meet. In the meantime, Hays is central."

"Sure thing. Can Josie make it by then?"

"Yes, so can John Winthrop from Russell County; Justin Harold from Copeland County; Scott Smith, sheriff from Bidwell County; and his deputy, David Hayes; Harold Sider, who's retired FBI and now teaches at K-State. You probably remember him. Josie's friend. He helped figure out who murdered Zelda St. John."

"I remember. Good man."

"And Sam Abbott, of course."

"Of course," The pace of the thrumming picked up. Sam and Dimon were oil and water.

"Me and Josie and your new psychologist. That's plenty. Keith and Dorothy are going to stay here in Carlton County. So that will be just two Fienes at the meeting. Josie and me. That won't look too bad."

He grunted.

"Are you coming, Frank?"

"No. That's a good team. Well-balanced. With sheriffs or deputies from several different counties. Keep me up-to-date on everything. And I do mean everything. But for this first go-round I want everything to look like it's on your shoulders as regional director. Not just *look* like," he corrected himself hastily. "I want it to *be* on your shoulders. This is your show. If the KBI is there, too, it will look like we're in charge. And we're not."

"Except for one outsider."

"Yeah, well. But this guy is really sharp."

"In forensic psychology? Josie has just been board-certified."

"I know. I can't cite all of Ferguson's credentials right off the top of my head, but I'll fax his résumé. He's won multiple humanitarian awards too."

"He's welcome to join us, Frank. The sooner we find the killer, the better. I just feel more comfortable with people I know."

"Don't we all."

• ● ● ● •

We all arrived at within fifteen minutes of one another. My sister looked stunning when she and Harold Sider blew in. She wore a full-length down coat with a faux-fur ruff bordering the hood. Normally we would have hugged but she simply nodded, said "Hi, Lottie," and promptly took a seat at the table. She had e-mailed before the meeting that she wanted to keep everything strictly professional and minimize our relationship.

Amused, I'd replied that I thought it was a good idea, but honestly! A body would have to be totally blind not to see that we are twin sisters. On the other hand, she indulged in beauty treatments and routines that I never seemed to find the time for. There are days when I look a good ten years older than her.

Enviously, I glanced at Josie. A little touch of Restylane, an occasional shot of Juvéderm. It does wonders. No Botox yet, because she once said her clients needed for her to show a few frown lines. I'm lucky if I remember to apply hand lotion. And the Western Kansas wind can dry out a watermelon. Eastern Kansas was like living in a perpetual spa treatment.

Harold Sider would fit in anywhere. I had never seen him in anything but khaki Dockers and scuffed loafers. He is of medium height and a deceptively pleasant man who keeps his keen mind hidden behind soft cocker-spaniel eyes.

Dr. Evan Ferguson arrived alone. My first impression was that he could compete with Harold for being the least memorable man in the room. Tall and lanky, he wore jeans and a camel-colored turtleneck sweater that thrifty shoppers could find at any mid-price department store. His hair was sandy, parted into a little too obvious a comb-over. His lined face held a slight dust-ing of freckles. He quickly took the seat second from the end of the table, glanced at his watch, and looked at me with concern.

"You're not late. We haven't started. We all seemed to allow a little too much time for bad roads."

"That's good to know. I would hate to be late for the first meeting."

"You're not. Cup of coffee before we start?"

"Sure."

His manner, his dress, his automatic beeline for the least powerful seat available was quite a contrast to Josie's well-tailored black cashmere suit and grooming that would be the envy of movie stars. The contrast made me uncomfortable, but at the time I couldn't have said why.

Most of us knew each other, but I introduced everyone, just to make sure.

Dr. Ferguson turned to Josie. "I've heard a lot about you. In fact, I've read a number of your papers."

"I'm looking forward to becoming better acquainted," she said. "We'll have to talk after the meeting."

I laid out all the facts quickly. There had been two bizarre deaths with no obvious connection whatsoever. The investigation was coming under the jurisdiction of the newly formed regional crime center. "Before we are really equipped to handle it, I might add. In addition to finding the killer or killers, it's important to do the best possible job without depending on the KBI or other agencies. I don't have to tell you the toll budget cuts have taken on this state. Our funding depends on how we handle this."

"But finding the murderers come first, I assume," Evan coached. "Even if we have to call in other people."

Startled, I gave him a sharp look. "Yes, of course. Of course. Finding the killer comes above everything else. I didn't mean that we would limit personnel to make a better financial impression."

"Good to know," Ferguson said.

"Now that it's clear that we're not in this for the money," I said lightly, "I would like to hear the questions or concerns of everyone here. And ideas. Especially ideas."

"The paper is calling this guy The Ghost Baby Killer." Justin Harold was the first to speak up. "Any truth to that?"

Damn, damn, damn. I went into first-class tremor control, but it's hard to fake self-confidence when you don't know the right step forward. "I'm afraid so. For once the papers are right. It's dead babies. Plural."

The heat vent pushed out warm air and the room had gone so quiet the noise sounded like a tornado roaring through.

"But the good news along that line is that there are only these two. The KBI has done a thorough search of statues of women in Kansas and these are the only two that have been the focus of babies left to freeze to death in the arms of female statues. This is loaded with psychological implications, of course." I swallowed hard. It was still hard to talk about it. "Any questions relating to that? Or any ideas? Right now we are grasping at straws. Any old rumors you can remember?'

"The first one was about ten years ago, wasn't it?"

I nodded. "Yes, the one in Hays."

"My mother wouldn't let my sister go to school the next semester. Either that or my sister just didn't want to go."

The buzz started. Odd tales. Some were urban legends. Or I should say rural legends out here. For that matter, one of my history professors insisted that the Elizabeth Polly Park was dedicated to a woman who never existed. We were good at that sort of thing here in Western Kansas. Substituting fiction for fact.

It was a delicate dilemma in family histories. Someone would turn in a story filled with bald-faced lies that they sincerely believed. I learned the hard way they did not want them straightened out by me or anyone else. Early on, I had decided on a policy of never allowing a family member to correct another's version. They could write another story contradicting every word, but they could not correct anything turned in by their relations.

"We don't have much time." Dr. Ferguson glanced at his watch. "This is supposed to be a four-hour meeting. Two this morning, then a break for lunch. If we are going to be out of here by two, I think we might benefit from a more focused approach."

I blinked. He was right, of course. It was easy for free-form thinking to go nowhere. Josie clicked the tip of her pen in and out. Swift disapproval. She kept her eyes down.

"You do have a point there." I kept my voice pleasant. "But all the men here today have lived in their communities for a long time. The people who elected them trust these officers will have their best interests at heart and I've found bits of information can be buried in gossip that didn't seem to be important at the time."

I looked at my sister who continued to keep her eyes lowered. I hoped I hadn't sounded defensive but I couldn't allow

Dr. Ferguson to sabotage my agenda. No matter how many degrees or battle ribbons he held.

"Let's spend another half hour going around the room and collecting whatever we want to call this. Then after lunch we'll give Dr. Ferguson and Dr. Albright time to discuss any insights they might have. After that I'm going to pass out a sheet with relevant information. If we all lived in a central location, we would have a whiteboard like our city cousins where people could follow the development every few days as a group. The best we can do out here will be to come together once a week or every ten days. One of my first organizational jobs will be to figure out how to transmit information that unauthorized persons can't hack into."

"I can hack into anything," David Hayes said flatly. We all turned to look at him. The new undersheriff in Bidwell County didn't look the stereotypical young genius or the brand new exotic female variation on TV. He was heavyset with an ill-fitting uniform and puffy eyelids. He had moved slowly when he came into the room and had to do a little manipulating to settle his overweight body into the seat. If there was a quick brain hidden there somewhere, it had eluded me.

"Will you have time to visit with me after the meeting?"

"If it don't take too long. I have to get back in time to do chores before it turns dark."

Our visiting psychologist gave him a tolerant, courteous smile.

Harold Sider and Josie exchanged glances at the look on Dr. Ferguson's face. Ah, the joy of introducing the good doctor to rural ways. Where half the time no one was what they seemed.

"Any other special skills anyone would like to volunteer?" These would go into a database later.

"Depends on what you're looking for." Justin Harold's ears turned bright red. "I can name plenty of stuff I'm good at, but I can't see where any of it has to do with a regional crime center."

"I know that. This isn't the way I had planned to start the regional organizational meeting. It's falling to us because the state says so. I wanted to start with a solid development plan. With sketches of the proposed center. Beginning with a state-of-the-art communication system. Unified radios, and cell phones that are on the same channel in all of the units."

It was no secret that in the beginning Dimon thought the center should be under state control. Last summer Sam and I had outwitted the state agency. It hadn't set well. We were so unprepared to deal with an investigation this complex that it had a payback feel.

"It's odd that you would be thrown something of this magnitude with so few resources," Evan said, as though he had read my thoughts.

"Lottie has had an unusual breadth of experience," Josie said. Everyone guffawed.

"Carlton County has had more murders per capita than any county in Kansas." This came from Sam who had sat quietly as usual.

"You bragging Sam?"

Sam twisted in his chair to look at Justin. He chuckled. "Just saying."

On that we broke for lunch. Four went off to a fast food place. Sam, Harold Sider, Josie, Dr. Ferguson, and I headed for the Mexican café next door.

●　●　●　●　●

We beat the others back to the meeting room. I went to the hotel desk and asked the clerk to arrange for more pitchers of ice water and more coffee. When I came down the hallway, Dr. Ferguson was standing by the heavy glass outside door staring at Josie's Mercedes SUV. No envy in his face, but something there that made me uneasy.

"Is that your sister's or Harold Sider's?"

"Josie's. Are you a car buff?"

"No. And it's a good thing. I've spent the last two years in Afghanistan dealing with soldiers with severe psychological issues."

I must have looked bewildered.

He noticed. "What I mean by that is that if I had a grand passion to own a beautiful car, I wasn't in a very good place to make good on it. My goal was to stay alive. And help others stay alive." He shrugged and his lips lifted in a self-mocking smile. He shuddered. "It's good to finally be back. I've got a lot of things I want to do."

My curiosity went into overdrive. I knew very little about this man. I was looking forward to what he had to say about our murderer. Ferguson brought a definite asset to the meeting. Coming from a war zone he wouldn't shock easily. My worry was that he would be dismissive about murders that paled in comparison to what he had witnessed on a daily basis.

As to Josie's Mercedes—we grew up in a beautiful house in the elite Mission Hills area of Kansas City, Kansas. Our father had inherited real estate that formed the foundation for the County Club Plaza. I was used to parrying off envy. But sometimes I was blind to the misery around me.

Josie had married a man even wealthier than our father. This was as expected. I married a Western Kansas farmer, a man twenty years older with four children. This was not as expected.

Elizabeth, Keith's oldest daughter was a year older than me. Two of his daughters, Bettina and Angie were reconciled to this second marriage, but Elizabeth and I had clashed from the moment I arrived.

We all took our seats. "Because of the unusual nature of these murders, we're going to give a lot of thought to what our psychologists have to say. I'd like Dr. Ferguson to speak to us first. He's coming to us from the military with the rank of lieutenant colonel where he's seen about everything in the way of violence. He's done two tours in Afghanistan and is now visiting rural Kansas communities to treat veterans with mental health issues."

When Ferguson walked to the front of the room the men stood and applauded, not because they knew anything about him other than what I had just told them, but because of their respect for veterans.

"Thank you for accepting me into this task force." He proceeded to give a grisly account of his murdered comrades, the trauma endured by men he had treated and suffering he had personally witnessed. His voice was well modulated, like he had had training in giving presentations. Just warm enough. Just the right inflection in describing the more terrifying events.

You could have heard a pin drop.

"But enough of my back history. I've been called because of my expertise in profiling killers and you have had a shocking event in this community. So, on to what I'm here for. This is a disorganized killer," Ferguson said solemnly. "Acting impulsively. Someone with a troubled relationship with his mother and an absentee father. Placing the baby in the arms of a woman carved from stone indicates his yearning for a mother's love. He has low intelligence and probably is a manual laborer who is socially inept."

Before he finished, he added that he predicted the killer would begin acting in nine-month intervals because that was the normal gestation period. He called for questions but he had covered nearly everything the men had gathered here to learn about today.

Josie clicked her pen robotically and Harold Sider looked at Ferguson with a veiled expression that disguised his thoughts. Sam stabbed for the missing tobacco pouch he normally kept in his pocket.

"Dr. Albright, do you have anything to add?"

She surprised me. "No, not at this time."

"Harold, how about you? Any insights you want to add to Dr. Ferguson's ideas?"

"None at this time."

"All right. Let's get down to the nitty-gritty, then. Sheriff Winthrop, please canvass the neighborhood around the Garden of Eden and see if anyone noticed anything unusual the night Brent Suter died. The rest of you, investigate in your own counties. Visit anyone that might remember something. Justin, find out what you can about the reasons your sister didn't want to start school." I passed around handouts of very specific jobs based on what I knew about their abilities.

"What about me? I just moved here last year." Scott Smith had replaced Sheriff Deal in Bidwell County.

"You're to help David set up his equipment. Then check with the task force members in the other counties to make sure we have reliable communications. David, please stay a few minutes after we dismiss to discuss the computer work. As for the rest of you, use your computers to keep me posted. We'll have a private newsgroup set up by next Monday. If that's possible?"

David nodded his head.

"You are to let me know immediately if you think of anything else. Keep it private—my eyes only—and I'll decide if the whole group should be informed."

After the meeting, Josie and Harold were driving on out to my home, Fiene's Folly. The remaining men straggled out, clearly pleased to be leaving before the weather turned colder. It took me about five minutes of discussion with David Hayes to determine that he was sharp as a tack and might very well be as good as he thought he was.

Josie had boarded her little shih tzu, Tosca, at a daycare kennel. She and Harold were leaving to pick up the dog when I called them back.

"Okay. Just what in the hell was that all about? You two are mad as hell about something. And I was expecting you to contribute something, Josie. What in the world came over you?"

"Everything that pious son of a bitch said was wrong, wrong, wrong." Her voice was low and furious. "And I'm not only referring to the profile. It's like he's some stupid little college freshman who has gotten drunk before a mid-term and is winging the test based on what he knows from TV shows. Or an amateur psychologist who has watched too many episodes of *Criminal Minds*."

"Do you agree, Harold?"

He nodded. "To the last detail. Not only is it stupid to give a profile this early, what he did say was clearly wrong. For one thing, anyone who can figure out how to get a baby up that high without a boom lift is not disorganized. That's takes some serious planning."

"But why would he give a superficial analysis?"

"Beats me."

Beneath her icy exterior, I knew Josie was in a white hot rage. She didn't say another word.

Chapter Ten

Dorothy was sitting in my favorite chair when I walked in the door. It's by a large bay window so it's ideal for reading. Earlier, she had put a roast in the oven and delicious odors wafted through the kitchen. Cedar logs had been mixed with other woods in the fireplace and sage candles were burning on the mantel. She had made pumpkin pies.

Every home has an aura and every time I walked into mine I felt a deep sense of welcome. I've always appreciated beauty, and the combination of woods and colors would thrill any interior decorator, although Keith's first wife, Regina, was the one who had put it all together.

The kitchen is part of a massive great room. At the end is a huge fireplace large enough to hang pots. The only thing I have done to this room is add leaded-glass inserts to the doors of our kitchen cabinets. They frame embedded emblems of Kansas: a meadowlark, a cottonwood, a man with plow, a sunflower, a spray of little bluestem, and a box turtle. Keith had drawn the line just short of the Great Seal.

Deep brown leather chairs and an oversized sofa assure family and guests that they will fit right in. Not to worry if they spill a drink or doze off. They are still welcome. My only contribution to this area was a decent reading lamp wherever I could stick one. I overruled Keith when he had commented that the bulbs were so bright airplanes would mistake our house for the local runway. I didn't care, but added dimmer switches, just to keep the peace.

Parts of this massive three-story house are over 100 years old and came with the marriage as did the farm and the step-children and the family complications. This is a suicide's house, so by rights, no one should be comfortable here. Keith's unstable tormented first wife was an artist who couldn't survive Kansas. Instead I've always felt that Regina's ghost applauded my efforts to survive the isolation and devastating winds that sweep across the prairie.

Aunt Dorothy was reading the commonplace book. I had left it on the table next to my chair.

"I hope you don't mind," she said. "This is fascinating."

"Isn't it? The poor child."

"What became of him?"

"I don't know. My mind has been on other things, as you well know."

She laid the book aside. "I'm so looking forward to meeting the famous Josie Albright. I often refer to her work for information about abnormal psychology."

"She is quite well published. I'm awfully proud of her. She's a fan of yours, by the way. She's read everything you've ever written and is quite excited that you will be here this weekend."

"She's very kind."

"Can I help with this wonderful meal you've put together? We don't intend for you to be a live-in cook, you know."

She rose. "There's nothing for you to do. We won't start eating until your sister gets here." Her eyes were alight with curiosity but I forestalled any questions about the meeting.

"My sister and Harold. Her friend from Manhattan. He teaches too."

"Friend? No romance?"

I shook my head. "No. Just friends. He was included on the task force because he's helped in Carlton County before. So he knows some of the people here. Plus, he's retired FBI and very sharp."

She didn't follow up on this thread and I was glad. I still felt a deep pang when I thought of Josie and romance. She and Keith's son, Tom, began a doomed affair last summer that threatened to tear the family apart. Josie had called it off when she realized the impossibility of making it work on a permanent basis.

Headlights brightened the lane leading to our house. "They're coming now. Wait until you meet Tosca."

We went to greet them and to my relief, Tosca sized up Dorothy immediately and allowed herself to be picked up. The little dog is an infallible judge of character. She even greeted Dorothy with a lick on the face. After the exchange of introductions, Dorothy put Tosca down on the floor and bustled off to the stove. Keith collected coats and took drink orders. He and Harold settled in chairs by the fire and Josie and I joined Dorothy in the kitchen. We sat at the table while we watched her work.

"Are you worn out?" I asked, because Josie looked exhausted. I knew she was not in the mood to talk and I hoped Dorothy wouldn't push her.

"I'm fine. But can we just eat here in the kitchen? Then I'm going to hit the sack. It's been a long trip and a long day."

I nodded. "I want to go to bed early too. Is your violin still in the car? I think you should bring it in so it won't get too cold."

"Good idea. But the last thing I want to do is play tonight. I can't even stand the thought of it."

Dorothy told the men supper was ready. I smiled. She usually said "dinner." I had to give her credit. She had adapted to Kansas ways already.

"Well, does someone want to fill me in?" Dorothy's question seemed to hover heavily in the air. No one spoke.

Then Josie cleared her throat and began, "Keith, Dorothy, I know you both want to hear about the investigation from a psychological viewpoint but..." Her voice faltered. Her face went pale. "Excuse me, I'm not feeling very well." She took a few sips of water, then rose from the table, apologized again and headed for the stairs.

Dorothy looked bewildered.

"We've had a rough day," Harold explained. He proceeded to tell her and Keith about Dr. Ferguson. "Josie is an expert in her field and she didn't want to jump up and contradict every word the man said, but short of that, there was no stopping him. He's taking everything in the wrong direction. The hell of it was, people believed him. We could see it in their faces."

"His being in the military, and a lieutenant colonel at that, added to his credibility. It always does. Doesn't mean officers are always are right, though." Keith spoke from experience, having been in Vietnam.

"Harold is right about everyone believing Dr. Ferguson. I had the feeling the team would follow him anywhere." I rose and collected their plates and carried them to the sink.

● ● ● ● ●

I was still in my robe when Josie came down the next morning. Usually professional down to the last strand of glossy hair, I was surprised to see her in worn jeans and an old sweatshirt. She had swept her hair up in a careless bun.

Dorothy planned to come over later. Outside my kitchen window the world was solid white. The bottom of the pane was covered with frosty snow crystals. Steam from the heat in the kitchen clouded the view.

I was conscious of Josie's every movement, but mostly her quietness.

"Sleep well?"

She answered with a slight shake of her head. I felt like I was trying to engage a stranger. There were faint blue shadows under her eyes which no amount of concealer could disguise.

Josie is more logical than I. But beneath her logic is the heart of an artist, and in fact, she had once considered a career as a concert pianist. Ultimately, she recognized that she had too many varied interests to spend hours and hours every day practicing, which is required to reach the top.

She walked to the window and began tracing hearts on the steamed windows. Then rubbed out the drawing and stood staring at the branches of the snow-laden cedar trees.

"Coffee?"

She continued to stare out the window as though she hadn't heard. I shrugged. It didn't matter. I knew she was overwhelmed. On edge. Josie's clientele was elite and well-educated. She was the most fashionable psychologist in the state for people who could afford the best. I suspected her first foray into chasing down a serial killer was a hell of a lot different than reading about them in college textbooks or treating well-heeled matrons with carefully cultivated depressions.

Her one-eighty-degree turn into forensic psychology made no sense whatsoever. I could not see her fighting monsters. It was a gross misplacement of her talent. Like showing up yesterday wearing diamond earrings and a cashmere suit. On the other hand, she had always insisted on being herself, no matter what the circumstances. And if "herself" meant diamonds and designer clothes, and it bothered other people, it was their problem and none of hers.

Her "real self" had caused some complications with Keith's family. However, the only one of Keith's children she actively clashed with was his oldest daughter, Elizabeth.

Elizabeth, a lawyer, lived in Denver and was a passionate advocate for abused women. She wore clothes made of cloth woven by women in impoverished countries and drove an ancient Volkswagen. Elizabeth was quick to chastise Josie for any and every display of ostentatious wealth.

I poured Josie a cup of coffee anyway and placed it beside her on the windowsill. She picked it up without comment, sipped, and then made a wry face. She went to the pantry and located my lone box of overpriced nutrition-deprived cereal which I kept just for her. Smart choice. It went well with her cigarettes.

"Did you tape any of yesterday's meeting?" she asked suddenly.

"No. I didn't think it was necessary."

"Did you write down any of that man's idiotic profile?"

"No." Taken aback, I glanced at her face. Technically, she should have been the one to get Ferguson's analysis on paper.

"I asked him to send me a written report so I could send it to all the men."

"Just my luck." She took a couple of sips of coffee. "Then I'll have to go by memory until we get it. I don't want to make any mistakes with this. I assume he'll either use e-mail or perhaps the fax."

"E-mail. Until we get everything set up. Right now, my little corner in the sheriff's office is the headquarters for the regional center."

She turned. "*Your* little corner? Don't tell me you are still the undersheriff?"

"Not exactly. Just in title only. Until the center is in full operation."

"And what exactly does 'not exactly' mean?"

"It means I'm sort of on call, but when Sam isn't there, the office is manned by a couple of deputies and some reserve deputies. Most of the time," I added lamely.

"And the historical society?"

"Margaret and Jane Jordan have taken over most of the jobs. They bring anything to me they think needs special attention."

"And Angie? Does she still live here with you and Keith?"

"No. She's kept busy helping Father Talesbury run the foundation and sanctuary. She decided to live in one of the empty houses on the compound."

Last year, I became embroiled in solving a grisly murder in Roswell County. In the process an ancient Spanish lady ended up willing me her priceless collection of books, a wealth of herbal wisdom, a hidden heritage of natural resources, and a lawsuit that would probably go on forever. Angie, Keith's youngest daughter, oversaw the cultivation and sale of the plants and rare herbs that financed the work of the Francesca Diaz Research Foundation located on the land I had inherited. Researchers there studied the effects of natural healing methods in combination with traditional medicine.

Father Talesbury, the Episcopal priest who operated a shelter for recovering African child soldiers, was chairman of the board of directors and a worthy adversary against the greedy reach of the United States government.

"Dorothy is renting a little house in town. She comes out here sometimes. But basically, she's on her own. And doing well. More than well. She might as well have hung out a sign at The Coffee Shop: Writer in Residence—Come tell her your story. She's collecting information that people would never tell me. Maybe because I'm the undersheriff, or maybe because she just has a special way about her."

The sunlight on the kitchen table altered, shifted briefly to a flickering shadow, then steadied.

"Whoops! Speaking of town dwellers, I think we are about to have company. Here's Dorothy now." We watched through the frost rimmed windows as she parked and cautiously made her way up the walk. Keith had shoveled it this morning, but it was still slick in spots.

"Hello, hello," I called. I took her coat and hung it on a peg in our mudroom.

"I'm so glad to get inside. My house is fine, but the heat in my car is a bit spotty."

She stomped her feet to remove excess snow, and started to take off her shoes.

"No need to do that."

"Perhaps. But I brought extra slippers just in case. I'm eager to talk with your sister and go over a few thoughts I've had about the case."

"Go right on in. She's just finished breakfast." Such as it was. Sugar and cigarettes.

When she entered, Dorothy glanced at the commonplace book lying on the table beside the bay window chair. Since I hadn't officially logged it in as an acquisition at the historical society, I carried it back and forth between home and the sheriff's office.

"When we've finished, I want to read that poor boy's book some more. Did Lottie tell you about it, Josie? I think you will be really interested. It's the most fascinating reading I've come across in a long time. And that's saying something." She folded both hands on top of the walking stick and surveyed the room.

Dorothy missed nothing and there was a quickly disguised flicker of interest when she looked at my twin who simply did not look well. "And I have some questions to ask you about the child in the book too."

"The case first, please," Josie said, ignoring Dorothy's attempts at small talk. "I was too mad to talk to anyone last night. I apologize if I seemed rude. And as for Harold, he agrees with everything I am going to say but he's beyond mad. He's absolutely livid. We talked about it all the way on the drive back from Hays"

"Really? He didn't look that upset when he came in last night."

"No, he didn't. He makes a point not to." She filled Dorothy in on her background. "I've just now passed the board for my degree in forensic psychology, but Harold is an old pro. I have a large private practice and have been focused on helping people, not solving crimes. But Harold can extract information from serial killers without a flicker of disapproval on his face. He said he had never been put in such a bizarre situation before."

"You mean the crime?"

"No. He's seen about everything. He means a psychologist acting so inappropriately." She dug her lighter out of her purse and looked at Dorothy. "Do you mind if I smoke?"

She no longer bothered to ask me. She already knew I minded and just didn't give a damn. She smoked anywhere she chose anyway.

"No. I don't mind." Dorothy managed a little smile and I suspected she was a reformed sinner. "And by the way, would you and Lottie like some privacy?"

Josie rose and went to the cabinet containing our one and only ash tray. Out of Dorothy's line of sight she shot me a quick questioning glance.

"No privacy needed," I said. "Anything Josie has to say about the case, you can hear too." With these words I had just issued Dorothy a full acceptance into the team. Beyond her formal status, she was now privy to unofficial speculation. All barriers to information had been removed. I hoped that was wise.

Dorothy's eyes flickered with quiet gratitude. She had read me right from the very beginning. There had been a reluctance on my part to fully include her because I wasn't sure if she could be trusted to keep her mouth shut. And I was uneasy over the number of people who were now members of the regional team investigating this case. People like Ferguson that I didn't know from Adam's off ox.

Josie went to the window and looked at the snow-covered cedar trees again before she sat down again. "There's so much we need to tell you about that I hardly know where to start. First of all, what Dr. Ferguson did yesterday was so wrong that Harold had trouble just sitting there."

"Like what?" Dorothy fished her tea bag out of her cup before she took another sip.

"Let's begin with the profile. One never, never gives a profile this early in the investigation. I mean never. Plus, what he did give was wrong, wrong, wrong. He said the killer was disorganized when he clearly isn't. He said the suspect had low intelligence and was a manual laborer. Is he kidding?"

"Why?"

"Why? That's it in a nutshell. What in the hell is he thinking? His jumping up and giving an immediate profile is the most bewildering thing. But that's not all. He tried to take the meeting away from Lottie. He smirked during everything she had to say. Smirked."

"Believe me, I'm used to dealing with men who make power plays. In this county there are many who thought a female shouldn't be the undersheriff. Then they decided it wasn't that big a deal since I was subservient to Sam. But when I was put in charge of the regional crime center all hell broke loose. The general feeling is that a woman should not be bossing men around. Especially all the sheriffs in nine counties."

"I simply can't believe the mentality out here." Josie blew a large smoke ring.

"And Ferguson may not have been smirking. He has this scar at the corner of his mouth that makes him look like he is." They both turned and stared at me. I might as well been talking to them in Greek. "Smirking. Not."

"Oh, for God's sake, Lottie. You would defend the devil if he came at you with a hand ax." Josie rose and crushed her cigarette. "I'm going for a walk."

"I don't think you can. Too much snow. And I wasn't defending him. I'm just trying to keep my emotions out of this for once. He does have this scar."

This was a fine howdy-do. I'm usually the one who is whipped around like a kite in free fall and Josie is the one who keeps things in perspective.

She immediately lit another cigarette. "Sorry," she mumbled, but directed her next words to Dorothy. "That's not all. You should have seen the reaction of the men at the meeting. They looked at Ferguson like he was Jesus Christ come to save them."

"I saw a taste of that when we were at the Garden of Eden. Lottie was not the one the men wanted to follow." Dorothy moved her chair a little to keep the sun out of her eyes. "They wanted Sheriff Winthrop to take the lead. She had to put them in their place."

I was very, very quiet. I know exactly when to let my sister rant, but was surprised she would do so in the presence of Keith's aunt.

"Where are you from, Dorothy?" Josie asked suddenly.

"New York."

"Another complication is having to drive to Hays to get us all together just because it's a regional KBI location." She carried her half-eaten cereal to the sink and dumped it down the garbage disposal.

"There wasn't another place available that would give us some privacy," I pointed out. "I couldn't have us meet in the courthouse. That place has a thousand ears."

Dorothy's tea kettle shrieked and Josie lifted it off the burner and carried to the table. The hot water released the sharp odor of Earl Gray. Josie continued her rant. "Let me enlighten you about law enforcement's tacky grid of technology systems out here. Some of the county sheriffs just barely know how to operate a fax. Even Lottie has to go to the historical society to transmit some files."

I said nothing.

"And see that goddamn snow?" She waved her hand toward the window. "See? That means powerlines will be iced over. Or down. On the ground somewhere. With understaffed crews busting their asses trying to get everything up and running again. Some of the lines will be brought down when trees or posts topple over. The crews will take care of the hospital first. Which makes sense. But still."

"We have great systems here in this house. State of the art. Nextech put in everything Keith asked for." I was tempted to drag her to the cable box and make her look.

"So what makes the power out here any better?" Dorothy asked. "It snows here too."

"Keith's generators." Josie walked over to the ash tray and crushed out her second cigarette. "He could run Manhattan on all his substitute systems."

"Keith doesn't want to take a chance on his vet clinic freezing," I explained to Dorothy. "He has a fortune tied up in medication and equipment. And he can't risk having power go off during surgery."

"Under the best of circumstances, the only place in town that gives a nod to the twenty-first century is the historical society. And Lottie paid for everything there." Josie reached into a purse and pulled out another cigarette and helplessly looked around for her misplaced lighter. Spying it on the windowsill, she walked over and retrieved it. She turned the lighter over and over, then placed it beside the coffee pot and her still unlit cigarette. I stared. She never misplaced things and normally, she immediately put her lighter back in her purse.

My sister is an unusually mindful person. It unnerved me to see her so rattled. Her face had a grayish cast. Her glossy hair was coming unpinned.

"Won't that be fun? Interrupting the 'girls' at the historical society to call the KBI and transmit confidential information?"

"It won't be that way forever," I protested. "We are going to have state-of-the-art equipment in the new regional center."

"Are you sure of the funding, Lottie? I've heard budget cuts in Kansas have been very severe."

"I've been promised. That's all I know. Dimon said so."

"Another thing, Dorothy. Have you noticed there aren't any women on the team other than Lottie?"

It was the last straw. They were on the team too. They were women.

So this was how it was going to be. Not only was I going to have to put the menfolk in their place, I was going to have to take on my sister—an arrogant psychologist—and a mystery writer who was undoubtedly planning a new series based on these crimes. Plus, a crazy killer.

Whether due to frustration or being cooped up or our anguish over our helplessness to find a murderer, we were getting on each other's nerves.

I refused to contribute to their bitchiness. "Excuse me, I'm going to get dressed." I headed for the stairs before I said something I would regret.

Chapter Eleven

Keith had left a note by the phone saying he was out doctoring a sick horse. I went into the master bathroom. There were large his and hers walk-in closets at one end. I raked through my clothes and pulled out a pair of cranberry corduroy slacks, and grabbed a blouse in a companion print. I slipped into my Danskos and headed for the mirror. I winced, then opened my makeup cabinet and proceeded to do my best.

I made a mental note to make an appointment at a spa in Hays. The works, I decided, as soon as they could get me in. At least microdermabrasion. Maybe even a chemical peel. In the meantime, a layer of moisturizer and foundation and taking care with my eye makeup did wonders. A touch of blush and some lipstick did even more. Pleased, I decided that I looked just right. Professional without being affected.

I straightened my shoulders and went down the stairs and back into the kitchen to take charge of the investigation. Keith came through the back door. Tosca wriggled off of Josie's lap and headed for his arms.

"Everything go all right with the house call?"

He nodded and rose from his haunches holding the ecstatic little shih tzu.

"Good. You're just in time for the fireworks." I phoned Dimon right there from the kitchen where everyone could hear and put the call on speaker phone.

"Frank, I've decided in the future all meetings will be held here at the farm until the regional center is built and fully equipped."

There was absolute silence on his end. Then, "Why would you make such a stupid move, Lottie? It's not suitable. You can't meet in a goddamn farm house. There's no precedent for it. Besides it won't look good."

"There's no precedent for this kind of case either. But I don't have anything to work with. My job is to actually stop a killer, and I really don't care what things look while I'm doing it. We have state-of-the-art electronics out here."

That thrum again, but I didn't give him a chance to marshal his thoughts.

"Also, our farm is central. I've gone to great lengths to include someone from all nine counties in this investigation. You've approved my list. Not that I need your approval since you gave me full autonomy. This is where we're going to meet until the legislature funds a building and equipment."

"Your place isn't central for everyone. It will be damned inconvenient for Dr. Ferguson. He'll have to drive all the way from Topeka."

"Yes. I used to drive all the way *to* Topeka. Same distance." I slammed down the phone.

Harold had joined the gathering around the table. I whirled around to face them. "Now that the gang is all here. We have a great deal to take care of before the next whole group meeting so let me get to your assignments right away. You first, Keith. As painful as this is going to be for you. I want you go back out to the Suters' and figure out why that kid was in the Garden of Eden to begin with. There has to be a reason.

"Victimology," Harold nodded his approval. "That's always the first step."

"And why would anyone want to kill this apparently perfect kid?" Josie said. "That's been bothering me the most."

"Not apparently, Josie. Is perfect—was, rather, damn near perfect." Keith didn't bother to disguise his sorrow. "No one's perfect, I guess. But Brent came awfully close. Not perfect in a goody goody sort of way, either." He looked out the window.

"Dorothy, we'll have a thorough report about the crime scene today. Copies of all the photographs the team took in addition to the pictures you took before the team from Topeka got there. You are very, very good at noticing details." *To say the least.* She was like having a live-in spy satellite in my house. "Go over this report and compare it with the photos. See if you can spot anything we need to zero in on."

"Harold, included in the autopsy reports Topeka is sending over will be lots of photos. I want you to go over those and let me know if you have any questions before Brent Suter is buried. And the baby also. We don't even know whose baby this is. Was. For the time being she will be held in the morgue at Topeka while we try to find the mother."

Alone in a morgue. Taken from the arms of cold statue to lie on a cold slab. I shuddered.

"And that leaves you, Josie. I want you to find out everything you can about the members of our team. We need to start compiling a list of strengths and weaknesses. For instance, is David Hayes the computer expert he thinks he is?"

"Right. And I want to know more about Dr. Ferguson." A faint smile crossed Josie's face.

I grinned. "I don't think he will be around too much longer. A couple of trips across Kansas to this farm and I kind of think he's going to want a new assignment." I made another note on my planning list. "Also, I want you to meet Merilee Suter. Either on a visit with me or by yourself. Whichever you think would be best. I want your professional opinion on the state of her mental health."

"Okay, but it will be a little hard to tell without running some tests."

"I know, but I'm worried about her."

"What about Sam?" Keith asked.

"I want him and Sheriff Winthrop to put their heads together and figure out how someone got that baby up into the arms of *Reaching Woman*."

"Will Sheriff Winthrop be included on the regional team?" Dorothy asked. Clearly she had enjoyed his attention.

"Just on this specific case. His county is outside the proposed jurisdiction. But obviously he wants it included. If I let that happen it's hard telling how many other counties will want to be part of it. Then we might as well be a satellite of Topeka taking orders from Dimon or God only knows who."

Harold nodded thoughtfully. "You'll have your hands full with nine counties."

"It's a load."

"What's the next step after we finish the work you just assigned?

"I want written reports. Not just the facts, I want your insights and opinions and gossip and old wives tales. Everything. I mean everything."

A fax tone shrieked in Keith's office. He rose and came back with a large stack of reports and copies of photos. "From Dimon," He walked around the table and gave the crime scene photos to Dorothy, and the autopsy information to Harold. "Looks like Lottie is going to keep busy figuring out the next steps while Josie sorts out how crazy we are individually instead of just in a group. As for me, I'll be at the Suters helping them figure out who would want to kill the all-American boy.

● ● ● ● ●

After Keith's car disappeared down the lane, we cleared the table and went to separate areas of the house to concentrate. Dorothy went to her car and retrieved her laptop computer.

Josie collected a list of the team members from each of the nine counties then disappeared upstairs to see if anything on the Internet popped up about persons involved in the investigation. It didn't take her long. In a little over an hour she was back downstairs with a preliminary report. "They are all bland, bland, bland. Except for Dr. Ferguson. And guess what? His military records are sealed."

"Okay. I'll bet there's no way to get access to them. Go ahead and finish. We'll compare notes when we're done."

"When will that be?"

"Probably later today. Everyone is going lickety-split."

Dorothy came into the kitchen. "All done."

"Everything written up, too?"

"Sure. I'll find something else to do while everyone finishes. I imagine the last person will be Keith since he's making a physical call instead of just looking at photos or using a computer." She headed for the bay window chair. "Back to my favorite pastime." She plopped down and picked up the commonplace book.

Josie headed back up the stairs to finish writing her report, but Dorothy called after her before she got to the top. "I need to know something from a psychologist's point of view. What does it mean when someone suddenly starts writing in free verse?"

"I honestly don't know. He hasn't done it before?"

"No. I just think it's odd, that's all." She flipped ahead in the notebook. "The writing gets really messy for a while. Which is strange because before this, he had an immaculate hand. Almost calligraphy. It goes on for about five more pages."

Josie shrugged and didn't come down again until it was time for supper.

Keith didn't come dragging in until after four. "Still want a written report?" he asked.

"Yes."

"It will take a bit."

"I'm ordering in pizza so take your time. No need to rush." I glanced around the room at all the exhausted faces. "In fact, I think we need a break. We'll start again tomorrow after we've had a decent night's sleep. Dorothy, you're welcome to stay here tonight it you want to."

"If you don't mind, I think I will."

When I got up to use the bathroom in the middle of the night I noticed a light shining from the bottom of the stairs. I went to the landing. The lamp beside my chair was still on. I went downstairs to check and found Dorothy fast asleep with the commonplace book on her lap. Jeans clad, she wore one of her seemingly endless supply of heavy cable sweaters. She exuded a faint aroma of lavender. Head drooping on her chest, she snored gently. Her heavy plain features complemented her pleasantly stocky body.

I had a sudden insight that she had been born into the wrong century. It was easy to imagine her on a homestead gathering cow chips for fuel, bearing children, wringing out the weekly wash, and cooking all the meals over an old stove. It was much harder to imagine her on the streets of New York.

Shamelessly studying this human enigma as though she were a concrete statue I wondered about her road less traveled. Did she regret never marrying? Had she taken lovers? Did writing make her happy? I switched off the lamp and turned on a dim night light next to the stairs. At some point she might want to go up to her bedroom and I didn't want her to stumble.

Curious about the variation in handwriting, I carried the commonplace book to the sofa and began to read.

> *Someone left a* New Testament *and a* Book of Common Prayer *outside St. Helena's Episcopal Church. It was going to rain so I rescued them. I know about the Bible and all that stuff but Biddy has never taken me to church. She says it's not for the likes of us and I would be an embarrassment to her.*
>
> *I skipped back and forth between the two books and checked off the things I thought were a good idea.*
>
> *I believe in God the Father, the creator. Knowing about God makes some things a lot clearer. Like where the Earth comes from. I had already figured out before I found this Bible that in the beginning there had to be something that always was. It's the only thing that makes sense. Believing in God is easy.*
>
> *But Jesus! I believe in Jesus but I don't like him. According to a creed in the Prayer Book he became man. But why would he want to? I've never known anyone—male or female—who is kind. I would never want to be like Jesus. If I saw him coming down the road I would cross to the other side.*

And then there is the Holy Spirit and I love the Holy Spirit with all my heart. He's what makes my heart glad when all my little animals are around me. He's what makes the leaves greener and shimmery some days. Some days I lie beneath my tree so filled with joy I become one with all the creatures and the land and sky and I'm over-whelmed with tenderness for everything living.

On one of the days when I felt like that, I held a Com-munion service for the animals. The right words are in the Book of Common Prayer. *I used a stump for an altar and covered it with leaves. On it I placed a couple of nuts for the squirrels and seeds for the birds. They all came. Even the crows gathered.*

We made a joyful noise unto the Lord.

The Father, the Holy Spirit. Sorry, Jesus, but two out of three is plenty good enough.

• • ● • •

The next morning we were all a mess. Keith cussed a blue streak when he spilled some of his coffee. Dorothy dashed over to clean it up like she was an indentured servant. I overcooked the scrambled eggs. Josie chain-smoked without a single "I'm sorry." Most surprising of all was Harold. After wandering from window to window and gazing at the ice-clad horizon, he ate a couple slices of toast then announced that he was "going for a stroll" before we got started.

By the time he got back Sam had arrived. I had called John Winthrop and invited him to sit in if he liked, but he begged off saying he had plenty of snow-related emergencies of his own to contend with. "Just give me the bottom line," he said. "I'm still busy asking around to see if anyone saw anything."

"Okay. We'll have a meeting with everyone here in a couple of days." I explained the reason for the switch to our farm. "We're technology paradise. The Hays location is not. Maybe meeting here will light a fire under the state budget committee. We've tried pleading and logic. Now we're going to apply shame."

"We both know who is not going to like this one," Winthrop said after a long pause. "Two whos, actually."

"Yes. Dimon and Dr. Ferguson."

I made a fresh pot of coffee and we all gathered around the large cherry table in the family room. "Dorothy, you go first. What did you find in the crime scene photos?"

She rose and walked around the table passing out copies of her report. "Please check the upper right hand corner. See all the footprints leading to the mausoleum? Those were made by the ineptest first-responders on the planet. They destroyed any credible evidence. Unless the crime scene investigators from Topeka find something having to do with fiber, we're hosed."

"So nothing we need to follow up on?"

"No, but I included some recommendations in my report. Obviously, these two murders, the boy and the baby are our immediate priority, but I believe you need to be improving the system as you go. The regional center is yours to set up any way you like. You need to start by going to every single town and training response teams so they won't screw things up again. But you have a real advantage right now. No one knows what a regional center should look like."

"If this works, I think Kansas will be divided into regional multi-county law enforcement centers." I made a follow-up note of Dorothy's suggestion for first-responder training. "Josie, you're next. What did you find out about the team members?"

"No red flags for any of them No criminal records. Not even sealed juvenile records. I hit a little speed bump with Dr. Ferguson because he was in intelligence in the Army. There were some things I couldn't access, but that is usually the case with the intelligence branch. He taught here at Hays one semester before he was called to Iraq. Did you know that?"

"No, but I know his life was interrupted a couple of times. No surprises, then?"

"Just one. Our computer expert, the undersheriff from Bidwell County, David Hayes. He's more than an expert. He's a superb hacker. He was hired by the government to help break some coding used by a white collar crime team." Josie passed around her report on the team, then reached for Tosca who was waiting patiently for access to her lap.

"Hacker?" said Harold. "That's ominous. Means he doesn't mind going to the dark side."

"Well, he didn't." Josie looked at him curiously. "Go to the dark side."

"He did," Harold rose abruptly, his hands extended like he was on the verge of making a speech. We couldn't take our eyes off of him. Then snapped his pencil in half. "He did go to the dark side. Or the government wouldn't have enlisted him. I'll bet my supper they offered him some kind of plea for his assistance and that's why he doesn't have some kind of a record."

"But he's good?" Unnerved by Harold's tension, I made another note. "He'll be able to do whatever we need him to do?"

"Oh, yes. He's goddamn good. You can bet on that."

"So, about the autopsy report. That was your bailiwick, Harold. Did something jump out at you?"

"No. Except there wasn't a trace of any kind of drug in the baby's body. The killer didn't even have enough compassion to put the little girl asleep before he put her in the arms of *Reaching Woman*. Cruel son of a bitch," he said softly. "The Suter kid's death was pretty clear-cut. A handgun at close range. Hollow point bullets. Can't get any deadlier than that."

"Do you think Suter showing up took the bastard by surprise?" Sam asked.

Harold began to pace as he jingled some coins in his pocket. "No, I don't. Why would Suter be there if someone didn't coax him to come? Or threaten him. Merilee Suter said Brent got a phone call before he left and he seemed excited. I want to know who called him. And why."

"Any recommendations, Harold? For proceeding?"

"None."

"Keith, you haven't said a word. Did you learn anything new at the Suters?"

"Like why anyone would want to kill Brent? No, the only thing that's changed is that no one in the family is holding anything back. So that leaves all of us racking our brains for a motive."

He glanced at Dorothy and then at the report in his hands. "Under the 'suggestions for proceeding' category that Lottie keeps prodding us to come up with. Our first job should be to find the crime scene."

"It's the Garden of Eden," I blurted.

"Only Brent. He was killed there. I'm talking about the baby. Not the one in the Garden of Eden. The one before that. The Blue Light Baby. Were there others? Killed by a different method? Dorothy has done a lot of investigation. There were no reports of a pregnant woman missing around Kansas. Did he snatch the mother from another state? Did he cross state lines? If so, it's a federal crime and we can call in some really heavy guns whenever we wish."

"No. That's not going to happen." I slapped his report down on the table. "We can do this. Local investigation is more effective. We can tap sources that are closed to the KBI. We know our own communities. Every person. Every rock and tree."

"Okay, then where is the mother? Is she alive or is she dead? Is she the only one? How can we find a killer if we can't even find the mother?"

No one said a word.

He spread his fingers wide apart and studied them as though there were an answer there somewhere. "I went to the Suters' to see if I could learn something about their son that might help us. Pat and Ernie hung on every word I said. Trying to reassure them sucked." He punched his fist into his palm. "I'm not putting any of you down, but we're simply not getting anywhere."

I looked around at their faces. Clearly everyone agreed with my husband. I drew a deep breath. I had to act fast. Just two more days before the total task force would gather. We couldn't bring this attitude into the meeting.

"Okay, point taken, Keith. But if we aren't true believers in our ability to find this killer you can bet no one else will be either."

There was a subtle sigh of relief that I wasn't offended. "Anyone else care to share your reservations with the group?"

No one spoke.

"Okay, I want to meet with each of you individually. Keith, you first." They started shoving back their chairs.

He waited in our bedroom. His shoulders were squared and his strong legs braced. We were both spoiling for a fight. My fists were clenched against my thighs. I tore right into him. "What's up, Keith? 'Not getting anywhere?' Seriously? You haven't even given me a week? Were you expecting clues sprinkled like bread crumbs? You knew when you were deputized this was going to be hard."

"The Suters is 'what's up.'" He looked at me with his troubling sharp-eyed way. Willing me to understand. "We've got to get up to speed fast. That family is broken. They will never be the same. I'm going to find the bastard that did this if it's the last thing I do. By whatever means it takes."

Whatever more he had to say I didn't want to hear it. I knew that look; unswerving, barely controlled tension pulsing at the base of his rock-hard jaw, teeth clamped. I knew what he meant by "whatever means it takes." He intended to step outside the law if it was necessary. The law as it is written, that is.

He is a very moral man with a strong sense of right and wrong. Thank God he is a thinker too. If it weren't for his compassion he would be unbearable and a righteous zealot. Keith's as fair as they come, but he has an unwavering sense of justice. And to him natural law as it is written on the human heart trumped the regulations written on paper.

Once he had retrieved a kid's 4-H calf that had "strayed" into his neighbor's pasture. He blatantly drove into the man's farmstead without so much as a wave to the astonished farmer, loaded the calf onto the pickup, and drove right back out. Wordless confrontation. No need to involve the law.

We've both sworn the same oaths. Bound to the same standard. I intended to adhere to it and play by the book. He wouldn't hesitate to burn the book if it was necessary.

I splayed my fingers across my face and closed my eyes against the memory of the many, many incidents when he'd decided there was 'no need to involve the law.' Justice was clear-cut.

I pretended I misunderstood his intentions. "Of course. We will all do whatever it takes to find this monster. We all will do our best. Did you think we wouldn't?"

Barely able to contain my fury I turned and headed for the stairs.

He called after me. "Lottie, I owe the group an apology. I was out of line to challenge you during a meeting."

"Sorry won't restore the damage your doubts did."

"I'll do what I can do to make…"

I paused on the landing. "Harold is next. We need to keep things moving."

Chapter Twelve

Harold came up to the loft five minutes later. His face was red like he had been outdoors during the time I talked with Keith.

"What's on your mind?" I asked bluntly. "Something is. You looked like you wanted to say more during the meeting."

"Keith has a point, Lottie. This whole investigation is a bunch of crap."

I stiffened. Him too?

"This whole setup is a farce." Harold didn't take his eyes off my face. "You don't have a thing to work with. I want to know who is responsible and I'm going to get to the bottom of it. At warp speed."

It's hard to look professional when you've been slapped down hard. Even Ferguson had commented on the lack of resources at the first meeting. "No one, I mean no one, would block us from catching this monster."

"Would Dimon?"

"No way. I know that man."

Harold walked to the window and jingled the coins in his pocket while he stared at the snow. Drew out a quarter and tossed it into the air. Caught it and repeated this action a couple of times before he returned to the table, braced his arms and leaned forward while he gazed at me intently.

"We're talking about a son of a bitch who freezes little babies to death. You've been thrown into a major atypical case without one bit of training. You don't know a goddamn thing about crime scene investigation. Or interrogation. Or even conducting a decent law enforcement meeting."

"What was wrong with the meeting?"

"It was far too informal. Too much discussion. All those written reports weren't necessary. Don't encourage hunches and impressions. Emphasize hard evidence. Anything else will screw you up. Task force meetings can't be show and tell. You have to lead."

I felt for a strand of loose hair straying from my French roll and tucked it back while I organized my rebuttal. "The whole point of creating a regional center, Harold, is because no one, and I mean virtually no one on the local level, has had any training out here. Not in investigation or interrogation techniques. And I conduct perfectly adequate meetings when I'm dealing with issues I know something about."

"That's just it. You don't know what you are doing. In fact, even I don't know what I'm doing. I'm glad the whole team wasn't here today."

I said nothing while my mind raced. Keith, Harold, how many others thought this regional team wasn't up to the job?

"No offense intended." He paused long enough to look at me to see how I was taking it, then didn't bother to soften his words. "But case in point, much as I love this setting it's not even remotely appropriate."

"But we have more equipment than anywhere else in the county except for the historical society."

"That may be, but no one is going to take a meeting seriously that takes place around the kitchen table like we are discussing a killer over a hand of bridge."

"Harold, driving clear to Hays is a waste of time. The facilities there are terrible. The equipment here at Fienes' farm is far superior."

"Then let's bring the sheriff's office up to snuff right away and bypass the state."

"Seriously?"

"You bet. I'm going to call in a few chips."

"We need to let everyone know you were trained at Quantico and were a regional agent in charge."

"No, don't. Not yet. There's something funny going on. It's almost as though someone wants you to fall flat on your face."

My stomach lurched. Dimon and I quarreled a lot but he was a good man. A decent human being. Certainly, I knew he wanted the regional facility under state control. Would love to see me back in my ivory tower. Where I belonged. Writing academic papers.

Dimon would put finding the Ghost Baby Killer first. Above everything else. I took a deep breath. First how? Was he actually working the crime from Topeka? Had the regional center been cut off and disposed of like an unseemly growth?

I put my suspicions aside and focused on Harold. I had to proceed as though everything was up to me. "What do you have in mind?"

"Postpone the team meeting until Friday. In the meantime, you need to figure out the next step for everyone on this task force. While you are taking care of that I'll import a team of experts who specialize in setting up technology systems. They'll work around the clock. Where will the new regional building be located?"

"About a half mile from the sheriff's office. Right on the outskirts of town. But for now, there is a huge room in back of Sam's office. We use it for storage. Some old evidence files. Old artifacts from the local museum. Banners for the harvest parade. Stuff like that. It's drafty with no heat. We could use it for whatever you have in mind."

"In short, you live in a very peaceful no-event county."

"Yes, until recent years, and then all hell broke loose."

Sam would be put out over having his office disrupted. It was like pulling hen's teeth to get him to agree to any change.

"I need your permission to make this official. You're the regional director. I can't just waltz in and make county property into a tech paradise unless you say so." Having made his case, Harold stood in total silence watching my face.

I was not unnerved. I had used silence as a tool plenty of times myself.

But I needed a ten-minute break to think. The key word was "county property." People donated stuff all the time, I reasoned, and we didn't need to get the commissioners' permission to put small stuff to use. A microwave here, an office chair there. The last time the office had been painted both the supplies and labor were kicked in by the local lumber yard. The same reasoning should apply to a large contribution to a regional setup.

My gut took over. No one had the authority to take this investigation away from me, and letting Harold intervene to this extent could be viewed as a sign of weakness. Or intelligence. Hard telling. People skew facts to support their opinions.

A gust of wind rattled the window. I shivered. *Face it, face it, face it.* As Harold pointed out, we were up against a stone-cold monster who froze little babies to death. I didn't have enough expertise. Or equipment

I'm not a fool. My job was to catch a killer by whatever means possible.

Besides, Harold was FBI, KBI, a by-the-book man at heart—retired or not—and I could only screw up so much before he blew the whistle on me. I trusted him, but bottom line, he would do the right thing. Make a call to Dimon. Put a stop to too much blundering. I didn't know whether to be furious or grateful. I could only go on one thing right now. He made sense. He was telling me the appearance of ineptness would so affect the troop's cooperation that he didn't dare let it go any further. The kitchen table approach was impossibly amateurish.

"Okay. Set up any and everything you think is necessary at the sheriff's office."

"And Sam? Can you square this with Sam?"

"I can tickle him into it. It will take some talking."

He smiled.

"I want the men to know more about your credentials, Harold. You can certainly take a more active role at meetings."

He shook his head. "No way. It's imperative that I stay in the background. I have already been tagged as FBI. Everyone knows Josie. She's a rising star in the forensic field. But the good ol' boys out here think she's too fancy to be taken seriously. Lucky for us, I'm just known as a harmless little old worker drone who's become a criminal justice professor after I retired."

Surprised, I looked at him. *You mean he wasn't? Just who was this man?*

"The team I have in mind will oversee the physical remodeling of the room so it's comfortable and functional."

"Oh, no way in hell. You can be in charge of technology installation, but that's where I draw the line. I want wood laminate floors that won't absorb spills. Enamel paint that's stain-proof." My list went on. It included a decent coffee pot.

"Done," he grinned. "Then you are going to get some fast training on running a law enforcement meeting."

"No. I'm not giving an inch on that. I want written reports that include hunches and impressions. Facts are only a small part of any story."

He raised his eyebrows. "I'm telling you, it's unprofessional and a waste of time. You need an iron fist. Order. Hierarchy."

"I agree on hierarchy and order. But I'm not giving one inch on the composition of reports. Just the facts, ma'am, are what I relay to Dimon. And look where that's gotten him! The most important information is that Merilee Suter is on the verge of a nervous breakdown and we don't know why for sure. But that's an observation. A hunch. Not a fact. So Dimon doesn't want to hear it. We think the call Brent got had to do with his old girlfriend. But we don't know that for a fact. It's based on intuition. So Dimon doesn't want to hear that either."

He listened.

I was just getting started. "And don't tell me how reports should go. I don't care how they're done back East. I blended historical research techniques with criminal databases to solve the Herbert Swenson case. A cold case. Dead over fifty years. My format stays. History plus mystery."

He said nothing.

"But the farm goes. Point taken."

"Okay." He threw up his hands in surrender. "Facts, and hunches, and impressions, and old wives' tales. All thrown into the same pot."

"And gossip and family myths. We'll sort it out later."

"Okay."

"Think about it, Harold. I'm not sprinkling fairy dust. It's no different than a tip line when a police station is working a major crime. You sort through a lot of junk. Crank calls."

"I said okay. You win. Call a meeting of the team for Friday morning. By that time Sam and you won't believe what can be installed for communications. It will make what you have now on a par with smoke signals."

"In the meantime, I want Josie to keep on checking up on the team members. I know she doesn't like Dr. Ferguson."

"I'm going to check him out as far as I can go. The military can be damned funny when it comes to releasing information. But he's not the one that concerns me. I want to know more about our boy genius before we turn him loose.

"David Hayes?"

"Yes. Our computer expert."

"And when do we start to work? On the building?"

"Tomorrow morning."

"I'll be there. And so will David."

"That's not necessary.'

I shot him a look. I had picked up a few tricks from Dorothy.

● ● **●** ● ●

That evening I left everyone to their own devices. I went down to the basement and slipped a martial arts training disc into the media player. I did some basic stretches and flexed my shoulders and went into a few preliminary punches. Back straight, fists up, I lifted my right knee and snapped off a quick kick. I alternated legs executing jump-snap kicks, then paused long enough to wipe the sweat from my brow.

My form and coordination were terrible when I moved to the tornado kick. I could not manage the jump-spin sequence. I was determined to master it. Dizzy from trying, I bent over to steady my queasy stomach.

I lifted my head. Keith stood in the doorway. How long had he been there? Ignoring him I walked to the player and reversed the disk to the sequence I did best. He walked over and stood to one side. Then watched. Proud of my form I alternated snap-kicks.

When I went through them the second time he lunged forward and easily caught my leg throwing me off balance. But before I hit the floor he squatted and his powerful hands slid under my back.

I could not avoid looking into his eyes but I could not fully read his expression. It was somewhere between mockery and tenderness. He gently set me on my feet.

"Don't get yourself in a position where you'll ever have to use this, Lottie. The videos you see, the movie clips, showcase women who have trained with masters. Since childhood."

I burst into tears then walked to the player and started the disk from the beginning.

He walked away.

That night I laid as far as possible on my side of the bed without actually falling off. "Come here," he growled and pulled me to his chest.

Early in our marriage I'd come to realize that little marital sorrows would always float around us like ghosts in waiting. He hated my involvement in law enforcement. I hated his over-protective side. We would go to our fiftieth anniversary without coming to grips with this issue.

In the meantime, going to bed worked just fine.

● ● ● ● ●

The next morning the room in back of Sam's office buzzed like a beehive. David Hayes walked around all the equipment. "Hot damn."

"Bet you've never seen anything like this before." One of the men gazed at him as he straightened one of the computers."

"Actually, I have. Just not out here." He smiled and went to the man supervising the installation.

David was clearly in his element. He moved easily in the light-footed manner that some really heavy men seem to have. Confident in his expertise, he seemed taller. Less gangly. In a half hour he had conferred with every technician in the room and they were deferring to him.

He had arrived with a list of specifications and argued for programs that I'd never heard of.

"Too much for out here."

David easily won him over. "This will be a prototype for several regions in Kansas. I'm looking ahead. We have to prove we can use all these resources. And I intend to."

"Going to cost a shitload of money."

He grinned.

I had selected a soft gold color of paint. There was no reason to start off with the hideous institutional green that was slapped on the walls of all the rooms in public buildings. Or boring realtor's beige. The floor would come last and a bit of texture would aid with disguising scratches made by big dogs or cleats.

"I have one more idea, Lottie. It's an alert system for when something is placed in the evidence room."

Storing evidence had worried me from the beginning because we were so short on manpower. In fact, none of the setups I'd looked at were very impressive. They were too easy to pilfer by both authorized and unauthorized personnel.

David's method relied on the pagers he was giving to everyone on the team. There would be simultaneous notification when evidence was entered or removed and the door was unlocked by a revolving code that renewed daily.

"Terrific!" We high-fived. Harold noticed and came over. David gave him a demonstration.

"That's ingenious. What are you doing out here?"

"Farming."

"What a waste. I want the FBI to know what you've worked out."

He managed a rueful smile. "Naw. I think they would just as soon I stay out here and tend to my crops."

• • ● • •

Keith and I arrived at the storage room early Friday morning. When we pulled up we saw a brand new entrance and a sign over the door: "Northwest Kansas Regional Crime Center."

"Well, would you look at this," Keith parked a couple of places down from the area reserved for handicapped persons.

I assumed we would be the first ones there but when we opened the door, there sat Sam looking like he had acquired a whole new kingdom. Warm air whooshed through a new central heating system. A huge conference table dominated the center of the room. A bank of electronic equipment was installed on the west wall.

The floors were covered with a high quality wood laminate and the walls would withstand regular scrubbings. Floor-to-ceiling cabinets with adjustable shelves housed forensic equipment and laboratory materials. In the back of the room was a small L-shaped kitchen. Someone had already started the coffee urn. I headed for it.

Sam stood when the rest of the task force arrived and gave the group a guided tour as though the whole installation had been his idea. I turned and looked at Harold who gave a small shrug and smiled. He had obviously coached Sam extensively.

It was time for the meeting to start, but Dr. Ferguson hadn't arrived. The coffee drinkers went to the mini-kitchen and grabbed doughnuts and a cup of regular or decaf. I went to the head of the table and laid handouts on the broad surface. There was a large whiteboard and I rolled it closer to the conference table. I laid a copy of the agenda at each place.

Then the door blew open and bounced against the wall. In walked Dr. Ferguson who strode to an empty seat bringing the odor of winter-fresh air with him.

He glared at me. "Don't interrupt. Go right ahead." He nodded to the rest of the group. "Sorry for the delay. Ran into some construction on I-70."

"Don't worry about it. We'll catch you up during the break. I'm sorry you missed Sam's tour." My words were calculated, implying that this room was Sam's turf because it was attached to his office. "David Hayes can tell you all about the electronics too."

David's face was alight with excitement. Harold had "checked him out" but did not give me any specific information other than to say our young computer guru was A-okay. I certainly didn't have any doubts about his ability after observing the reaction of the men who had installed the systems.

I walked over to the whiteboard and listed all the members of the team with specific assignments for each of them. Then I listed all the relevant facts we had compiled so far.

"Why are you using a whiteboard instead of a PowerPoint presentation?" Ferguson snapped.

"Because PowerPoint slides can't be seen all at once and depend on a projector. I want any and all of you to be able to walk into this room any time Sam is in his office and be able to get the big picture at a glance. Whiteboards are the best for that purpose. Sam will have the key to this room and be familiar with updates."

Ferguson looked around the table, rolled his eyes, and settled on a look that could only be described as a sneer, inviting the group to go along with his evaluation of the set-up. But unlike the last time, the men weren't cooperating. The room had turned the trick. They were proud of it.

"I can't believe this."

"Believe what, Dr. Ferguson?"

"Using whiteboards when you have all this equipment. Why not just send out a composite e-mail to a distribution list? If someone knows how to create such a list, that is."

David froze in his chair, taking quick umbrage, but easily keeping a lid on ill-timed comments.

"I'll send out e-mails when I need to inform the team of new developments or if I've decided to take the search in another direction. But I'm going to keep this whiteboard updated. I value the judgment and opinions of each person in this group."

I turned my attention from Ferguson to the men in the room. "Drop by the office when you're in town. Your minds are more important than your use of electronics."

Ferguson scoffed.

"Maintaining electronics is David Hayes' job. Most of the men here don't have time to take a computer course just to tell me they've had a new insight. They don't need PowerPoint for that."

"What's PowerPoint?" asked Justin Harold.

"It's like a cattle prod," the Bidwell County sheriff quipped. "Only harder to use."

There was a ripple of laughter. Josie and Harold Sider exchanged amused glances.

I turned back to Ferguson. "The Northwest Kansas Regional Crime Center is going to approach problems realistically and give a lot of consideration to our limitations. There's a lot of 'make do' out here. Now, back to the business at hand." I rubbed my palms together. "Sam and a few other men will figure out how someone put a baby in the hands of *Reaching Woman*. Keith will concentrate on the Suter family, and so on. Your assignments are all on the papers I'll pass out at the end of the meeting."

"It would be easy for someone to come in here and sabotage this equipment," Ferguson wasn't going to let this go. He quirked an eyebrow and his expression said that I was too dumb to have considered that.

"Yes, it would. That's the beauty of having all this set up in back of the sheriff's office instead of a separate building a couple of miles away. Someone will be here to guard access at all times, day and night. Sam and I will no longer just switch the phones over to our homes. Either he or I or a reserve deputy will be here twenty-four/seven. But David will be the only one using the more sophisticated equipment. He's also trained to use the ViCAP database."

"ViCAP? Jesus Christ." Ferguson's outburst—coming from a psychologist—was unexpected. "ViCAP? Are you nuts? There's so few people in Western Kansas that you would be lucky to get the money together to buy a decent supply of dry pens for the whiteboard. And that's if there is a sale going on. Why would you be using such a sophisticated program? What's the point of all this stuff out in the middle of nowhere? It took forever for me to get here today."

"Yes. Driving forever to get here is the point. The personnel in Topeka don't like having to drive out here for every little whip stitch. They want us to solve our problems on a regional basis."

Justin Harold rose and walked over to the coffee pot and began rummaging through the cupboard for a tray. When he found one, he arranged an assortment of doughnuts on it and carried it and a carafe of coffee back to our table. I suppressed a smile, knowing his interruption of Ferguson was deliberate. "Warm up?" Justin moved around the table, dissing the frustrated psychologist.

"But ViCAP, why?" Ferguson's voice was filled with cold fury. He pulled a notebook from his worn leather briefcase and began taking notes.

"This case in particular is a good example. Some other state might have entered the facts about similar crimes."

"It's a dumb-ass program rarely used. Not worth wasting our time on."

"I agree that ViCAP has been hindered because not enough law enforcement agencies take the trouble to enter information. But this crime center is going to enter every last bit of data. It might help in other areas."

The Violent Crime Apprehension Program was a tool of the FBI that compared entered data for similarities. It coordinated investigations. A similar program works beautifully in Canada where entering information is mandatory, but was slow to take off in the United States because the original entry system had been too complicated and local authorities didn't bother to use it.

Saddened by Ferguson's scorn, I looked around the room knowing from all he had said and the looks that crossed his face how he probably viewed these people: Josie a thin-flanked weeping beauty who would develop a headache and scurry back to Eastern Kansas at the first hint of trouble. Aunt Dorothy, a prideful old mystery writer who rarely spoke. She had even brought her knitting today. Keith protectively guarding his turf like a range bull warding off wolves.

And Sam, with his large Roman nose—an elegant bump in the middle—set in his ways and ineffective, cultivating his Old West image by growing his hair a little too long and usually sporting a cowboy hat and a leather vest undoubtedly seemed like a caricature to Ferguson. In fact, the whole group undoubtedly looked like the most unlikely inept collection of law enforcement officers he had ever worked with.

His assessment was wrong.

I glanced at my watch. It was time for a break. The smokers headed outside. Ferguson left too, then in a few minutes stepped back inside. "Something has come up. I need to head back to Topeka." He picked up his brief case and left.

"He called Dimon," Harold said when he heard Ferguson start his Volkswagen.

"You eavesdropped?"

"Nope. But only because I wasn't able to. I only heard the 'Hello, Frank.' Then he saw me and moved away."

"There's a chance. Just a chance," I said slowly, "that Dimon wants this center controlled by KBI personnel. You brought it up and I've been thinking about it. He might want Sam and me out of here. And I ain't gonna go."

Chapter Thirteen

I was done in and not up to cooking supper. As usual, Tosca made a beeline for Keith the moment we walked in the door. He laughed and picked her up and began stroking her silky ears. "How's my best girl tonight? Been lonesome today?" Tosca licked his face. If dogs could talk!

Josie and Harold Sider would bring Dorothy with them when they came out to the farm. "It's a good night to order pizza," Keith suggested.

"Oh, that's right. It's Friday." Our local café only offers it when the high school has a home game. Even though we give them a large tip to smooth their feathers, they are very reluctant to deliver this far out from town.

Keith awkwardly balanced Tosca in the crook of his elbow while he dialed the phone. Josie, Harold, and Dorothy arrived fifteen minutes later. After the pizza was delivered, we ate with perfunctory attempts to carry on a conversation. There was an unspoken reluctance to discuss Ferguson's derision of the regional center.

"You have no idea how different this house usually is." Determined to inject a bit of cheer, I directed an onslaught of small talk toward Dorothy. "Lots of people around and music. You can't imagine the music. Josie and Keith play beautifully together and stay up half the night. At least one of the daughters is usually around. And when Bettina's little boys are here it's just heavenly. This place jumps."

No one can top Josie when it comes to scornful looks, and I resented it.

"Murder doesn't make for lively evenings," she said haughtily. "Especially when babies are involved." She stood before the fire warming her backside.

I persisted. "And I *can* cook, Dorothy. Honestly. Normally I would be stuffing you with pie and you've been in my kitchen more than I have this past week."

"I love having someone to cook for." She gave a little no problem flap of her hand then looked at Harold and Keith who weren't bothering to disguise yawns. "I think it would be a good night to turn in early." She rose and collected her knitting.

"Sorry, Sis, I didn't mean to run everyone off." Apparently ashamed of her churlishness, Josie tried to get back into my good graces. "Dorothy, don't go to bed yet. Tell you what. Lottie and I have both caught up to where you placed a marker in the commonplace book. Why don't you read it aloud?"

I had planned to tackle *The Crime Classification Manual.* I couldn't afford to take evenings off but I could study after everyone else went to bed. "Okay. Not that Franklin Slocum is much easier to think about than the Ghost Baby Killer."

Josie's face tightened with indignation. "I could just weep. After we find that man, I want to find out what became of that sad little boy."

Harold wandered over to our row of floor-to-ceiling bookcases and plucked a history book from one of the shelves. Keith picked up this latest copy of *Veterinarian Practice News.* They each headed for a recliner. Josie and I settled into wing chairs beside Dorothy and she resumed the narrative. She had a splendid reading voice. But even if she were a poor reader, it wouldn't have mattered. We were all three quickly bound up again in this tragic account of a small boy's life.

I found piles and piles of books with the covers ripped off in the landfill. Which I think is just terrible. I would never hurt a book.

"Returns," Dorothy said. "A bookstore has to tear off the covers and return them to the publishers to get credit on its account. Some of the books are offered to customers anyway, but that is illegal."

"What about hardcover books?" Tosca lifted her head as though she, too, was interested in Josie's question.

"They are sent to wholesale markets at drastically reduced prices."

Dorothy cleared her throat.

"Sorry. Go on. Didn't mean to lead us off-track."

Dorothy began where she had left off.

They are all Westerns and I love them. I have read some of them three times. Especially the ones by Mr. Louis L'Amour. Sometimes there are pictures of him on the back. I wish I had a father who looks like him. I cannot change the way I look but he has helped me understand what a man is supposed to act like. I know what a man is supposed to do. There is another book called The Virginian *that makes it even plainer. I have decided to make a list of all the things a manly man should do. I'm also going to add where I have room for improvement like I do on my list of animal accomplishments.*

And I found a bag that isn't too girly that I'm going to use for a possibles bag. In the Westerns all of the men carried a possibles bag. They kept stuff they would need during a day but I'm going to keep treasures in it too. I started off with a beautiful stone that I'm sure will bring me good luck, and a feather from a lovely blue bird. And I'm so thankful.

I have a special friend. A squirrel. He has been coming very close and this morning he left a nut right at my feet and he looked at me. He did. He stopped for a moment after he dropped this nut right by my foot. He sees me. He actually knew he was leaving me a nut.

I have to admit that I did an unmanly thing and shed
some tears. No one ever, ever really sees me. I put the nut
in my possibles bag. It is one of my greatest treasures.

Dorothy paused, took off her glasses and rubbed her eyes.
"He's double-traced some of the letters. It has the effect of bold-
ing the words."

"This project was very important to him then," Josie said.
"That and the animals. He wants to know what men should be
like. He could do worse than L'Amour. But go on. No one is
ready to go to bed just yet."

A Manly Man:
1. **Does not cuss when there are ladies around.**
   This is not a problem because I never get to be
   around anyone.
2. **Removes his hat when he walks into a room.**
   I don't have a hat so this is not a problem either.
   I keep checking the landfill to see if someone
   has thrown one away. I want a hat more than
   anything.
3. **Does not talk too much.**
   I win that one. I never talk if I can help it. People
   cannot understand me anyway. They could if they
   would listen. But they give up right away.
4. **Is always fair and true.**
   I never have a chance to be. I would always be fair.
   Always. Because I know how much unfair hurts.
5. **Always stands up for what is right.**
   I will do this. I pledge my honor to this. I will.
   This is easy for me to say because I never have a
   chance to stand up for anything. I practice in my
   head with a beautiful gun with pearl handles. I say
   "when you say that, smile." More than anything
   in the world I want a chance to show people how
   brave I am.

"Oh that poor neglected child." Tosca was lying in Josie's lap and anxiously looked up at her face. She laughed and scratched the base of the little dog's topknot. "I'm fine, Tosca Nothing to worry about."

"We're at a good stopping place. That's the end of his list. Time for me to turn in."

"Me, too. I'm sure I'll get some feedback tomorrow about today's meeting and I need a good night's sleep so I can keep my wits about me."

Dorothy put the commonplace book on the table. I checked the kitchen and put remaining slices of pizza into zip-lock bags and headed upstairs.

The phone rang before I even reached the third step.

"Hi, Lottie. David Hayes here. I got a hit."

"A hit from ViCAP?"

"Yup."

"A case like ours? You mean in additional to the ones at Polly Park and Garden of Eden?"

"The very same. I know it's hard to believe and it was a long time ago—well, about fifteen years—long enough, but the same thing. Exactly."

"Where? And how come we didn't know about something that shocking?" My fingers flew to the pulse in my throat.

"Well, that's the weird thing. You know what you told Ferguson about local law enforcement not using ViCAP enough? There's been a big campaign by the FBI to get some of the sheriffs to turn over old records and get them entered into databases by paid FBI personnel. Their documents are returned to them, but the center has the benefit of the data for profiling. In fact, when the local boys can see all their stuff online a lot of them are getting with the program. Everyone wins."

"About the one you say is similar to our case? Details?"

"I didn't say similar. I said exact. It happened in Liberal, Kansas. A baby was found frozen to death in the arms of a statute called the *Pioneer Mother of Kansas*. Here's the thing that adds something special. She was already holding a baby against her breast. This one went undetected because it was on the opposite side like she was holding twins. It seemed to fit in. It was three days before anyone noticed and that was because of the stench. The town is very proud of the statute and the newspaper kind of kept a lid on all the gory details. The article said that 'the body of an abandoned baby was discovered in the grounds by the library by two children who had been playing hide and seek.' No more details given than 'every attempt is being made to locate the mother. Persons seeing any suspicious activity were to report to…' and so on, and so forth."

"It has to be the same killer." Although I could control my voice, make myself sound rational, analytical, like a person qualified to be in charge of a complex investigation, I could not control the sudden lurch of my stomach like I had taken a plunge in a roller coaster and was falling, falling. I wanted off of this world that was plummeting into evil.

"I'm going to start entering all the data we have so far on our case."

"Okay. You might hold off clicking Send for a couple of days. Something new might turn up. But why didn't Dimon find this?"

David cleared his throat. "I have special ways."

• • ● • •

When I finally climbed into bed beside Keith I could not fall asleep. Eventually I gave up and put on my quilted chenille robe and sheep's wool-lined slippers and went downstairs. I brewed a cup of valerian root tea and went into the family room. The fire had burned down but I dug around in the woodbox and located kindling and brought it back to life. When it began to leap and fill the room with the pungent aroma of cedar, I tossed in more logs. I headed for my leather chair where I wrapped myself in a heavy quilt. Content to just watch the fire sparking then ebbing in the dark room, I waited for the tea to work its magic.

A born list-maker, in a few minutes I switched on the lamp and reached for my pad and pencil and tried to write out what was bothering me the most. After a few minutes I slapped the writing material back down on the table. I couldn't even do that.

I was stuck on determining the next steps. I absolutely did not know what to do next. Didn't have a clue as to what to do next.

Unless Sam and his men could figure out how someone got a baby up in *Reaching Woman*'s outstretching arms.

Unless Dorothy spotted some piece of evidence in the crime scene photos that we had overlooked.

Unless Dr. Ferguson or Josie could work some kind of a miracle and come up with a genius analysis that would help us find a person so clever that he could murder three little babies and one grown man and not leave a trace behind.

But Harold and Josie had contempt for Ferguson's abilities.

I gave up thinking and reached for the commonplace book. Poor Franklin Slocum had far more troubles than I did. Dorothy had left off reading at the point where his greatest wish was to be a brave person and stop evil. To stand up for what was right. It was a noble goal. Maybe some of his courage would rub off on me.

A car came through the trees yesterday and a boy and a girl got out. I know who they are. They were in high school and are seniors. Anne was a cheerleader and Timothy was homecoming king. He spread a blanket on the ground and they both laid down and I'm too embarrassed to explain what happened next even in this book. I know all about it from the pamphlets the doctor gave me but I had never seen it with real people just with the animals. It made me feel very, very shy and unhappy because it will never happen for me.

All kinds of things happened to my body and I could hardly breathe and I wanted to be Timothy so bad I could not stand the aching. Anne made all kinds of noises and then they both laid really still and kept whispering to each other.

The animals that I can act like the best are the prairie dog and the possum. I can hide quick as a flash and that's what I did and I played dead like a possum. But I have not found the right spell to turn myself into a wood frog so I can make myself invisible and stop breathing.

After they left I cried and cried. I know that no one will ever love me. Not like that. And I've started feeling sorry for Biddy. Poor Biddy. I went back to the house that night and watched Biddy through the window. She cries sometimes when she goes to bed and now I know why. I wonder if my father ever loved her and who he was and if he will ever come back. Poor poor Biddy.

Other cars come here. I always watch. Even though it makes me miserable. I watch. I'm a super good hider. It's about the only thing I do really well. My clothes are so dirty now that I look like I'm part of the woods.

● ● ● ● ●

The next thing I knew Keith was gently shaking me and held a cup of coffee in his hands.

"Morning, Sunshine."

"Morning? You're kidding."

"I'm not. You slept here all night."

Chapter Fourteen

I was glad to take my turn manning the sheriff's office. I carried in a stack of books about psychology including the new version of the *Diagnostic and Statistical Manual of Mental Disorders*. Harold and Josie could and would fend for themselves when it came to meals. Dorothy had returned to her own house in town.

At about ten o'clock Merilee Suter drove up. It was a school day so I was surprised.

"Sam here?" she asked as she headed for my desk.

"No. I'm the only one today."

"Good. I wanted to catch you when you were alone."

"Have a seat. I think I can dig up a can of pop or do you drink coffee?"

"Nothing, thanks. And I can't stay long. I cut study hall and the class I should be in now is Geometry and I do just fine in it. Mr. Latimer is covering stuff I already know. Not that I'm a math whiz, but Brent was and he made a game of teaching me stuff. Sometimes I had to calculate grain ratios just to prove to him I could do it. I didn't do so well with quadratic equations, though. But then I doubt if I ever need to master that."

She fidgeted, then put her hands beneath her thighs and bounced her legs like they were driven by a little motor. I knew I was going to have to put up with a lot of small talk again. Talking in circles instead of diving in to why she came. She still looked like hell. Dark circles under her eyes. A tic now. A little side jerk when she talked. Her lean jeans, intended to be super-tight, sagged through the legs and buttocks. Her long shag needed trimmed. She was furtive, like a little wharf rat.

A hard chair was the best I could offer in the way of seating. Sam's office was simply Sam's office and no prize. We had the new swanky room in back, fronted by this office that still looked like it had been snatched from a set for an old Western. Like this place was a disguise covering up the real thing. We had an old scarred desk and an office chair with splits in the leather that Sam had patched with duct tape. The walls were peppered with literature racks and wanted posters.

There was a dispatcher's room through the door to the left. Another door led to rather bleak restroom facilities with small black and white hexagon tiles. To the right of the main office was a cloakroom with a cabinet and plugins for our coffee pot and an assortment of brooms and cleaning supplies. Next to the cabinet was a broken down old fridge with a tiny tin bin at the top that was supposed to make ice. It usually held a six-pack of Diet Coke and a supply of apples. Nevertheless, the office was immaculate because Sam kept it that way. Visitors were always accosted with the odor of Pine-sol and tobacco.

"Something important must have come up for you to cut classes." My gentle prodding stopped her rambling narrative.

"You're going to think I'm crazy, but I've been thinking about why Brent would go to the Garden of Eden that time of night. There's only one thing I can think of that would draw him out without him letting me know what was going on."

"What Merilee?"

"Someone told him Joyce was still alive. Even there, maybe." Her big eyes followed my face to see if I would take her seriously.

My fingers tightened around my coffee cup. *Of course.* Everyone on the team should have hit on that immediately. The lure wasn't just information but the person herself. Whether true or false, Brent would have gone there to see for himself. "That's solid, Merilee. And I appreciate your coming up with that and then knowing it was important to pass this along. Good for you! There's a number of people I'm going to tell."

"Like who?"

"Well, Harold Sider, for one. And my sister, Josie, and Keith, of course, and his Aunt Dorothy, and Dr. Ferguson. He's the psychologist from the KBI. They will all kick around that idea."

She managed a cautious little smile. "I was afraid you would think I was crazy."

"No way." But there she was again checking to see what I thought about her mental health. It was never that we would think she was wrong or stupid or arrogant for making suggestions. It was always that we would think she was crazy. "I think you've made a very astute deduction. I appreciate it."

She rose and picked up her backpack from off the floor and checked her watch. "Guess I'd better get back to school. It's lunchtime now and then I have an English class." Her carriage was awkward, her body a long slumped curve, but she blushed with pleasure over my encouragement. "See you," she said as she walked self-consciously toward the door, turned and gave an awkward little wave. Then her mouth opened in a perfect "O" and her hands clasped the side of her head. She looked like the figure from the haunting painting, *The Scream*. Only she was not standing on a bridge with a dark figure advancing. She was standing in a bare bones sheriff's office on a bright winter day.

I could not get to her before she collapsed. I lifted her head from the floor and cradled it on my lap and stroked her hair for a moment before I lifted her to her feet. There was a cot in the dispatcher's room. With starts and stops we wobbled toward it. I laid her down, shoved a pillow under her head, and covered her with a blanket. There was no point in calling 911 because I was it.

I called Josie and asked her to come immediately.

"I'll be there in a flash."

"I can't go home. I don't want to go home," Merilee wailed. "Please."

Waif-thin, she looked like a wisp of a ghost that would disappear into the first wind.

"Merilee, what is the matter? Tell me." Was something terribly wrong in that perfect 4-H household? All the tales Josie had told me were whirling through my mind: Incest where it was not obvious, psychological warfare that was unbelievably cruel, undercurrents concealed by impeccable behavior. Something that required training to unearth. But for the life of me, I could not see Ernie or Patricia as the type who would do anything to damage a child.

"Tell me," I demanded again. Coping with Merilee's mental condition would be Josie's bailiwick. Mine was to find out if there was a criminal situation right under my nose.

"I did tell you." Her voice was weak, but defiant. Faintly hostile.

"Merilee, is there something going wrong with your parents? Something I should know? There are all kinds of support systems out there."

Clearly shocked, a surge of blood gave her the strength to sit up. "Don't you dare. Don't even think about blaming my parents for any of my problems. My folks are two of the finest persons you are ever going to meet. Bar none."

The door flew open and Josie walked in. Merilee's face drained of its last dollop of color. She gave a little cry and edged away from both of us.

"It's fine. Everything is okay." I reached for her and held her against my chest while I smoothed her hair. "Shh. It's fine. Josie is my twin sister. You're not seeing double."

Josie stood quietly while I calmed Merilee.

"How did you get here so soon?"

"Tosca needs dog food. I was already in town when you called. Now what's going on?"

Relieved, I grappled for the right explanation that wouldn't distress Merilee even more. "Merilee, has had, is in…"

"I don't want to go home. Please don't make me go home." She buried her face in her hands.

Josie gestured for me to stand back and she took over. She knelt in front of Merilee and removed her hands from her face. "What's going on? You're safe here. You're with friends. You can tell us anything, but we've got to know."

"I told Lottie. She just ignored me."

I started to protest. She hadn't told me anything.

"I hear voices. They aren't in my head. They're real. And I see things. Out of the corner of my eye. I can't turn fast enough to see what's going on. Someone is trying to drive me crazy."

"I didn't ignore you…" But my voice broke off when I realized I had. I decided she was unstable the first time I met her.

"I'm taking you seriously." Josie looked her in the eye and patted her hands. "We're going to get to the bottom of this. But before I take other steps I need an honest answer, Merilee. Are you afraid of your parents?"

"No, I swear to God, no. They wouldn't hurt a fly."

"So, it's just your home?"

"Yes."

"When did it start?"

"Right after Brent died."

"Only at your house? Not in school or anywhere else?"

"No, just there."

"Okay, before I do any testing, I want to check something out." Josie stood and gestured for me to follow her into the main office. "What is Dorothy up to? Would she be available to stay at the Suters' for a couple of days?"

"She would be glad to." I didn't have to ask her first. Dorothy welcomed any kind of involvement. "What do you have in mind?"

"It's my policy. First I always take the patient's words at face value. I learned that lesson the hard way early in my practice. A lady came in who claimed her husband was trying to break her leg. I zeroed right in on her underlying paranoia. Then one day she showed up with a broken leg and, needless to say, filed charges against her husband. Ever since, I've checked the validity of a patient's story first. *Before* I venture a diagnosis. After that I check out physical factors. Blood counts, brain scans, etc. That's the sequence: truth, then physical tests, then analysis as a last resort."

"But first impression?"

"First impression, Merilee's in terrible shape."

"I'll call her mother right away and set up the logistics for Dorothy spending the night there. Or several. In the meantime, you can arrange any necessary physical tests."

"Merilee isn't in any shape to drive herself home. Will you take her out there?"

"Sure."

"Good, then I'll send Dorothy out in Merilee's pickup."

"If I were her parents this would freak me out. What are you going to tell them?" Josie asked.

"The truth! Patricia already knows Merilee is not well and until you can arrange for testing, you've suggested that having a member of the team stay at their place will help calm her and give them some rest. They know she isn't well, but I don't think she's told them about the voices." Together we glanced at Merilee lying curled in a fetal position.

"I wish I could prescribe some medication." Josie's glance was full of pity. "Psychologists can't and I doubt if your family doctor would appreciate a call from me telling him what this girl needs."

"I think Patricia has already taken her to Dr. Golbert for something to help her sleep. But it's clearly not working."

"No. It's not," Josie agreed. "I want you to stay with Merilee and see if you can rummage up an extra blanket and keep her warm. Try to get some food down her. I think there's some orange juice in the fridge in the Regional Room. And I'm going to run over to Dorothy's and make sure she's willing to do this."

Josie called back in fifteen minutes. "It's all set. She's collected her knitting and everything else she needs and understands that her job is actually to listen for voices. And we are to come by and check on her every day. She also wants to know if you would bring the commonplace book by."

"Nope. I have to keep it here or at the historical society. Besides, I don't want to risk Merilee reading it. It's too strange. Poor Franklin Slocum has managed to upset the three of us and I can just imagine the effect it would have on someone who barely has body and soul together."

"One thing is for damn sure. If Dorothy hears voices, there *are* voices."

• • ● • •

Dorothy called the next morning. I hadn't even had time to brush my teeth.

"I don't know if this is good news or bad news."

She hadn't even bothered with a "hello."

"The child is not hearing things. The voices are real. And they are set off by an inexpensive motion-sensitive player someone tucked under her pillow. That's why her parents couldn't hear anything. She would only hear it when she laid down at night."

Stunned, I just stared at the receiver. "Just a minute. I want Josie to hear this."

I yelled upstairs and ordered Josie to pick up the extension. She pounded down the hallway and listened to Dorothy's account of her night.

"I don't know what we're going to tell Merilee." I was on our landline and twisted the cord into a bow. What would be more reassuring? That some bastard is messing with her mind, or letting her keep on believing that she might be losing it?

"I've already taken care of that dilemma," Dorothy assured me. "I showed her the device when she got up and told her there wasn't a thing wrong with her. There actually were voices and I heard them too. I ordered her to get out of bed immediately and get ready for school. And that we would find the evil-doer post-haste."

I cringed. "And that made her feel better?"

"Most certainly. Yes. Anything is better than thinking you are going crazy. And we *will* apprehend this cruel devil and bring him to justice."

Her dramatic phrases make me feel like I had stepped into one of her novels where all her endings were happy and swift and sure. On the other hand, there was something about Dorothy. Just her solid self-assured presence in a room made one feel that "evil-doers" would get their just desserts. Every time.

"Where is Merilee now?"

"Ernie drove her to school. I don't think it's a good idea for her to get behind a wheel just yet. We need to find out a little more about the kind of kids she's going to school with. I don't think anyone there would be trying to 'gaslight' her but I think you should take a look at them. Ernie will pick her up when class is over too because I don't think she should take the bus either. I'm driving the pickup. It's quite impressive, actually. Excellent for traversing these roads."

Chapter Fifteen

I caught Sam up on Merilee's problems and the reasons Dorothy had stayed with her last night. The Suters' pickup pulled up in front of the sheriff's office. Dorothy walked in and triumphantly handed Sam the plastic bag containing the recording device. She'd had the presence of mind to wear rubber gloves.

"Well. Good job, Ms. Mercer." He held the bag up to the light. "In fact, I don't know of another lay person who would have handled this so well." They both blushed.

"I didn't let Merilee touch it." Her face glowed with quiet pride at Sam's complements.

"This here recorder is dirt cheap." He viewed the bag from all angles. "Doesn't even cost ten bucks. You can buy it anywhere. The local truck stop has a bunch of them. They work on the same principle as talking dolls or those safety gadgets that bark like a dog when someone tries to break into a house."

"Can anyone think why some sadistic s.o.b. would want to torment that poor child?" I wasn't expecting a reply.

"It's such an obvious device. That's what floors me. There was no real attempt to disguise it. All she had to do was move to set it off. It would have been found when she changed her sheets." Dorothy looked at Sam. "I'm not as brave as you think. The first time I heard it I froze. Then I realized the sounds were coming from beneath her pillow. Merilee didn't wake up. I'm sure she is exhausted."

"She probably was more relaxed and felt protected knowing you were there."

"Perhaps." She modestly ducked her head. "I'm sure her parents would have been right by her side if they had known. But she didn't tell them about the voices because she thought she was losing her mind. She didn't suspect anything else."

"Did you get any sleep at all?" Sam gently patted the back of her hand.

"No," she said bravely, looking deeply into his eyes. "I hadn't planned to anyway. I was in a recliner next to her bed and started knitting and simply listening. That's all I had planned to do. Just listen. But when I heard the voices and Merilee turned over, I felt under the pillow for the device and fumed the rest of the night. I'm still mad. Who would do this kind of thing?"

"You didn't wake Patricia or Ernie?"

"No. Merilee hadn't told them about it. She's very protective of her parents. There was no need to wake them in the middle of the night. The Suters have had all they can stand. They are dead on their feet, both from the death of their son and their daughter's state of mind."

"Good for you, Dorothy."

"Merilee told them about it this morning. They seemed relieved to know there was a basis for their daughter's nerves."

"Did you hear anything else?" All business now, Sam reached for a legal pad lying on his desk and started taking notes.

He was not a habitual note-taker. He caught my puzzled look. "These will be transferred to the whiteboard in the Regional Room."

In that instant it became apparent to me that Sam believed Merilee's issues were tied to the macabre "Ghost Baby" case.

No. They couldn't be. Not directly. Indirectly, sure, because of her brother's death. But I had convinced myself that the voices were a vicious high school prank. Some twisted kid exploiting this tragedy. Widening the fracture in this family's hearts. We hadn't made one speck of progress in finding the killer. How could we decipher another layer of complexity?

"Mind if I record this too?" Sam fumbled around in a drawer for a tape recorder. "I'm not as fast writing stuff down as I used to be and I want to get your very first impressions exactly right."

Dorothy nodded. "Other than the night sounds that are usually there on a farm, there weren't any other strange noises. It's an old house. Floorboards creak. There's a loud old Regulator clock that chimes the hours, but nothing unusual. I think I finally dozed off a little toward morning, but I'm beat."

Sam picked up the little bag and gestured for us to follow him into the new Regional Room. Anything that was classified as evidence in this case had been transferred to Topeka when the state forensic team first came out. This was the first piece we could officially log in here at the center. It was a sobering feeling.

Sam went to the main computer and punched in a password that generated the daily code. He filled out the chain of custody slip on the screen, then walked into the evidence room and placed the bag inside the first locker.

"No one can take this out now, even you, Lottie, without again using a rotating number that will be dispensed by the computer." He went to the phone and called David. "Good news," he announced after he hung up. "His pager chimed just like it should to let the team know when someone has entered evidence. He's in town and will come by the office to double check my paperwork."

"Wow. I didn't expect you to have the system in place this soon. When did this all happen?"

"A couple of days ago. David told me what you two had worked out. I watched him set everything up. Had a few ideas myself."

I shot him a quizzical look. When had Sam become a computer genius?

"Getting things to work wasn't my doing. But David and I did a little brainstorming and I told him what I was worried about. He came up with solutions and then I shot them down. Then he countered with some kind of an answer until we came up with something that suited us both."

"Awesome." And it was. I had urged members of the team to do their own thinking. And they had!

"There's even a camera inside that closet and each auxiliary member of the team will have a special gadget—sort of like a pager—that chimes when a person logs stuff in or out. He has set up something for the mainframe computer too."

Dorothy gazed at him with admiration.

"This was all David's doing of course, Ms. Mercer. I merely pointed out where people could beat the system."

"I'm sure your suggestions improved the design enormously. Your wisdom and pragmatic approach would be a valuable asset for any law enforcement agency," she said in the stilted manner she used in her books. Sam blushed.

Beaming, David walked in the door. "All the systems up and running according to plan." He walked over to the mainframe and logged in.

We told him about the buzzer. "Why in the world would someone do something so bizarre? It makes no sense whatsoever. Merilee was losing her mind. It was such a cruel thing to do."

"I'll tell you why." David stood and shoved his hands in his pockets. "Some people love to torment others. Like a cat toying with a mouse. They study ways to destroy people. Starting in junior high and on through high school there was this kid…"

His voice trailed off and he swallowed hard to steady his breathing. I thought of the little Duck Boy and the pleasure his classmates took in tormenting him.

"I was a perfect mark. Fat. Bad skin. No friends. Not good at anything. Grades weren't anything to brag about. No reason to single me out other than I took everything harder than anyone else. That why the Suters have been singled out. I'll bet on it. The family is in more pain than most folks will suffer in a lifetime. Especially that frail teenager. She's ideal." Sadly, he gazed at me. "Better hustle, Lottie. This man isn't crazy, he's evil. And evil beats crazy every time."

● ● ● ● ●

Two days later, we had another regional meeting and started at one p.m. so Dr. Ferguson would have plenty of time to drive out. The day was cold and uninviting but there was no snow on the ground.

The first thing on the agenda was individual reports. I had asked David Hayes to go first. He looked like the Pillsbury Doughboy approaching the front of the room and immediately hid behind the podium I had placed there. He wore a uniform shirt with his undersheriff's badge and the buttons were strained across his ample stomach. His jeans hung limply below where they should. His pasty face was moon-round and pock-marked. I turned and looked hard at Harold who gave me an amused smile like he knew I was struggling to make sense of this man, this unlikely alleged computer genius who proceeded to tell everyone about the state-of-the-art equipment protection system.

His presentation was rat-a-tat-tat without a single unnecessary word. When he finished he distributed specially programmed pagers to every one of us. Then he explained the different kind of chimes and what the sounds meant.

I glanced at Dr. Ferguson who smiled when smiles were called for and applauded with the rest of the team when David finished.

But then Ferguson rose to his feet. "I join everyone here in expressing my appreciation for all your hard work. And your skill. Let's give him another round of applause." He turned to the rest of the table. "Before you take your seat I have a few questions. Mr. Hayes, is it?" He said this like David's role was too unimportant to bother remembering his whole name.

David turned awkwardly and faced him.

"So here is my main question. Have we actually accomplished anything with all of this fancy new equipment? Found a person of interest? Tangible clues?"

David's mouth tightened. He shook his head. "Not at this time, no." He lumbered on back to his chair.

Dr. Ferguson's gazed around the room again. He paced with his hands clasped behind his back then addressed the startled group. "Has Dr. Albright developed some theories about the assailant?"

Josie shook her head then studied her nails. The jubilant mood present during David's presentation vanished. No one spoke.

"Then I would suggest this Star Wars knock-off." He paused and made a sweeping gesture toward the row of electronics. He studied the gleaming new machines thoughtfully with an elbow propped in his hand and a finger against his lips then slowly shook his head before he continued.

Anger surged through me like a bolt of lightning.

"All of this is worthless unless it helps us track down people to interrogate about this crime. Or crimes, I should say. A young man has been gunned down. Babies have been left to freeze to death in bizarre places. We are no better off than if we lived in the 1800s." His hand swept the room. "What good does all this do?

"You are entirely out of line, Dr. Ferguson. Sit down. Let the rest of the men give their reports." Surprised, he spun around to face me. "Take your seat, please." Ladies have more authority than street fighters but maintaining the façade was tough. I wanted to deck him.

I studied the cowed faces of all these men who looked like they had just been dressed down by General Patton. David headed to his chair like a prairie dog ducking into his hole. Josie was the most self-confident person I knew, yet even she was silent. Her eyes were concealed behind a professional glaze that hid her thoughts.

Sam's eyes narrowed. Next on the agenda, he strode purposely toward the podium. He drew his white handkerchief from the pocket of his leather vest and gave his sheriff's star a little polish as though to remind everyone that this was his office, his building. He was still the main man. Duly elected year after year.

"Well now," he said to Ferguson. "Them's mighty discouraging words there, son. It's clear you come from the city and ain't used to applying a little energy to make things work out. Things are different out here. We're used to things not going our way. In fact our state motto is *Ad Astra per Aspera*. Means to the Stars through Difficulties. Most generally we come out on top. But don't worry. We still think kindly of you."

I looked at Keith who was covering his smile with his hand. We had seen Sam's John Wayne act before. Moreover, he could switch to well-educated English at will. My gaze switched to

Dorothy who had caught on at once. She began the applause that echoed around the room.

Sam gave an acknowledging dip of his head. "Now, on to the business at hand. As far as 'tangible clues' go." He paused long enough to shoot Ferguson a hard look, then put a photo under a projector, switched on the light, and threw up an image on the screen. "I would like to offer this explanation of how someone managed to put a baby in *Reaching Woman*'s arms."

He picked up copies of the picture and starting passing them down the table with the sequence ensuring that Ferguson would be the last to receive a paper. "Now, I want you all to pay attention to the marks on the area next to *Reaching Woman*. She's only reaching with one arm. Her other hand is clinging to a bar that links some of the sculptures. She's in a hell of a mess because an octopus has a tentacle wrapped around her. By the way, she's one of the prettiest of the women with a little pink in her cheeks. This wasn't discovered until the Kohler Foundation started removing all the crud from the concrete."

"Do they own the place?"

"No, they deeded it back to the community. To Old Man Dinsmoor, by the way, the octopus represented the trusts and monopolies that were wrapping its tentacles around the globe. *Reaching Woman* has to step right careful to keep her balance. She don't know where she's goin'."

"I've been there." Scott Smith, the Bidwell county sheriff thumped his fist on the table.

"Not knowing where you were going or the Garden of Eden?" asked Justin Harold. The men guffawed.

"Both, smart ass. The highlight of the whole display is the Liberty Tree Sculpture. Bankers and lawyers and politicians crucifying labor on a cross of gold. Lady Liberty is spearing a trust in the head while voters are attacking its flank with ballots."

"You don't say," Justin Harold snorted. "Too bad it's just symbolic." The meeting devolved into a raucous discussion of the presidential campaign where the issue of hard money was once again a hot topic.

"Business at hand," I ordered. "Business at hand."

Harold Sider was laughing openly but Dr. Ferguson refused to join in.

"Sam, about those marks. Were you going to tell us something relating to the investigation?"

"Yes, the marks are how the killer managed to get to *Reaching Woman*. See those little scraped places. He didn't use a boom lift or a ladder, he climbed up there. It wouldn't have been easy, but it tells us something. Whoever did this had to be young and agile enough to get this done and know something about climbing. I'll ask one of the state boys to check for rope marks and I'll bet there will be fibers left that might even tell us what kind of rope he used and if there was rappel equipment involved. Kind of think there was."

"Good job, Sam."

We went around the table but there wasn't anything else to report. There were a lot of questions for David. He came to life when he discussed technology.

Then Keith noted that there might be a weather change and some of the men had chores to do and if Dr. Ferguson was going back to Eastern Kansas he had better get started.

"I am," Ferguson replied. "Well, this certainly has been worth my time. I thought this would be a total waste."

Talk about attitude adjustment.

He sounded friendly enough. Remarkably so, actually, for someone who had been slapped down hard. It was okay with me if he was just faking it. I'm a great believer in civility in any form. False, sincere, insincere, whatever. Just so we could come together long enough to get some work done.

• • ● ◉ •

We invited Sam to follow us home and stay for supper.

"Can't promise you much. Just chili and cheese and crackers. And some popcorn afterwards."

Having no family of his own, Sam loved the warmth of our household and was one of Keith's closest friends. His wife had died of cancer and he had lost his only child in Vietnam. Too stern to cry, the old man usually gruffed out a polite refusal of our hospitality. Then we coaxed. It was our ritual and we all understood what it meant. That he didn't want us acknowledging his loneliness, didn't want to impose on our good will. That we were not to mention the fact that he would be going home to an empty house. That he was one sad son of a bitch.

Sam turned to Dorothy. "I expect they are inviting you too, Ms. Mercer."

"Of course," Keith and I said at once, stumbling over each other's words. "We'll have a party to celebrate the successful opening of the uber law enforcement center of the High Plains."

And we did. Or at least we tried. Keith opened some of his infamous home brews, and Josie and Dorothy and I dug around through our bottles of wine. None of it was stellar, but it would do and I made a mental note to hit the liquor store the next time I shopped.

For the first time since this nightmare of an investigation had started, there was music in our house. Keith was an excellent musician and Josie was outstanding. All of Keith's daughters were musical except for Bettina who was usually too busy chasing her little boys around to improve.

Dorothy's eyes sparkled. "I had no idea," she murmured after Josie began to play "Turkey in the Straw" and Keith joined in with the guitar.

"There's someone missing." Sam contentedly waved with his pipe. "Old Man Snyder. But you might never meet him. We can't tell when he's going to show up."

Josie laughed. "He lays me in the shade. Honestly. You would have to hear him to understand."

But the playing was off. It was very subtle. Josie's fingering lagged no longer than the flutter of a butterfly's wing, but it was there. Keith's notes weren't as clearly separated as usual. Like his fingers had gotten thicker overnight.

Not all the popcorn kernels had popped. And Tosca didn't want to sit on anyone's lap. Instead she laid in her special bed resting her head on her paws like she had gotten hold of a bad bone planted by some evil adult and she planned to punish us all until the culprit confessed.

We were bone tired and discouraged even though the meeting had ended on a positive note.

The phone rang. "I'll get it," Josie said, putting down her fiddle.

She came back two minutes later, her face beyond white. We stared at her. Trembling she grasped the door jamb of the music room.

"Merilee Suter is missing."

Chapter Sixteen

Keith and Sam and I left for the Suters' immediately. When we pulled into the yard Patricia was waiting as she held open the screen door. Her frail form was thrown into shadows by the looming yard light. Obviously hoping we were bringing Merilee home, she watched the three of us come up the walk. Hope died when she could make out our faces.

"Any word?" Keith asked.

"None. I was hoping you knew something."

"We're here to get some information before we start looking. Given the circumstances we don't have to wait before we put our full resources behind this."

Patricia crossed her arms over her chest as though she could ward off evil. "My God," she whispered.

She waved us through the kitchen and into the living room, talking as she went. "Merilee wasn't here when I got home from work. I thought she was with one of you. Or Ms. Mercer. She thinks the world of her. Do you think the person who pulled that malicious trick with the thing under her pillow is behind this?" Her voice shook and her tongue seemed to have swollen to the point where it garbled her words. Vexed, she swallowed hard and pushed her fist against her mouth.

Ernie sat on the sofa, his hands clamped between his legs. "I just hope to God it *is* that person and not the one who killed my son." He did not get up but scanned our faces to see if we were withholding information.

"It may be that she is at a friend's and lost track of time," I said lamely.

Ernie scoffed. "She calls. Always now, because she knows we worry ourselves sick over stuff that didn't bother us before."

No one had to tell me what he meant by "before."

"When did you find out she was gone, Ernie?" Keith's voice was cold and steady. Putting all his feelings in a box so he could focus.

"I was in the field but had my cell phone with me. Patricia called after she got off work. Thought maybe I'd given Merilee permission to go somewhere. But I had no idea where she was. I came right in from the field and we started calling around. Her pickup is here. That's what gets me. She had been to all her classes and then drove home from school. Patricia and I drove back to town because there's a girls' volleyball game tonight. I thought maybe one of her friends picked her up and took her to the game. She likes to watch it sometimes."

"So you and Patricia have already looked into the first things that came to mind?"

"Yes." He stared at his shoes. Ashamed at his ineptness. Like a decent father could have prevented having his kid just disappear. A decent father wouldn't have racked up two tragedies.

Sam gazed at the wreck of a man, then looked away. Ernie Suter was ruined. Sam suppressed his fury and turned to me. "Lottie, I want you and me to look over Merilee's room. Ernie, do we have your and Patricia's permission to search the house?"

They both nodded. I followed Sam's thinking and was sickened. He was worried about foul play.

"Keith, I know you are familiar with any questions that need to be asked. Please proceed with that while Lottie and I go upstairs. Pat, Ernie, stay here and talk to Keith. Every detail will help."

"I want every square inch searched," Sam said as we headed to the second floor. "No stone left unturned."

"Okay." The Jon Benet Ramsey case jumped into the mind of every law officer west of the Mississippi. The missing six-year-old beauty lay murdered in the basement of her home, which the police had neglected to search. She was found there by her own father eight hours after she had been declared missing.

"And that includes the barns, the machine shed and the workshop and garages and seed and grain bins." Sam's voice was tight with rage. "Everything. Inside and out and under. Check beneath tractors and combines and mowers and rakes and wagons." His face drooped. "Don't know if this is local or regional business, Lottie. Just know we don't have time to sort this out."

"Agreed. But we don't have the manpower for this kind of search, Sam."

"The hell we don't. Call David and ask him to get ahold of every member of the team and get them here right now. Then call Winthrop and ask him to send extra men."

"I want Dorothy to go over Merilee's room too. She sees things other people miss."

"And Dr. Ferguson? Can that smart-ass add anything special?"

I glanced at my watch. "We can call him but he will be nearly to Topeka by now. By the time he turns around and comes back we'll be finished here."

"Have Dave call him anyway. I don't want him saying that we left him out."

• • ● • •

We all went back to the Regional Room later after a twelve-hour search of the Suters' farm and the entire one hundred-sixty acres of homestead land the house set on. We added what we could to the whiteboard. Five bleak lines of everything known about Merilee's disappearance. All of that had been contributed by the Suters.

"Dorothy went through Merilee's room, but she will go back and look again when it's broad daylight. Josie will take a look too." I looked around at the men. We were a dismal lot.

"Did you get ahold of Ferguson?" I asked David.

"Yes, but like you said, there was no point in his turning around."

"He called me," Josie said.

Surprised, I waited for her to report. We had come to the sheriff's office in separate cars so she didn't have time to tell me this until now.

"He told me how sorry he was over the latest development. He wanted to know if I had any ideas because I had more experience than he had in clinical psychology. His specialty was counseling persons with Post-Traumatic Stress Disorder and helping track down serial killers."

I wanted to ask her if he had belittled the team again, but we were down enough without bringing up controversies.

"He said he would call you later. He suggested that everyone get as good a night's sleep as they could manage because he thought it would take a while to get to the bottom of everything."

I nodded and managed a weak smile. "I appreciate that. Anyone else have anything to add?"

There was dead silence.

"Okay. Time to pack it in. Everyone is dead on their feet, including me. Go home. Get some sleep. David will page all of you when we need to meet again as a group. If you have a good idea, call me." I glanced at my watch. It was already morning. "I'll be back here at about one o'clock tomorrow afternoon."

Justin Harold volunteered to stay at the Suters. I persuaded Dorothy to come home with us. It didn't take much. Sobered by the effect of participating in a real life crime instead of making stuff up, she seemed to be more comfortable staying on the farm. Whether she was in town or in the country, her walking stick was always within reach.

We dragged ourselves upstairs and I put on warm pajamas and crawled under the covers. Keith reached for me and we clung to each other. His anger seeped into the air and if he had any words, he choked them back. I shivered and reached for another layer of quilts.

The phone rang. I sprang out of bed and answered it with a sense of dread.

It was Sam. "I didn't want to get into this at the meeting, Lottie, but I'm ready to throw in the cards."

My heart started beating like a kettle drum, not sure of what I was hearing. "What do you mean?"

"I mean we may have wanted to solve these murders through regional resources, but it's not working. Ferguson is right. It's time to admit it. Especially with the disappearance of Merilee Suter. We're over our heads. It's time to turn this over to the KBI."

"Oh, Sam."

"Nothing against you or any of the rest of us. We've given this our all but we keep getting in deeper and deeper. A dead baby, a son that any parent would be proud of murdered in cold blood, now a teenage girl missing."

My heart sank. What if he was right and we had no business trying to solve a major crime? What if a regional center really wouldn't work? Arguments marshalled in my head but I was too tired to give them voice.

"We have no business taking on one major crime case, let alone three."

I swayed with fatigue. *No shit. Welcome to the club.* At that moment I believed we couldn't do it either. We were a bumbling collection of amateurs. He'd nailed it.

"Wait a day or so before you call Dimon, please. I want to sleep on it."

"It's my call as sheriff, Lottie. This is county business."

Was it? I hung up the phone and crept under the covers and huddled against Keith.

• • ● • •

I dragged myself into the kitchen the next morning, then noticed someone had already made coffee. I poured a cup and smiled at the first taste then headed for the bay window to watch the sunrise. Dorothy was already poring over the commonplace book. She started to rise.

"No, don't get up," I protested. I saluted her with my coffee cup. "You're a quick learner. I can't stand most people's idea of coffee. I would just as soon drink weak tea."

She gave me a wry smile. "I noticed."

There were footsteps on the stairs and Keith and Harold came down together. I sighed and went back to the kitchen to prepare scrambled eggs and pancakes. Josie emerged about an hour later and we were all too subdued to discuss Merilee's disappearance.

There was a faint cry from Dorothy and we all froze. She came to the doorway. "Lottie, Josie, come in here. I want to read you something." She looked around at our anxious faces. "Sorry to startle everyone. This has nothing to do with the here and now. It's sad, that's all. Poor Franklin Slocum."

"I'll take over in the kitchen." Keith sounded annoyed. "You two go listen to your soap opera."

Josie's face said she was dying to bawl him out, but she tightened her lips and we got the hell out of the kitchen.

"Listen to this." Dorothy started reading immediately:

I'm so ashamed, so ashamed, so ashamed. I can't even do what I swore I would do. My blood oath. That I would always act like a manly man and stand up for what is right and true.

A girl came here by herself yesterday. She comes here a lot and takes off her shoes and just sits where the bank is low and sticks her feet in the water. She looks lonely. A man came and watched her a while. In this journal I want to record lovely and true thoughts. I know what he did because my paperback books talk about it, but I was so terrified that I thought I would melt into the earth.

When he was done he just left her there and I didn't know what to do. After a long time she rolled over on one elbow and tried to get up. Finally, she did. I know she lives close around here because she always walks to the creek. What he did was so evil and while he was doing it I didn't make a sound. I didn't try to help her. Instead I turned myself into a wood frog and stopped my heart and floated above her and listened to her cry. Then I pulled out my six-shooter and swooped down and told her it would never happen again.

The next morning, I hid in the woods next to the school and didn't see her go in or come out. I watched for her a whole week and when I had a chance I read any newspaper I could find. There was nothing about it in them so I knew she had not gone to the police. Then a week later I saw her go to school. But I'm still ashamed that I didn't try to stop it.

Stunned we all three looked at one another. "He witnessed a rape," Josie said softly. "And his response was to berate himself for not trying to stop it."

"Which he could not have done. The most likely result would have been for him to get hurt."

"Or killed," Dorothy added. "Or even more maimed than he already was."

"Wait just a minute here," Josie said. "On the other hand something else might be going on. He might be making all of this up. He's a young boy entering puberty. And filled with anger. Reading old Westerns and badly needs to feel like a hero."

Dorothy and I looked at her.

She shrugged. "To tell you the truth, I can't tell whether this is a fantasy or one of the saddest true stories I've heard. Either way, he isn't handling it well. The floating above would indicate that he disassociated."

"And the shape-shifting?" Dorothy asked.

Josie snorted and crushed out her cigarette.

The telephone rang and we all jumped. Harold answered and stuck his head around the corner. "For you, Lottie."

He handed me the receiver.

Sam again. "What did Keith think about our turning everything over to the KBI?"

"I haven't had a chance to talk to him."

He grunted. "When are you coming in?"

"In about an hour. I've been doing some thinking myself. We can't take this back once we call Dimon. We'll be washing our hands of the whole thing. I want you and me to slug this out before we take the final step. Between us we can come up with every reason why this is a good idea or bad idea. Pros and cons." We did this often on matters far less important. "Meet you there in an hour."

I grabbed a piece of toast to eat on the road, and told Keith and rest of the group that Sam wanted to talk. I drove to town, my mind half on what it should have been thinking about and the other half grieving over Franklin Slocum's sad life.

● ● ● ● ●

"Did you change your mind?" I asked. He sat behind his old desk and I pulled a chair in front of it then headed into the ante room to grab a bottle of orange juice. Sam lit his pipe and gestured for me to sit down.

"I slept on this too." He shook out his match and laid it in his ashtray. "Goddamn I hate to just give up."

I marshalled my arguments. "Here's the thing. What can the KBI do any better? The agency does all our forensic work now. You know they couldn't round up the group we did to search for Merilee Suter."

"That's for damn sure."

"And they couldn't have stopped whatever happened from happening."

He listened to every word I said.

"The only benefit to washing our hands of this operation would be political. We could say we did everything we could from the very beginning and that would just be to make us look good. That's all."

"In short, we would be turning this over to the KBI because we have no guts." He blew a smoke ring into the air, then absently poked it with the stem of his pipe breaking up its perfection.

"Yes," I said softly. "No guts. Nothing at all to gain by turning this over to the state boys as far as solving these crimes go. We wouldn't gain expertise because we already have Ferguson, Josie, and Harold, and people with a great deal of common sense."

"And David," he added. "Unlikely though he seems."

"We wouldn't gain manpower and God knows the KBI would lose the kinds of community connections where people come forward with little tidbits of information. There's already community pride in this regional center and generally folks out here don't like state agencies. We hold all the cards. We've got the KBI beat."

"Maybe."

"Oh, Sam." I groaned knowing he was still on the fence. I pressed my hands against my head, hoping a little pressure would forestall a headache. "Okay, your turn." I peered between my fingers. "What are your arguments *for* doing it?"

"You've got me there, Lottie." He spilled some ashes on the front of his shirt and quickly brushed them off, taking no chances that there was a live ember.

Gloomily, I watched as he fanned the debris onto the floor. The place hadn't burned down yet.

"After I got a little sleep I realized I would be doing it for all the reasons you mentioned. None of them very honorable. What it amounts to is that I'm so upset that all this happened that I just wish this whole tragedy belonged to someone else."

"This doesn't belong to us, Sam. We've done nothing to bring any of this on."

"I know that. But it sure feels like it.

I rose. "Okay. We've got everything out of our system now. I'll call Dimon with the latest case details, but we've agreed to keep this under regional jurisdiction. I'm going home and you do the same. That's an order. Get some sleep. I'll call Betty Central to come in and take over the dispatching. Turn off your phone. If anything else comes up, she can transfer calls to my house. There's enough people there to make a small hotel prosperous."

"David fixed it so Betty couldn't get into our computer." He smiled. "My suggestion."

Betty Central has many good traits, but discretion isn't one of them. She is heavy-set, with tight blond curls that looked like they belong on a Shirley Temple doll. But for all her incessant chattiness, she treasures her job and comes whenever we call. She can be handled and coaxed into anything, but she is exhausting. When I got home, I simply waved at Harold and Keith. "Answer the phone, please. I'm going to get some sleep."

"Okay," Keith called after me. "Dorothy and Josie went back to bed too. When they wake up and are in shape to answer the phone, I'll hit the sack."

By four in the afternoon we were all awake at the same time. I took a ham out of the freezer and began preparing a sweet potato casserole. Dorothy made a slaw and we all looked forward to a decent evening meal. I glanced at Josie who had swiped her hair back into a loose ponytail and hadn't bothered with any makeup. Clearly she was in no mood for small talk even if I could have thought of anything to say.

Afterwards there seemed to be an unspoken agreement that we all would more or less retire to separate spaces. Dorothy went back to her own place. Keith and Harold found a football game and Josie went upstairs to download old movies on the set in the rec room.

I was worn to a frazzle from having extra people around. I had reached the place where I simply wanted everyone to go home and was becoming a worse hostess with each passing day. But I couldn't afford to slack off. I had too much to learn. I headed for my stack of books on abnormal psychology and forensics.

Chapter Seventeen

Two days later, on a bright, white winter morning, I called a regional meeting to coordinate any information that had been gathered.

Right before we began searching the Suter homestead, Sam had sent out a request alerting all law officers throughout the state to be on the lookout for Merilee Suter. We could provide a current picture of her but we couldn't issue an Amber Alert because we weren't sure Merilee had been abducted. All the counties organized search teams and reported back to the regional organization. The western half of Kansas had been picked to pieces.

Everyone but Ferguson was present. Five officers from Wilson County in addition to Sheriff Winthrop came over too.

Harold Sider went over to the window and stood there jingling the coins in his pocket. "Should we wait?" he asked finally.

"No, I'm sure Ferguson will get in touch with us if he isn't coming. We have a lot to cover and need to get started. Everyone is especially anxious to hear what you and Josie have to say. Even if you don't have a complete profile yet."

"So much is atypical that it's sort of a quarter profile."

I made a few introductory remarks. Then Justin Harold reported that everything had been quiet on the nights he stayed at the Suters'. "They are taking it awful hard. But I can't do nothing about that. They want their daughter back. Can't do nothing about that either."

We had kept a member of the team at the Suters' for comfort. For kindness. But beyond a certain point there really wasn't any point to keeping up a pretense that they needed guarding because they had not received any threats or ransom requests. Nothing that required an active police presence.

"Harold, Josie, as psychologists, do either of you have any special insights? Or at least some ideas on who we should not be looking for?"

Harold rose and walked to the front of the table. "Josie and I have been taking our time in developing a profile." He looked around the table. "As you might have noticed." He smiled. "I've hesitated because some of my ideas are in direct conflict with those offered by Dr. Ferguson. For one thing the unsub is not a disorganized killer. He has high intelligence and is capable of thinking through complications."

Troy Doyle, the new sheriff of Copeland County elbowed Scott Smith, the Bidwell County sheriff, in the ribs. "See, I told you this son of a bitch ain't no dummy. And another thing, he ain't no ordinary crazy. He's got everyone fooled." He spoke loud enough for everyone to hear.

"Go on," Harold coaxed.

"Sorry. Didn't mean to butt in."

"No, really. I want to hear what you have to say."

"Well, he's rich. Or at least rich by Western Kansas standards."

"And you know that how?"

"Sam talked about all that rappel equipment. They don't just give that stuff away. And he's a smooth talker because he managed to get Brent Suter to leave his house and drive to the Garden of Eden at night without telling his folks where he was going. The kid took off. Just like that."

"No evidence that Merilee put up any kind of a struggle either," Scott added.

"Right," Troy sat straighter in his chair. "And smooth talkers usually aren't laboring men. They can do better. And so they do. Doctors and lawyers and teachers and such. But he's not from around here because people capable of killing babies don't just drop down from the clouds. Folks out here pretty well know their neighbors."

"Not necessarily," Justin Harold said. "Remember Dennis Rader. Folks didn't have a clue."

"That's different. That was in Wichita, where no one knows anybody else. Out here we most generally know if someone is crazy."

Smith hooted. "You have to be sane yourself to know."

There was a brief spirited discussion about Troy's ideas and the nature of Rader's savagery. Rader, the BTK killer who had tortured and murdered ten persons, had eventually provided the clues that led to his capture.

"But I don't think he was a doctor or lawyer or teacher less he's from Colorado. Most of those folks go soft out here and he would have to be pretty athletic to climb up to where *Reaching Woman* is." Troy furiously chomped his gum. "He's from out of state too. Hard to become a top-notch mountain climber out here."

"'Less he sought out Mount Sunflower." Justin said with a straight face. There were snickers all round.

Gently sloping Mount Sunflower, the highest point in Kansas, was on privately owned land, and used to sport a sign "On this site in 1897 nothing happened." It was just fifty miles from the lowest point in Colorado.

I splayed my fingers across my face and shook my head, unable to keep a straight face. I might as well have been a substitute teacher dealing with naughty school boys.

Josie stood and walked to the head of the table to join Harold. "I don't have anything to add to that," she announced, grinning broadly. "Do you Harold?"

He shook his head. "Amazing. You've nailed the major points of the profile Josie and I came with up by simply using common sense." He turned toward the board and quickly made a list. "This is incomplete, but it will keep you from wearing yourself out looking in the wrong direction. This isn't much."

1. Intelligent
2. Articulate
3. Probably in a profession

4. Athletic
5. Possibly from out of state
6. Prosperous

Harold stepped back and looked at the list. "That's it. That's all we can say for sure. And you'll notice we haven't added one thing that you haven't figured out yourselves. One correction. He doesn't have to be rich to have the rappelling equipment. He's not poor, but stuff for mountain climbing costs far less than some of you spend for guns."

"So what's our next step? Time's a-wasting."

"The bad news is that there is no apparent new step. You've proved today that your ideas are as good as us so-called experts. I want you to follow up on any ideas you might have. Let David know what they are and if it involves active investigation, he will alert all of us. As you well know this is not like living in a city where there is always backup. And we can't go racing to someone's side every time they step out of a house."

We all sat there studying the board. I glanced out the window as a Dodge pickup sailed past our line of vehicles and parked at the end. It was a 2500 and well-equipped to pull the attached U-Haul trailer.

The door flew open and Dr. Ferguson walked in. "Sorry I'm late," he said. "I'm not used to the vehicle I'm driving. Or the trailer I'm dragging, for that matter."

He nodded at Harold and Josie then removed his newsboy cap and thoughtfully studied the board. "Sorry you've already wasted so much work. Especially since so much of it is off the mark."

Harold's eyes narrowed.

Ferguson turned to me. "Sorry, Lottie. I'm taking over this investigation. Or perhaps I should say that the KBI is taking over this investigation and I'm in charge. I'm going to pick up all the equipment and take it back to Topeka. Can't do anything about the money you've spent remodeling this fancy room because it's attached to the sheriff's office. You and the state will have to work that out."

The only sound was that of the wind whistling down the street and the thump of a tumbleweed whacking against the building.

I rose and stood by Harold. Stunned, I folded my arms across my chest. "No," I said flatly. "No. You're not."

A mocking smile spread across his fact, but I didn't give him a chance to speak. "Papers. You would need papers to do this. All kinds of orders signed. Do you think I'm just going to let you ruin everything we've done so far? In a few minutes' time?"

Josie casually readjusted a hairpin anchoring her chignon to the base of her skull and stepped forward to line up with me and Harold. "By whose authority are you doing this?" There was a softly mocking tone to her voice as though she were dealing with a preschooler who wanted to swipe another kid's blocks.

"Trying to do this." Harold corrected her with a knowing smile. "Trying to take the equipment. He hasn't gotten it done yet." His tone was casual and detached. Conversational, even. He caught my eye urging me to go along.

I took my cue from the two psychologists. "Ah, shucks. He's misplaced his papers. So sorry, Doctor. You'll have to come back another day. Tomorrow, maybe?"

Ferguson's face flooded with fury. Harold had sized him up correctly. The man could not tolerate any kind of mockery.

He struggled to gain control over his physical reactions. "Authority? I'm here at the behest of Frank Dimon, of course. I told him about all the colossal blunders made by this Mickey Mouse task force, the problems out here, and we agreed that the regional center isn't working out. It's time to shut this place down and turn this nightmare of an investigation over to the big boys."

"Ah, Dimon. I might have known." Josie's voice was slow and perfectly reasonable. "However, you can't take this equipment. It's mine. I own it. I have receipts for every bit of it."

Ferguson drew a slow deep breath. "What do you mean it's yours?"

"Just what I said. I own every piece."

"That doesn't even make sense. The regional center was voted in by the state legislature. There's no reason for you to spend that kind of money on a state-of-the-art facility in this flea trap of a town."

"What the state legislature votes for, and what it actually provides funding for, are two different things," said Josie. "We would have to wait until the next grasshopper plague before they would throw some money out to Western Kansas."

Harold placed a hand on Josie's shoulder to show his solidarity. "And furthermore, even if you could claim this equipment, you wouldn't know how to run it. David set everything up. The main server is programmed to wipe the entire hard drive clean if anyone but him tries to use it."

"Oh, I hardly think that Mr. Hayes can beat the best minds of the FBI." Ferguson's mouth curled in a disdainful smile. "Although I'm sure he is quite good." His condescension could not have been more obvious.

"This ain't no flea trap either," Troy Doyle asserted tardily, as though he had needed time to process the insult. "No need to call us names."

Other men recovered from their shock. Scott Smith rose from his chair. "It's time for you to leave. Go on back to Topeka before there's trouble."

"And don't let the door hit you on the ass on your way out," piped up Justin Harold.

"And the horse you rode in on," piped up one of Winthrop's deputies.

"And good riddance to bad rubbish."

They vied with one another to hurl more clichéd taunts. The room filled with jeering laughter. I shivered at the degree of hostility. Just a few weeks ago they had admired Ferguson's credentials as a decorated soldier. But he had insulted them and implied that rural people simply weren't as smart as their city cousins. That there was something crazy wrong with all of us or we wouldn't be living here in the first place.

And underneath it all was raw grief over crimes so hideous the whole region was paralyzed and living in a frustrated purgatory.

Their normal civility had given way to gallows humor, sick and filled with self-loathing over their inability to help their neighbor.

Ferguson's face flamed. He whirled around and left.

My ears rang when the door slammed. Not bothering to disguise my anger, I whacked the whiteboard with the back of my hand and addressed the men. "Look. I don't have a clue as to why we were subjected to this outrage. But we have to keep our heads. Before we dismiss, I want to call your attention back to the points Harold listed and that you figured out yourselves. Don't lose sight of the fact that we are looking for someone who is a professional man, a good talker, athletic, and probably from out of state."

Troy and Scott began to list the points.

"In the meantime, I'm going to find out what's going on. I'll head to Topeka the minute we leave this building. Frank Dimon has got a lot of explaining to do."

"I'm going with you." Keith rose to his feet. A muscle leaped at the base of his jaw.

"Okay. Meeting adjourned."

We headed for Keith's Suburban. I was glad he was along. Dimon respects both of us but he doesn't hesitate to hold back some of details from me, and he knows Keith is capable of beating the truth out of him if he has to.

● ● ● ● ●

Five hours later Keith and I were facing the man who was a dead ringer for Aaron Hotchner on *Criminal Minds*. He has the same dark coloring, and low heavy dark brows accenting his penetrating brown eyes. His perpetual five o'clock shadow was at odds with his pointed elf-like ears which hinted that there might be a sense of humor buried very deep.

Only Frank Dimon was no actor. I suspected he was simply born this severe. I thought he never would loosen up enough to call me "Lottie" instead of "Ms. Albright." Last summer when he had apologized for a fatal error regarding the rights of an old Spanish lady, he sounded like he was squeezing the words out of a throat so constricted he was in danger of choking. "I'm sorry. It was all my fault," were words he had never said before.

Keith was still hopping mad over Ferguson's actions. We waited for Dimon to explain to why the KBI would rush in intending to strip the Regional Crime Center of all its equipment.

"Oh, Ferguson completely misunderstood me." Dimon's eyes widened and he rapidly drummed his pencil on the top of his desk. "In all fairness, you need to know that Dr. Ferguson and I actually did discuss the lack of progress you were making." His face reddened with the effort of being totally honest. "It is quite obvious, you know. And, frankly, the newspapers are having a heyday. And until we have all the funding sewed up it's critical to appear as though we are doing everything we can."

"No *appear* to it," Keith snapped. "We *are* doing everything we can."

"I didn't mean it that way," Dimon said, looking miserable. "I know how hard you are working. But as you know, Lottie, you're a part-time historian...." He paused long enough to scan my face.

"Fulltime, sometimes."

"And a part-time undersheriff."

"Fulltime, sometimes."

"And Sam is getting up there in years."

"*Is* up in years. Not just getting there, and duly elected year after year over men half his age."

"And Keith is a part-time farmer and part-time veterinarian."

"And a part-time reserve deputy and you're forgetting part-time musician. And Josie has a private practice and teaches too, and now she's gone into forensic psychology. So? It's the way things work in the western third of the state."

"But there was a baby left to freeze to death by a..." He broke off suddenly and reached for a glass of water. "Be right back. I'm going to get you a cup of coffee and give Ferguson a ring. Do you want anything, Keith?"

Keith shook his head and Dimon hustled out of the room. Keith and I looked at each other with amazement. It was such an obvious ploy to get himself back under control. For a moment I thought I had seen tears in Dimon's eyes. God forbid that he lose his professional persona when we were sitting right there. But his movements, his expression said his frustration over being this helpless was as hard on him as it was on the rest of us.

He returned with our coffee. "Couldn't get him," he said. "Went straight to voice mail."

"Just what did you tell that man to do that he would decide to grab everything he could get his hands on?" Keith's voice said there would be consequences if he didn't tell the absolute truth.

Dimon looked away then took several sips of coffee before he began to tell us about his conversation with Dr. Ferguson. He was obviously determined to be as transparent as possible but he seemed quite puzzled. "He came in yesterday morning and said your team was meeting today. He wanted to know if there was anything I wanted him to talk about. I told him that we were mad as hell over the lack of progress. Nothing I didn't tell you a few minutes ago. And that the press was keeping everyone riled up."

Keith's gaze was relentless. And contemptuous.

Dimon shifted in his chair. "This whole fiasco shows what a mistake it is to give information to the troops before all the facts are known. I treated Ferguson as an equal and talked about all of my concerns, without taking into account his military background. I said maybe the regional center wasn't a good idea, after all. I was thinking through options. That's all."

Ironically the Regional Crime Center had been Dimon's idea to begin with. But he had wanted the director appointed by the state.

"I said perhaps we needed a strong leader used to giving orders."

There was no doubt my approach utilizing a collection of farmers and part-time law enforcement persons was driving Dimon nuts.

"At no time did I say he should be that strong leader and that things should be put in place that very second. He misunderstood."

"Well, *was* he the 'strong leader' you had in mind?" Keith pushed for the truth. Dared the man to lie.

"I was thinking about him," Dimon admitted. "He does command respect."

"And women don't," my husband said flatly.

"Hey. I'm trying to be honest with you folks. Completely open. I'm just saying how it is, not how it should be. Let's not lose sight of my point that Ferguson completely misunderstood me."

He looked to me for help. I said nothing and considered the differences in our positions. He had agreed to inject a mediocre congressman's nephew into a major crime investigation for a half-baked promise of more funding, and was too exhausted to follow up on his suspicions that something was fishy. I no longer needing funding. None. We had state-of-the-art equipment, privately owned, and an enthusiastic team of rural sheriffs and undersheriffs. If we had a forensic scientist we would be totally self-contained. But until then, I needed the KBI's labs.

Dimon laced his fingers so tightly the knuckles were white and he thrust his hands onto the immaculate desk and leaned forward on his elbows. "Maybe I'm the one who didn't understand. I honestly don't know the man all that well and certainly didn't expect that kind of overreaction. But all we did was talk. Under no circumstances did I give him carte blanche to dismantle your operation."

"Frank, the man is a total narcissist. He's a disaster."

Dimon had thrust Ferguson on me. Representative Williams had thrust this outlier on Dimon. We had both been shafted. I had told Keith about Williams but we'd had both taken it lightly. We understand politics and compromise but won't play the game. When all is said and done, it isn't worth it. Sitting in the chair opposite us was a perfect example of a man who had been entrapped.

But he should have said "no" to Williams. I would have. Keith would have. And so I decided. He could just stew in his own juices.

"Maybe you didn't know what you were getting into, but there's something you can to do to set things right." I checked my watch.

"What?"

"I'm going to call David Hayes and ask him to set up a conference call to all the team tomorrow morning. It's too late tonight. Then I want you make a special apology to the whole group and make it clear just who is the A team and that I'm in charge."

Dimon splayed his fingers across his forehead. "Will Ferguson be included in this mass communication?"

"Of course. He can hear it from you at the same time everyone else does. It's going to be one hell of an awkward phone call. But that's your problem, Frank," I said sweetly.

He groaned.

"And with everyone listening, I'm going to kick Ferguson off the team."

Chapter Eighteen

Keith drove and I stared out the window. It would be after midnight before we got home. The snowfall had been heavier here and the rays of the setting sun overlaid the bright white fields with apricot and lavender shading. Some of the areas looked like a bolt of peach silk had been flung across the prairie. The snow gleamed like it was lit from within to show off winking sparkles. Beyond, the sky blazed with glorious hues of orange, blue, and deep purple. Kansas has the most beautiful sunsets in the world, I thought, as I patted Keith's thigh and put my seat in full recline. The hum of the tires lulled me to sleep.

I woke with a start when the OnStar equipment began to ring. Simultaneously, both of our cell phones echoed through Keith's Suburban.

Keith answered his before I could dig mine out of my purse.

It was Dimon. "Where are you?" he asked without any preliminary greeting.

"Just past Junction City."

"Turn around and hit fifty-seven. We've got another one. Head for Council Grove."

"Another what?" Keith slowed down and began looking for a median where he could turn in the other direction.

"Another Ghost Baby. I'll meet you there. Get a move on. Use your lights and siren if you need to."

Dimon hung up before we could ask any questions.

Keith made a fast U-turn through the flat median and flew down I-70 toward Highway 57, which was the fastest way to Council Grove.

"Guess we both know where we're going," His voice shook.

"Yes, it has to be the *Madonna of the Trail*."

The historic female statue clutched an infant with one arm and a rifle with the other. A little boy clung to her leg. The sculpture was one of twelve placed by the Daughters of the American Revolution along the Old Trails Road which reached from Maryland to California. There was one in each state the wagon trains had passed through. Council Grove was also famous for being the site in 1825 where the United States negotiated a treaty with representatives of the Osage and Kaw tribes. The Indians got eight hundred dollars, and Mexicans and Americans got safe passage along the Santa Fe Trail.

I dialed David Hayes. "Tell the team to meet us in Council Grove at the corner of Union and Main Street. As many as possible and as fast as they can get there. When they arrive they are to hang back and wait until the state forensic team does its work. Just look, that's all. It's a four-hour drive for most of them and if they aren't in a good position to get here don't worry about it. Keith and I will be there in less than forty-five minutes and Dimon won't be far behind. We'll brief everyone later. Everyone needs to be careful not to mess up the crime scene but I want to hear everyone's ideas. Be professional. Pay attention to details."

David asked what they should be looking for. "A statue." I said. "She will be holding a dead baby."

I didn't have to tell Keith how important it was for us to get there before anyone from the state team did, because whoever landed first would be setting the hierarchy. I expected the local law enforcement to cede the investigation to us immediately. If my regional team was first on the spot I would see to it that jurisdictional authority was handled well. But if the state boys beat us there, I couldn't count on being given total inclusion.

I grasped the safety bars on the side of the door and hung on. Suburbans can fly like a jet when they are pushed. We didn't slow down until we reached the outskirts of town. Then Keith turned off the light bar and slowed as we headed down main street.

It was deep twilight. Keith pulled up to the *Madonna of the Trail.* "Shit. Goddamn the luck. People have already heard."

We had spectators. He slammed on the brakes and yelled orders as soon as he opened the door.

"Everyone back. This is a crime scene."

I made a beeline for the police chief who was standing at the base of the statue and introduced myself. "I'm Lottie Albright, director of the Northwest Kansas Regional Crime Center. I'm in charge of the task force assigned to the so-called Ghost Baby crimes. I'm sure you've read about them."

He looked at his hand like he had forgotten what to do with it. Then realized he should shake my outstretched one. "Alex Summers."

His shake was lame and helpless. He was in a uniform. The population was only two thousand, and no doubt knew each officer personally. But I was willing to bet that the force needed all the authority they could muster and Chief Summers wouldn't be caught dead in jeans. Summers had a short white beard and droopy heavy lids that shaped his eyes into the triangles of a retired clown. His mouth looked like an upended canoe.

"Keith, go get the crime scene tape and my camera. Start securing this place."

Summers seemed relieved when I took over. He turned back to staring at the statue. His face said he was horror-struck. "We got this 911 call. And, so help me God, when I got here I was so dumbfounded all I could think of was to call Topeka. We're not prepared," he finished lamely. "I've never seen anything like this."

"No one can ever prepare for something like this. You did the right thing by waiting for people who are trained instead of messing stuff up. The state team will be here in about fifteen minutes. My husband and I were closer."

Keith returned with my camera. He started roping off the area. "Include the whole park," I hollered. "Keep out all the resident heroes that want to stick their nose in."

"What's the next step?" Summers asked.

"I'm going to photograph my footprints, then make a quick walk through the grounds to check for any loose evidence and take panoramic wide-view photos as I go. Then I'll come back and sketch off a grid and make a very thorough search.

He watched Keith. "Can't he just make people go home?"

"No. Not as long as they stay back from the crime scene. We can order them to leave, but it won't work. No more than ordering a news crew away. Legally they are on public property."

I speed-walked around the perimeter taking pictures at a manic speed, then returned to the eighteen-foot-high statue and began clicking from every angle.

"Can't you take that baby down?" Summers' eyes were still trained on the statue. His mouth opened and closed like a guppy gasping for air.

"No. We can't do that until the forensic team has done their job." My phone vibrated and I glanced at the incoming text. "They are just five minutes away."

"Thank God. There's simply no way to explain to people why we would wait around and leave a baby here in the freezing cold. They are going to think we are totally heartless. Even if it's dead. It seems unnatural."

I noticed he was careful not to say he or she. He probably wanted to keep his distance but his eyes said that nothing was working. His heart was right up there with the baby's.

Clusters of people edged down the sidewalk. Some moved uneasily as though they weren't sure they should be there. Others were making use of their iPhone cameras. Word was getting around.

A white van raced down the street. *Thank God.* The KBI forensics team would set to work immediately. They had moved out of their old building in November and everyone who worked there was enjoying their spiffy new headquarters on the Washburn University campus.

Dimon jumped out the door before his driver had put the car fully into park. His face dissolved into bull dog wrinkles, then he barked orders to the team descending from the back. "Do *not* sacrifice one single step for the sake of speed, I don't care if half the town is here watching. Do *not* miss a trick."

Joe Nelson, the senior KBI forensic investigator crossed himself and stood silently gazing at the tiny body for a moment, as though he was struck dumb at the sheer depravity. Then he hollered at his men and got to work.

Dimon turned to me. "Is Josie coming?"

"Yes, she and Harold both. We couldn't get ahold of Dorothy and she's really good at seeing details in a crime scene. Either seeing things or making connections. I don't know which, but she sure has a knack for putting two and two together. She'll be able to tell a lot from the pictures."

"Goddamn it, Josie and Harold should have some opinions by now."

"They are going back to Manhattan in a couple of days. Harold says he's been away too long now and Josie wants to take care of some business at the university. We've hit a wall, Frank. The regional team and your people too."

"Anyone else coming from Western Kansas?"

"Probably not. I think the work will be finished here before they can make it. But everyone on the team knew immediately, thanks to David Hayes."

A little green Volkswagen buzzed up, parked next to Keith's Suburban and Dr. Ferguson stepped out. He strode over to where Summers was standing. He read the chief's name tag, and shook his hand, then they both turned to watch the forensic team.

My blood froze. My throat tightened. Of course. Everyone on the team had been notified. As of tonight he was still on the team. The game changer would have been tomorrow morning when Dimon made the promised conference call. Tonight was business as usual.

● ● ● ● ●

In the cold freezing wind Ferguson's face was motionless and without color. His lips were too numb to move easily. He stared at the tiny form held in the arms of the statue, and shook his head. "I simply cannot understand why we can't identify some-one who is capable of so savage a crime." His voice was soft and low, but Dimon and Keith and I were close enough to hear every word he said. "The bastard. Who could do such a thing?"

I turned when I head the hum of a powerful motor.

As soon as Josie parked, Harold Sider stepped out and his face was as white as if he had just stepped off a monster roller coaster. There are many cars faster than a Mercedes but with my sister behind the wheel he had probably just received the ride of his life. She had bought this fully loaded SUV especially for trips back to Western Kansas when she realized four-wheel drives were essential for navigating mud and snow. Her "real" car, a Mercedes sedan, was back in Manhattan. Both vehicles were a shiny black and the top of the line.

My sister ran to me. She squeezed my hand. There was none of her psychologist's detachment this time. Her face was as anguished as my own.

The scene was being videotaped and cameras were flashing all around. The phone cameras from bystanders rivaled those of the forensic team. Josie and I watched as Joe Nelson carefully pulled the tiny corpse from the frozen arms of the statue. In a dramatic switch of policy from the days of J. Edgar Hoover, the bureau now encouraged public participation in solving crimes. Profiles were thrown right out there and it had proved to be an effective tool.

Carefully, carefully, Joe removed a corner of the blanket cover-ing a tiny knitted hat and a miniature body wearing a hospital-issued bunny-printed flannel gown.

Blue.

A boy this time.

Josie and I reached for each other's hands. Keith quickly turned his face away.

A news team from a national network arrived. Ferguson straightened his back and stepped forward into the mic a reporter eagerly thrust at him. Joyful at having found such a distinguished connection immediately, she looked at the camera.

"I'm standing beside Dr. Evan Ferguson, who is in charge of treating our brave men and women in Kansas who have served in the military. Dr. Ferguson is an imminent psychologist, one of the most prominent in his field. Would you care to say a few words, sir? What can you tell us about the perpetrator of this heinous crime?"

"Obviously he has a pronounced Madonna complex. Somewhere in his childhood he was totally lacking in mothering and developed a profound desire to be cuddled and loved. He wants to be the infant that we saw cradled there."

The reporter was rapt. She motioned for the cameraman to move a little closer.

"He has a compulsion to kill infants and put them in the place that he was always denied. He kills them so they will stay in the right place and won't move. He can't help himself."

Aghast, I stared at the ground. This was exactly the shoot-from-the-hip analysis that Josie detested.

Then I looked at Dimon. He was obviously flabbergasted. He honestly hadn't known what we were dealing with. He was as shocked as I was.

He understood before I did. I was too mad to think. "I can't make that call tomorrow morning, Lottie. Not now. That reporter thinks Ferguson is God Almighty. If we kick him off the case, he's going to go straight to the press."

Chapter Nineteen

The wind howled around the house like it was trying to take off the roof. The sound was eerie, discordant. Josie chain-smoked, so my kitchen stunk. Harold prowled from window to window jingling the coins in his pockets and stared out like he could will the damn weather to go away.

Harold and Josie were desperate to get back to Manhattan. It would have made the most sense to go on from Council Grove to their own homes, but they had to come back for Tosca and now were unable to leave because of the weather.

"What can you tell me about Ferguson, Josie?" I was poring over manuals about psychology. "Dimon obviously doesn't want to cross him because he will most certainly go running to the press and tear the regional center to pieces. Plus, he will undoubtedly blame Frank for turning the investigation over to us in the first place. You can bet your life he'll make sure everyone knows that he's far superior to you and Harold."

She scoffed. "So why hasn't he been making stunning progress if he's so capable?" She beat a little tattoo on her thighs. "Come on, Tosca. Come over here." The little dog looked up and snuggled down further in her bed. Josie straightened and made a face. Tosca sniffed.

"Ferguson obviously has a narcissistic personality disorder. As you know, I never, ever give a cut-and-dried diagnosis without proper testing. But in this case, I have no hesitation. I admit I can't stand the man, but that's not why I'm just spitting it right out. He's simply grandiose to the max."

"He craves the limelight, that's for sure." I laid my book on my lap and hoped she would sit down and talk to me about other criteria for diagnosis.

"Very few persons with this type of personality disorder come to me for treatment because they don't think there is anything wrong with them. They think they are incredibly gifted and brilliant. So superior that only very special people can appreciate how magnificent they really are. They need constant admiration. Their sense of entitlement is unbearable. I see their wives in my practice. And their children. But not them."

"Sounds like Ferguson, all right."

"Yes. He's textbook." She wandered toward the stairs. "Going to start a video. You interested?"

I shook my head. Disappointed, I went back to my reading and recalled the reception Ferguson had received when he tried to round up our equipment. In light of what Josie had said, he had probably been enraged when the men jeered. Ridicule from mere rubes that couldn't fathom his superiority. Had to be hard to take.

The afternoon wore on. I couldn't remember a time when there was this little conversation in this house. After watching two mediocre movies, Josie came downstairs and suggested that learning to knit or some other sort of hand work would help me handle stress better when I'm agitated, instead of reading books that were over my head. I countered that smoking was not the best way for her to handle stress when *she* was agitated. She could take up weaving or macramé. Then she blew a smoke ring right in my face and marched off with a book.

I began flipping through medical response charts, memorizing techniques for first aid. Keith was in the music room twanging around on his guitar, experimenting with chords that I'll bet would never work with any melody.

Dorothy was here too and, sensing the tension in the room, resumed reading the commonplace book. Which I was not in the mood to hear, in case she was planning on organizing one of her little story times.

Sleet pelted the windows and snow was piling up in drifts. Zola Hudson and Keith had done everything possible for the animals and we should have been snug as a bug. But we weren't. I laid down my book and looked around at our faces, seeing deep fear. All of us were adept at controlling our lives, and now we were confronted with the deaths of three tiny babies at the hands of someone so depraved it was beyond our imagining. The baby boy at Council Grove had enclosed our outrage in a shroud of grief. And we drew no comfort from one another. The killer had even left the same message on the same untraceable paper. "See how the mighty have fallen?" No fingerprints. Nothing misspelled.

We were ahead in only one way. This time we knew where the child had come from. The baby was taken from the hospital in Lawrence, Kansas. His DNA matched that of a newborn there. The baby had been a week old and the mother had already been discharged, but she came daily to hold the child and nurse him. She pumped her milk for feedings during the night. The father came twice a day during daylight hours. They were both there every evening. The hospital wanted to keep the little boy another week because he was underweight.

There were relations who came and went and peered through the viewing window. They were not allowed to enter, of course, but there was a bevy of people cooing at this precious child. It was the couple's first and they had been trying for a long time.

Hospital staff and certainly doctors and nurses streamed in and out of this special room where the infants needed intensive care. The man who took the infant masqueraded as a doctor in surgical clothes and was wearing a surgical mask. Because the little boy was undersized and kept in this isolated ward, a bevy of doctors and pediatric nurses were in and out. To run this test and that. Examine his heart, his lungs. Always some new worry originating from the results of this test or that. The "doctor" had simply plucked the infant from the crib, stopped a moment to greet the nurses at the desk, and walked away.

Now the mother was heavily sedated and the father walked around like a zombie. The nurses staffing the pediatric floor had sounded the alert as soon as they realized something was amiss. They all said the man came during the shift change when there was a lot of commotion.

Most infant kidnappings are committed by deranged women who want a child. Not by a doctor wearing clothing hospital personnel expect to see every day of the world. No one remembered what he looked like because his head was wrapped and he was wearing the kind of mask that was proper under the circumstances.

Lay people usually didn't know about the security bracelets the babies wore. But all the doctors certainly did. These bracelets set off an alarm if they aren't disconnected before dismissal. That was no problem for the man who took the baby. The bracelet never made it out the door. It was later found in a Haz Mat container.

The CTV tape showed a number of men coming and going that evening but no doctors that couldn't be easily identified. All the other men who showed up on the camera were visiting patients and had a right to be there. If the thief had disposed of the surgical clothing in one of the trash bins close to the hospital there might have been some forensic evidence transferred, but he had been smarter than that.

Due to being underweight and frail, this baby's chances of survival were much less than the average baby. The medical examiner forensics said the child didn't last an hour.

"Oh, no!"

Dorothy's sudden outburst scared me. Confused, I stared blankly at the fire before I jumped up and ran to her side.

"What's the matter?"

"Franklin Slocum. This book. Something happened."

Josie came too. She eyed Dorothy, this visiting aunt who was rarely rattled and usually managed to keep all her emotions under control.

"What?"

"I don't know," Dorothy said. "Not for sure. Listen to this."

I want to die. I want to die. Yesterday this terrible man carried a little boy into the woods over his shoulder. The boy kicked and kicked and had tape over his mouth. No one could hear him scream out here anyway. I heard his screams in my mind. The man dragged an old log into the center of this little clear place and then stripped off all the little boy's clothes and laid him over the log.

I cannot write what happened next. I did not know it could happen to boys. I could not watch it all the way through.

I did not make a sound.

I think I did not make a sound.

I may have made a sound.

The man looked up suddenly.

Then I shape-shifted into a little wood frog. They can still their hearts, their breathing. I can too now. When I need to.

Then he twisted the little boy's neck like he was a little rag doll. He left him there and when he was gone I came out from my hiding place and went to the boy. I knelt beside him and held my hand close to his nose. There was no breath.

He was dead.

I could not bear to touch him. I started to cry. I had to tell someone. Biddy. The police. Someone. I had to be a manly man. This time I would be. Not like I was when the little girl was hurt.

I picked up the handkerchief the man had used to wipe himself. There was a lot of blood mixed with stuff that smelled like the rubbers the teenagers left. The smell made me sick and I gagged, but I did not throw up.

Then my heart started beating so wildly I was afraid everyone could hear it in the next county.

He came back. The evil man came back. With a shovel this time. I heard him in the leaves when he was still pretty far away. I ran to my hiding place and did not move. He dug a hole for the little boy and it was very deep and he covered it with leaves. He did a very good job.

Then he started looking around. He started at one end of the clearing and tried to find something. I looked at the handkerchief in my hand and became a wood frog again. I didn't stir and didn't breathe. I could still hear the crunching of the leaves and while the man was still searching I heard a car coming.

Two cars drove up. Some teenagers jumped out with their fishing poles. He heard them too and slipped away before they got here.

When it was night I went home and sneaked inside. I was too nervous to sleep. The next morning, I decided to go to the police. My body was filthy and my clothes were dirty. I filled the bathtub with water. Biddy heard me and came marching in. She's used to my sounds and my hand signs so I told her to get out and then we got into a fight. She said she wished she had killed me when I was born and I told her that if she did that she wouldn't have gotten any money to take care of me.

Oh her face. Her face when I said that. The look on her face. And I knew what I had I said was her biggest fear in the world. That I would die and she would stop getting money.

Why didn't I think of it before? There were other ways to stop her from getting my money besides dying. All I had to do was to prove she was not taking care of me and the government would take me away and poof—she would lose her money. I told her this and she left me alone while I cleaned up.

I told her to find some clean clothes for me. She was so angry her hands shook. She opened the bathroom door and threw a pair of jeans and an old flannel shirt on the floor.

I told her I wanted clean underwear and she came back with a pair of shorts and some socks. She even found some old shoes. I don't know where she got them but sometimes the social worker gave her things for me.

I went to the police station. It was hard for me to walk that far and I was tired when I got there. I still can't talk right but I could write down what they needed to know. I practiced what I going to say/write when I got there.

There had been a murder. A terrible murder.

But the first officer I saw was Steven Avery. A boy I had gone to school with. He was about seven years older than me and just barely old enough to get this job.

I hated him. He was the meanest of them all. And he caused all the others to be mean.

Dummy. Duck Boy. Freak. Filthy retard.

Steven looked up and spotted me and I backed away and then turned and hurried home as fast as I could go. He would never listen to me. I could hear him laughing and calling. "Duck Boy. Waddle on back here, little Duck Boy." He could have caught me, but I doubt if he thought I was important enough to chase.

When I got home, Biddy was sitting on my bed holding the commonplace book. She was at the very beginning. I hollered and she dropped it on the floor. It fell upside down with the pages open to the ceremony of blessing for the animals. So she had only read the first pages.

I shook when I picked it up because I knew if I lived here she would destroy it and it was my best friend. I would die if I didn't have this book. But I could no longer live in the woods in my special place. What if that man came back? I went to the kitchen and found a plastic trash bag and wrapped my book and tied it with twine.

This wasn't fair. It wasn't right. This book is my best friend.

There is nowhere safe to hide it here where Biddy can't find it. And the handkerchief. I know it's important. There is blood on it from the little boy. Blood mixed with that smelly stuff. I brought it home with me last night but I know it's not safe here either.

Sometimes if I think a while I can figure out what to do. The police need to know what I saw.

I am going to think. I will take the commonplace book and hide it under my special tree and put the handkerchief in there too with the plastic bag holding all my other stuff. Then I will come back home and make Biddy do what she should. While I think.

I have a right to a warm house and a bed and some food. If she doesn't give me that, I will go to the social worker she is so scared of. They will take me away and give me to someone else and I don't care anymore. But first of all I'll got to decide what to do. If someone like Avery gets ahold of the handkerchief he will just throw it away will never let me talk or explain. He would never let me write anything down.

I will go to my tree tomorrow morning. Just after the sun comes up. I will figure out how to get everything buried. After that I'm never going into the woods again. I'm going to live here with Biddy.

A special prayer poem:

Goodbye little squirrels and thank you for teaching me to hide quickly.

Goodbye little wood frogs and thank you for teaching me to slow my breathing. Goodbye little possums and thank you for showing me how to play dead.

Goodbye little otters and thank you for teaching me to swim.

Goodbye my most precious little owls, for teaching me to think

Goodbye, goodbye.

I will be back someday.

We didn't make a sound. The sleet increased as it hardened and peppered the window like birdshot fired from a twelve gauge. The fire crackled and Tosca, sensing some change, padded softly into the room where we sat like statues. She jumped on Josie's lap and looked up at her face to comfort her. But Josie slowly rose and dumped Tosca on the floor and went to the doorway.

"Harold. I want you to read something."

He came to the room and glanced at all of our shocked faces. "What's going on? You all look like you've seen a ghost."

"Take this." Dorothy shoved the book toward him. "Read it. Right now. It won't take you long."

Josie's face was pale. Perhaps mine was too, because Harold slowly looked at all of us like we had become ghosts.

He carried the book back to his chair by the fire. When he finished, he came to the doorway. "Josie, I need to talk to you."

"Keep in mind, Harold, that this child might be just making all of this up. It's almost too improbable to be true," she said slowly.

"I know that and I'm confused too. But we need to talk."

She followed him from the room.

Chapter Twenty

Dorothy and I sat and waited while two of the finest psychologists I knew conferred about an incident that happened a decade ago. I was awash with grief for this lonely child, but Dorothy's face was impassive. Thinking, thinking, always thinking. Bewildered, Tosca transferred to my lap while Dorothy and I waited for instructions.

Then Dorothy grabbed her walking stick and pulled herself to her feet and began pacing. But her slow steady energy flagged as though the accumulation of tragedies were weighing her down. Once again she could not neatly work out a solution. One of her preferred happy endings.

"If this is all true," she said soberly, "if it is…"

I said nothing.

Harold returned and asked Dorothy and me to join him and Josie. He went into the music room. "Keith, there's something you need to know about. It's all here in the strangest book I've ever read. You'll need to read this section yourself, then I want us all together so I won't have to repeat everything. Josie and I need to ask Lottie some questions and I want you to hear her answers."

"Does it have anything to do with the Ghost Babies?"

"No, thank God, but it has to do with something that happened about ten years ago and Josie and I have a moral obligation to stay here and do what we can. We are both officers of the court and as such it's our duty to report a crime. Although this is way beyond the reporting stage. If what this child says happened is true, everyone would know about it. If this account is made up and none of it is true, there won't be a record of these events. Either in law enforcement records or in the newspapers." Harold's face darkened. "I'm beginning to think this damned county is the Bermuda Triangle for crime."

"Actually, there is another possibility," Josie said calmly. "The crime itself could be a fact and the account and details are made up. It might be a tormented crippled child's effort to fabricate circumstances where he can participate in real life. As a hero. Not as Duck Boy."

We found seats in front of the fire and waited for Harold to speak.

"Lottie, how did you come by this book in the first place?"

"Jane Jordan brought it to me. She works at the historical society. The staff is instructed to turn items like this over to me to decide if we are going to keep them. Our storage is limited and we don't keep very many artifacts. There's not enough room. But we try to keep documents. Especially anything that is classified as primary research. And the commonplace book falls into the document category."

"And how did Jane come by it?"

"From a local farmer. Martin Horn. He has taken up metal detecting."

"It's a thankless pastime," Keith said. "Most of the low cost ones aren't very good. I have a metal detector and mine is pretty high quality but it mostly locates junk. Martin thought he would find a lot of coins, but he didn't."

"His was good enough to detect the nickel binders. If the rings had been aluminum it wouldn't have happened. Franklin Slocum salvaged this one from a dump site and I have no idea where he found writing paper," I said.

"So Martin Horn realized the historical society might be interested?"

"Yes, we're lucky about that. His mother volunteers there and has served on the board."

"Okay. After Keith has had a chance to read it, I want to take it to Sam and after he's read it and lifted all possible prints I want David Hayes to run them through IAFIS."

"You have access to the Integrated Automatic Fingerprint Identification System?" For once Dorothy was truly impressed.

"David Hayes has access to everything. That kid is scary good."

I recalled Ferguson's scathing dismissal as though Hayes was a redneck with no ability.

"And, Keith, wear gloves. It's already contaminated as hell, but we can save one more set of prints being added. Actually it's less cluttered with alien prints than some of the evidence I've seen. There should be Franklin Slocum's, his mother's, Dorothy's, Josie's, Lottie's, Jane Jordan's, Martin Horn's, and of course the prints of whoever owned the notebook in the first place. Before they threw it away."

"Oh, brother." Keith looked at Harold with disbelief.

"I've seen worse."

"And there might be friends of the original owner of the binder," I added. "I can't see where running fingerprints would get us anywhere."

"Frankly, I don't think it will. But we don't want to leave any stone unturned. Our next step will be to take this to Sam, have him read it, and find out if he knows something about little boys being murdered."

"No, missing." Dorothy rested her hands on top of her walking stick. "Franklin said the man buried the child. The parents would have no way of knowing if the boys were murdered. They would be reported missing."

We looked at Dorothy.

"And there was another little boy. Remember I said they told me at The Coffee Shop that little boys had disappeared? And it totally changed the culture of this county. No more allowing kids to roam at will."

"There was a little boy that went missing here in Carlton County. Then another one in Bidwell County. About a year apart. I remember that well. No one who lived in Northwest

Kansas could ever forget that. We searched everywhere." Keith's mouth tightened. "Two more families that couldn't put themselves back together again."

Keith picked up the commonplace book and quickly read about the rape and murder. "I hope to Christ this is all fiction." His voice shook.

• ● ● ● •

Harold and Josie and Keith and I went together to the sheriff's office. Dorothy's car was at our house and she said she would come back to the farm after she shopped for groceries.

While Sam read the commonplace book, Harold strolled around the room, then stopped and studied the bulletin board. Keith joined him and looked at the wanted posters. I went into the Regional Room and straightened the chairs, dusted, and waited for Sam to finish. Josie fired right up because she had been around Sam a lot and knew he wouldn't complain about smoke.

"I'm done," Sam said in about thirty minutes. I glanced at the lines in his face. He looked ten years older than he had when the Baby Ghost murders began. And now the rape and murder of little boys on top of that. He entered the Regional Room and lifted all the fingerprints, scanned them, and sent them to Hayes for processing.

"Now I want you to witness the fact that I'm putting this notebook where no one can get to it." He went through all the steps to enter the codes into the computer that would allow us to put the commonplace book in the evidence room. The procedure alerted all the regional team at the same time that a certain piece of evidence needed extra security. Ferguson included. He was the least of my worries at this point.

"Get your coat, Lottie," Sam ordered. Keith reached for his, but Sam stopped him. "I just want Lottie with me this time. Lottie in her capacity as undersheriff. Right now we're going to keep all questions on a county level and low-keyed. The right protocol. Then I'm going to ask for help from the FBI immediately and that will allow Harold to join us. Lottie and I are going to Slocum's and I'm going to see to it that that worthless bitch never sees that kid again."

"Man. No longer a kid. He would be in his twenties," I reminded him. "Old enough to do what he pleases. Maybe he's reconciled to Biddy by now.

Sam stopped suddenly. "Need to check something first."

He went back into his office and phoned David Hayes. "Want you to do a search. Is Franklin Slocum drawing disability payments? Call me back."

The phone rang in about five minutes.

"That's just what I thought." He hung up and stroked his mustache. "That's just what I thought. Franklin is drawing disability and it's being sent directly to his mother's bank account, and to add insult to injury, she's also getting a check as his caretaker. We're going straight to the Slocum household and make damn sure he's actually getting the care that bitch is billing the government for. Then Franklin Slocum is coming straight to my office and I'm going to get some information from him if it takes all day and he has to draw me pictures."

My throat tightened at the thought of this person who had never gotten a break in his life being grilled like he was a common criminal. He had tried to do the right thing years ago. Did his best to be a "manly man." His trust in the human race had been broken. His models were gentle little animals, but he hadn't been allowed to live in peace.

I wanted to save him from a brutal grilling. Josie looked at me and sensed my anxiety. "This may be a huge relief for him, Lottie. We won't know until we see him. But at least he will be telling his story to people who will listen. One thing is for sure. His book ended with him wanting some time to think. He knew no one would pay attention to him. His mother hated him from the moment he was born. He only got love from little woodland creatures. Now he's going to be supported by those of us here who will show him some respect."

Maybe. Maybe this young man, once a crippled child who had captured my heart from the moment I picked up his book would welcome a chance to tell his story in person. He would finally get to be a "manly man" and Do The Right Thing. Perhaps Josie was right and it would take a load off his mind to talk to people who cared.

"Josie, I want you and Harold to stay here with Keith because this is county business and I don't want anyone saying we were overstepping ourselves." Sam put on his sheepskin coat and exchanged his Stetson for a fur-lined trapper's hat with earflaps. "But if everything isn't ideal out there, I'm going to raise holy hell and bring Franklin back here for questioning. Might be what I'm going to have to do anyway to get some answers."

"Are you positive this is under county jurisdiction?" Harold asked. "It sounds like pretty heavy stuff."

"Yes, technically county. At this beginning level. That's why I don't want you and Josie officially involved with this. Lottie can work either way. As my undersheriff or as regional director. Keith can go either way too. He's a reserve deputy on a county level and also on the regional team. But for now, I think if three persons showed up Franklin would find that intimidating."

"Sleet is picking up. Are you and Lottie going to be okay?"

Sam shot Harold a look and Keith laughed. "Don't worry about Sam. He's equipped for any kind of weather that comes up. Let's go on back to the farm. There's nothing we can do here."

"Okay. I'll bring Lottie home after we finish at the Slocums' and she can catch you up on what we find there."

●　●　●　●　●

The house was set back from the road. It was a white and plain rectangular box with no shutters or adornment to alleviate the starkness. The roof was nearly flat. There were bare spots in the siding. Plain unpainted sheets of vertical plywood joined by another piece of wood at the top jutted out on either side of the entry door to provide some protection from the wind. The light aqua blue paint on the window casings showed some signs of peeling but with a coating of snow on everything, the place looked neat. Somehow I had expected a shack. This was poor and plain, but not falling-down ugly. There was a faint stream of smoke coming from the stove pipe vent on the roof.

We pulled up and immediately saw that there was too much drifted snow to get to the front door. There was a lump in the driveway that was obviously a car but it would be virtually unusable until spring thaw. No doubt Biddy Slocum had plenty of food stashed away to see her and Franklin through the winter.

Like most people in Western Kansas Sam carried emergency equipment wherever he went. His face had flushed with anger after reading the commonplace book and now the bitter cold kept it bright red. There was no path leading to the house. He opened the tailgate and took out a shovel and set to work. When he had cleared the way, I followed in his footsteps. He marched up the steps and knocked hard at the door. Again and again. Making it clear that we did not intend to go away.

Finally, a woman answered and opened the door a crack. She did not ask us in, but simply stood looking us over. She was a tall woman with reddened masculine hands twisted with arthritis. Her face was swarthy and deeply freckled. She was wearing gray sweatpants with a goofy top sporting a Disney decal. Wisps of dark hair strayed from under a knit cap that was pulled down over her ears. The odor of Pine-Sol drifted from the living room. As though she had cleaned houses all her life and couldn't break the habit even after her hands had rebelled against scrubbing and wringing and polishing.

Through the crack I could see an old-fashioned coal and wood-burning stove with feeble flames lighting the hinged isinglass and cast-iron door. I doubted if the room was very warm, let alone the rest of the house, even though there was little square footage. There was a bucket of coal by the side of the stove and scraps of kindling next to the bucket to get a fire started again in case this one went out.

Sam braced himself against the wind when he realized she wasn't going to ask us in. "Morning, ma'am. I'm Sheriff Sam Abbott. We would like a word with Franklin Slocum. Are you his mother?"

"Yes. What kind of business do you have with him?"

"I need to discuss it with him privately."

She hooted. "Won't do you no good. My son is retarded. He can't answer your questions."

"I would like to see him anyway."

"He can't talk right. Won't do no good to ask him questions. He can't walk right either."

"I need to see Franklin, anyway."

"Yeah? Well you can just get right to it. He's with his father in Chicago."

"Chicago?"

"Yes. What do you want with him?"

"Just some information. I need his address."

"Told you. It won't do you no good."

"I'll write to him."

"He can't read or write either."

Anger surged. I looked at her steadily, recalling passages of the commonplace book. She did not flinch.

"How did he get there?"

She glared at me, her eyes alive with malice. "His father came and got him." Her face reddened. "About time he took some responsibility, too."

"I need his address," Sam persisted.

"He didn't give me an address. Just picked up the boy."

"When did this take place?"

"Reckon it was about three years ago," she answered quickly. Her eyes flickered with a hint of superiority. Confident that she could best anyone in authority.

We were not dealing with a stupid person. After all, I reminded myself, she had triumphed over how many school administrators and social workers? Not for Franklin's welfare, but she had constantly improved her own situation.

"Haven't heard from him since."

"What is Franklin's father's first name?"

"Franklin. Just like the kid's."

Most persons, innocent or guilty, were nervous when the sheriff knocked at their door. Not Biddy Slocum. Nor did she show the slightest bit of concern for her son. I had the feeling that anyone could have come and gotten him and she wouldn't have minded. I closed my eyes for a second. I felt like slugging her.

No one knows Sam better than I do unless it's Keith and there is an alert tension that comes over this man when his lawman mind moves into high gear. He switched to his professional best. I could tell by his voice, his face, and the set of his shoulders that he was like a bird dog on point. He was much too intelligent to say or do anything foolish, but I knew we would be coming back here soon.

"Thank you for your time, Mrs. Slocum. I appreciate it." He turned abruptly and we headed back down the steps.

"That evil bitch," he said as he started the car. He put the gear in reverse and very carefully backed out in the tracks he had created when we came. "I'm going to get to the bottom of this."

"Did you notice she didn't show any concern at all for his welfare?"

"Colder than a witch's tit."

From time to time Franklin had shown some concern for his mother. He realized how hard it was for her to have a son like him, but I had no sympathy whatsoever for Biddy Slocum. Especially after having met her.

"Well, you're the sheriff. This is in your bailiwick. What's the next step?"

"I'm going to go through the usual county channels. He's got disability money coming from the government every month. You can bet Biddy didn't switch it over to the father's bank account."

"If there is a father."

"Exactly. Then to cover all the bases, I'm going to see if there is a death certificate on file."

I slowly exhaled. I had been thinking the same thing.

"And if there's not—and you can be sure there isn't—I'll have grounds to file a missing person's report which gets the Feds involved. This man who is supposed to be living in this county because he's drawing welfare payments here is committing fraud."

"It's his mother's doings, not his. Franklin tries to do the right thing.

"Maybe so, but there's fraud here. And maybe a missing person. That's how I'm going to approach it, anyway."

"Which means Harold and Josie are back in the picture."

Chapter Twenty-one

Dorothy was waiting for us. In more ways than one. She stood when Sam and I came through the door.

"You should not have done that," she said immediately. She abruptly thumped her walking cane on the floor to emphasize her point. Hard enough to jolt the murder of crows and a small line appeared about four inches down. There was a flash of silver before the birds settled back down to roost.

A hidden umbrella? A concealed compass? Dorothy was the queen of nesting dolls and hidden things. Her favorite pen was actually a recording mic and a large pendant was a whistle in fashionable disguise. One of her lipsticks held a shot of mace. All were clever accessories for a best-selling murder snoop.

Dorothy frowned and gave a minute twist, forcing the crows back in line.

"I shouldn't have done what, Dorothy?"

"Sent out a group notification that you had accessed the evidence room."

"But why?"

"Why did you not stop to consider that one of your team might be responsible for all, or some, or most of the crimes we are supposed to investigate?"

I was literally dumb-founded. Surprised, I turned to Sam expecting him to find this accusation ridiculous too. But there was a gleam of respect in his eyes. As though he appreciated her different viewpoint. He was not offended. On the contrary he seemed to appreciate the very remark that I thought was paranoid.

"I'm sure of our team, Ms. Mercer," he said. "They are top grade when it comes to character."

"I have no doubt about the quality of those men, but they *will* talk. However much you might wish for their silence, they *will* talk. To their wives. Best friends. Significant others. Persons whose lives have not been examined."

"You have a point. A damned sophisticated observation, in fact.

"This whole town gossips about anyone and everything to anybody."

Sam reached for his pipe. "There are empty chairs next to the fire and if you will join me there, I would like to hear more of your thoughts."

"I'll make some hot chocolate first."

"Wonderful. I'm cold to the bone and more than upset."

"As am I, and I want to hear all about the Slocums."

We all gathered in front of the fire and Sam and I caught everyone up on our frustrating visit to Franklin's mother.

"I don't know if Duck Boy was deeply troubled, or compensating for a terrible life, or was actually a clear-eyed assessor of his environment with superior coping skills." Harold rose and walked to the fireplace. He picked up the stoker and jabbed at a burned down log. "I can't come up with a decent profile."

"Well, let's ring up Ferguson," Josie said, not bothering to keep the sarcasm from her voice. "He'll be happy to provide one in five seconds."

Harold grinned. "I'm open to any ideas."

Josie scoffed. Harold edged the log to one side and put on a fresh one. Then he added a few sticks of dried sage and the odor blended with that of popcorn and Sam's pipe. "And frankly, Dorothy, I think you have a point. We have been assuming that whoever is doing this is an outsider, but let's go back to square one and take a look at the people on our team."

We made a quick list and of course quickly eliminated the people in the room, which was the bulk of the team. The Wilson

County sheriff, John Winthrop, was well known and a temporary addition to the regional team. Then with the exception of Dr. Ferguson and David Hayes, the rest had lived in Northwest Kansas most of their lives.

Harold walked back to his chair and reclined with his hands clasped behind his head. "Let me be clear. I don't think for one minute that it's one of us, but Dorothy is right. We are taking everyone for granted. Let's give everyone a little thought first."

"They were all vetted regionally," Sam's tone said he didn't mind this, just that he considered it a waste of time.

"I know that. But by now we are looking for some rather strange things. Unasked questions we didn't know to consider in the beginning. Lottie? What can you tell us?"

"Okay. Here's who's who. Nine counties make up the region known as northwest Kansas: Carlton, Copeland, Ingalls, Bidwell, Rose, Speer, Tecumseh, Ewing, and Roswell. Two counties, Tecumseh and Ewing, don't want anything to do with a regional crime center."

"No kidding. I don't think any of us here are very happy with it either."

"Go on, Lottie," Josie said, with a reproachful glance at Harold.

"Roswell really doesn't count. It's a tiny little kite quadrilateral that's better known as the Diaz Compound. There's still a huge lawsuit going on to settle who exactly owns that land."

Harold smiled at Josie. "Don't I know. I've heard all about that place and that lawsuit."

"Nearly everyone has. In fact, all the states in the union are waiting to hear the results because water rights are involved. It's one of those cases that seems to be local and then turns out to have extraordinary implications. Anyway, Roswell County is still attached to Carlton County for judiciary purposes. They don't even have anyone to send here."

"That's three counties that didn't have a representative at our meetings. Roswell, Ewing, and Tecumseh. That leaves six," Sam said.

"Right. Our own Carlton County is just teeming with people on the team. Me, Josie, Keith, Sam, Dorothy, and you, Harold. You are an official consultant for Carlton County. The Copeland County sheriff is Troy Doyle. Troy is the one who gave that terrific profile by just using everyday common sense and logic. He's the one who replaced Sheriff Deal. Deal is the one who tried to kill me and Josie."

My sister managed to keep all emotion off her face.

"Bidwell County was represented by Scott Smith and his undersheriff, David Hayes. Justin Harold nearly always has something to say. He's from Ingalls County. He takes immediate and fierce umbrage when anyone insults Kansas or implies that we aren't bright because we live out here. And we all know about David by now."

Harold smiled. I was sure he knew a lot about Hayes that he hadn't told the rest of us.

"The other two counties at the meeting were Rose and Speer. Mr. Redstone never said a word. He's the retired sheriff of Rose County and they are supposed to replace him when they find someone new, but it just doesn't seem to happen. He's held that position for the last nine years."

"He's even older than me." Sam's eyes twinkled as he took a strong draw on his pipe.

"Leon Fleming, the Speer County sheriff, was the one who took furious notes. He wore every type of device that could be attached to his uniform and I'm willing to bet all his reports are impeccable."

"He didn't ask any questions, did he?"

"No. And it wasn't just because Ferguson interrupted us. He never does. I've been in other meetings with this man. He's a little unnerving. Just listens and takes notes. So I guess I really don't know much about him."

"I'll have him checked out and David will try to locate Franklin Slocum's father."

Josie reached for Tosca who had been very patient during the long stay at the farm. "We're taking off tomorrow, Lottie. The weather report says it will be clear and I-70 is supposed to be open. And the little doggie is getting a bit broody." She rubbed Tosca's ears, who looked up with gratitude. "Yes she is, now. Baby wants her own widdle beddie-bye."

Astounded, Dorothy looked at my sister like she had lost her mind.

"There's absolutely nothing more we can do here." Tosca jumped off Josie's lap and left the room.

Unspoken was that none of us could make a move until more information came in. We were blocked as far as locating Franklin Slocum, needed to find out more about Leon Fleming, and although we would follow up on every call and tip that came in about the Baby Ghost Murders not all the lab work had been completed.

●　●　●　●　●

The next morning Harold and Josie said their goodbyes and left for Manhattan. Normally I was sad to see my sister leave but today I couldn't wait for a chance to be by myself. I was exhausted both from the strain of trying to keep up a good front for sake of our budding regional center and sheer inexplicable horror of the crimes. I was on sensory overload and felt like I was going to crash.

Dorothy had gone to her own house too and after I saw Josie's car turn the corner, I grabbed a blanket and a pillow and snuggled down in the bay window chair. I grabbed Donis Casey's latest mystery, although I suspected that my ability to concentrate was nonexistent.

I dozed off, lulled by the familiarity of my little nest. And then the phone rang.

It was Josie, who didn't bother to say hello. "You'll never guess who I just heard from."

I waited.

"Dr. Ferguson."

I was fully awake now.

"He wants to talk and offered to meet me in Manhattan. He suggested a spare room at the university so it would be convenient for me."

"Why?"

"He says he has some different ideas that he wants me to consider regarding the Baby Ghost Killer and he wanted me to listen away from you because he knew you would reject them out of hand. He says he has some valuable information and as a psychologist I would be in the best position to understand it."

"So, what did you tell him?"

"I told him I would be glad to listen."

"And are you?"

"Hell no. You're the regional director. This is your case. I want you there too. I was honest when I said I would be glad to listen. I just didn't mention that I wouldn't be there by myself."

"And when will this meeting take place?"

"Day after tomorrow. Can you come? His so-called 'valuable information' might not amount to a damn, but it won't hurt to listen."

"That's true. And of course I'll be there. It's my job. At any rate I can't wait to see his face when we both show up."

• ● ● ● •

When we walked into the room together I wished I had a camera. A good one like Dorothy's to catch his exact expression. I expected visible shock or at least resentment. There was a flicker of something. Anger, I think. Quickly suppressed.

He gestured toward chairs then sat down himself and leaned toward us with his hands clasped and his elbows resting on the table. A perfectly earnest pose.

"I'm sure you are wondering," he said with a wry smile.

"Yes." Josie sat absolutely straight and the look on her face was not encouraging. "You said you have some special information."

"Yes. I do. And believe me I would give anything not to be the bearer of bad news. There are some things I think you should know about three of the members of your team: David Hayes,

Justin Harold, and Troy Doyle. I'm coming up with some serious psychological history."

I sucked in my breath. I felt like I had been kicked in the
stomach. I recalled Dorothy's scathing disapproval over letting the
whole team know that Sam and I had accessed the evidence room.

At least we hadn't told everyone that what we had deposited
was the commonplace book. And even if we had said we had
deposited an old three-ring binder, it would not have been of
any interest to any of them since it didn't pertain to the Baby
Ghost Murders.

Only our family knew about this book. Plus Sam. And he
might as well be family.

And as Josie had pointed out, everything in the book might
have been the outpouring of the mind of a troubled little boy. Or
a little boy who wanted to be the hero in his own story. He was
reading paperbacks. He wanted to be moral and upstanding. He
surely would have heard of missing boys. Were there subsequent
missing pages that might contain a happy ending? Had he led
the police to a burial site? We needed to locate Franklin Slocum
and verify the information.

Before yesterday, all we had put in the room was the goofy
little play-back device that had been placed under Merilee Suter's
pillow.

Ferguson directed his remarks to Josie, as though I was of
no importance at all.

"Let's begin with Troy Doyle. I understand that he was
responsible for the profile you had posted on the board when I
arrived the other day."

Josie said nothing.

"It's quite obvious to me that he fancies himself an amateur psychologist and they are always dangerous in a police investigation.
Especially when they've developed a theory they feel they have to
defend. I couldn't find too much on Doyle in any of the databases
at my disposal. No military history. No police records. Nothing in
any juvenile records either. So my first question would be where
did this man come from? And what are his qualifications?"

Astounded, I could only stare. That was all? Just another of his half-baked theories?

"Moving along to Justin Harold. The class clown. The cut-up. Always out to get a laugh." Ferguson's mouth pulled down even farther in disdain. "I mean who does he think he is?" he scoffed. Then seeing that we didn't join in, he frowned and looked down before he continued.

"The first clue I had that something was amiss with Hayes was the way he ducked his head and basically stared at his shoes when he was talking to you and your sister. In fact, Ms. Mercer got the same treatment."

I had planned to let Josie do all the talking but couldn't restrain myself. "Dr. Ferguson! You had just finished putting David down. Calling everyone's attention to his every flaw. Of course he looked at his shoes."

"Maybe he's just shy," Josie offered.

"Beyond shy." He looked at me triumphantly. Wicked pleased that he had drawn me in. "He's deeply uncomfortable around women. And at his age that isn't normal."

"It's hardly abnormal. And I would like to point out that he ducks his head and stares at his shoes when he is around men too. I'll bet he's introverted to begin with and then became hooked on computers sometime around junior high when young boys are awkward socially anyway. But that's speculation," Josie said pointedly. "I don't actually *know* that. And as I'm sure *you* know—it's very presumptuous to speculate about people. Psychologists are too often wrong."

Ferguson did a slow-burn and the scar at the corner of his mouth made it look like he was gearing for battle.

He went right on expounding on his theory. "Hayes obviously was short-changed when it came to nurturing relationships in his childhood." A vein throbbed in his temple as he picked up heat. "He has very low self-esteem and I suspect he's not nearly as intelligent as your friend Harold Sider gives him credit for. In fact, I would like to know more about Sider's involvement in this whole investigation because Hayes is totally fixated on winning affection from his mother."

"Dr. Ferguson, that's enough. You're maligning fine men. Without a shred of proof." Furious, I rose to leave. Maybe Dimon was afraid that if we removed him from the team he would go to the press, but I wasn't. I didn't give a damn what he told the press. "And furthermore..." But before I could officially fire the bastard, Josie stopped me with a warning shake of her head.

She held up a hand, pulled her cell phone out of her purse and glanced at it.

"So sorry to interrupt. I just had an important message and have to leave immediately."

Ferguson gave her a black look. "I have a lot more to tell you and would like to have your support for some of the ideas I'm presenting. Lottie, you'd better listen, whether you want to hear it or not."

"Sorry. Can't stay." Josie race-walked to the door.

I glanced back at Ferguson who was obviously furious.

● ● ● ● ●

"What in the hell came up that's so important?" I asked as we hurried to her car. "I was getting ready to lower the boom."

"What's important was me getting the hell out of that room before I flew across it and strangled Ferguson. Everything he was saying was a crock of shit. Not supported by anyone who actually knows anything. Plus, by the look on your face I knew all hell would break loose. You were about to make an enemy. And I want Dimon to be the one who gets kicked in the balls. Not you. He's the one who got you into this mess."

She was right, of course. "But the things he said! Ferguson doesn't even know David. He was attacking like a kid would in junior high. Using a kid's taunts. Fat. Sloppy clothes. Bad skin. Definitely not cool."

"Exactly."

"So why would he come up with these ideas about these three men like he's trying to discredit them?"

"Or more to the point, it's like he's trying to establish his own credibility and that's what I need to figure out. According to Dimon, Ferguson's got credentials out the whazoo so why would he be (a) trying to indict David? And (b) offer such half-baked ideas to begin with?"

"He obviously wants to be the big cheese. The main man who gets all the credit for solving the Baby Ghost Murders. He wants to be in charge of the investigation."

Josie frowned. "Duh. I'd have to be an idiot not to notice."

"I assume you noticed that all the three men he named were the ones who gave him the hardest time during the last meeting."

"You bet I did. I'm going to straight to Sider's office and ask him to pull a few strings to access Ferguson's military records. Especially anything that has to do with medical history."

"Medical?"

"Yes, I think he's nuts."

Chapter Twenty-two

Sider laughed at Josie. "Did he get the best of you? You hardly ever let that happen. I think you need to stand back and apply a little of your analytical skills to what that man was saying. As for checking him out. I've done that, believe me. There are some areas of his military records that are virtually inaccessible but I've been assured it's not because there is something sinister there. It's because of the classification level of some of his work in intelligence."

"I can't stand the man." Josie fished around in her purse for her cigarettes.

"That's very obvious, but what I want you to think about is his Madonna theory and why someone is killing these babies."

"I don't need to think about it. I'm not buying it."

"That's obvious too. But you know criminologists and profilers look at the human mind differently than psychologists who treat patients. I'm looking at this from a forensic standpoint and we need your ideas as a clinical practitioner."

"I'm forensic too," she countered.

"Just starting. So, what's up with this savage?"

"Savage?" She raised an eyebrow.

He grinned. "The killer, not Ferguson. Why don't you buy the good doctor's theory and look for someone who lacked a nurturing experience with his mother?"

"Because the idea is crap, Harold. Pure crap. Everyone's mother lacks something."

Then they launched into a heated discussion that was far over my head. I tried to follow the implications of quotes from the *Crime Classification Manual* and then the *Diagnostic and Statistical Manual* but got lost somewhere along the way. What did register was Harold's insistence that Josie's dislike of Ferguson caused her to ignore all of his input.

"I'm not buying Ferguson's Madonna theory either," Harold conceded. He rose and adjusted the light coming through the blinds. This morning he wore a beautifully tailored pin-striped suit. It was in striking contrast to the khakis he usually wore at the farm. "That sounds like the kind of psycho-babble I hear on TV talk shows. He glanced at his watch. "I have to leave for Kansas University in an hour. I'm lecturing at a conference."

"Don't let us hold you up if you need to be somewhere else," Josie said. "I came by to see what you could find out about Ferguson's vetting process."

"No problem. I've got plenty time. But there's one thing about the Baby Ghost Killer I'm sure of now. Whoever is doing this—no matter how he got started in the first place—his primary motivation is to show us how smart he is. That's the ultimate goal. To humiliate the police and show us his superior mind. He's taunting us."

"I think you're right. Absolutely. But as a clinician, I'll guarantee you there is something else terribly wrong besides a desire to stick it to the police. When we catch him we'll find someone who is legally sane. Brilliant, highly organized, but totally crazy from a mental health standpoint."

My eyes widened. Psychologists weren't supposed to call people crazy.

She tapped the end of a cigarette against her gold case and paused just long enough to fish her lighter from her purse.

"Another thing that is bothering me is the length between his first crime and the last two. The Ghost Baby at the Elizabeth Polly Park was over ten years ago. Now we are dealing with a Ghost Baby murder at the Garden of Eden and another one in rapid succession at Council Grove. Ten years. That's a long time between crimes. Was he locked up somewhere?"

Harold looked at her solemnly, his dark eyes sorrowfully mirroring his and Josie's grief at not being able to make a bit of progress. "It's a long time, but not unheard of. Look at Dennis Rader, the BTK killer. He waited thirty years before he started again. Or the Unabomber. It's ominous that the last two Ghost Baby murders—Garden of Eden and then the *Madonna of the Trail* are close together."

They were leaving something out. "And the unspeakable torture the Suters are going through," I reminded them. "It's easy to overlook that family because the images of little babies are imprinted on our brains. Like the after-burst of a bright light or the blindness from staring at the sun. Aren't the babies all we can see? That's true for me. Frozen babies."

Josie nodded and Harold looked away.

"But in some way the Suters are connected to the Baby Ghost murders. For that poor mother and father there is one child murdered. One missing. What did those poor people do that some maniac would focus on them?"

• • ● • •

We went to Josie's townhouse. I didn't intend to go back to Western Kansas until the next day. Josie rapped lightly at the door and it was opened by a middle-aged Hispanic woman who held Tosca in her arms. The little dog gave a faint yip and she transferred the trembling shih tzu into Josie's arms.

"She's had a good day." She looked intently at Josie and then at me.

"My sister, Lottie," Josie explained. "We're twins. Obviously." She made a face. "Thank you. Will you be available tomorrow if I need you?"

"No, I'll be sitting with my grandchildren. But I think Tosca will be just fine. There's nothing really wrong with her," she said disapprovingly. "Just nerves."

Josie managed a weak smile.

"Nerves?" I raised an eyebrow.

"Apparently. Her appetite is off so I took her to the vet here when we got home. He examined her thoroughly and said she just needed to be back in her own surroundings for a while. I think being in Western Kansas brought back too many bad memories of past experiences."

She was serious! I kept a straight face and tried to look concerned but I think Tosca sensed that I thought she should simply straighten up because she took one look at me, sniffed, and snuggled down further into Josie's arms.

"I need a drink. Would you do the honors, Lottie, while I tend to Tosca who obviously needs some special attention?" She buried her nose in the dog's fur.

Oh, boy. Gladly. If ever I needed a shot of good scotch. I carried my suitcase into the spare bedroom and then went back into the living room and walked over to her bar. There was a variety of alcohol but, as usual, only one bottle of scotch, a Glenlivet Nadurra Oloroso. I never knew what brand of scotch I would find.

Josie did not drink regularly and was an experimenter when it came to scotch. Only one bottle at a time, never decanted, unless she was entertaining, and I hardly fell into the honored visitor category. She has one of the most beautiful sets of crystal I've ever seen and I carefully opened the bottle and poured the amber liquid into thin glass tumblers.

To her credit, when she came to Western Kansas she never said a word about our motley collection of gift bottles, mostly presented by guests during hunting season and selected because the names were cute.

Once a grateful pheasant hunter presented me a bottle of Crown Royal and a quilt she had handmade from purple velvet Crown Royal bags, prominently displaying the gold embroidered label on every block. There was even a special entry class for Crown Royal designs at our county fair. Keith mostly drank his dreadful home brew instead of bourbon so the aging bottle still sat among the casual collection of misfits we referred to as our liquor supply.

I gave Josie a glass and smiled at Tosca nestled in her lap. Classical music came from magnificent speakers that were embedded somewhere. The centerpiece of the room was her antique Steinway concert grand piano. It had been restored, she told me once, and cost over one-hundred-twenty-five-thousand dollars. Although people in Western Kansas are awed by her ability with the violin—fiddle, when she switches styles—she is a stunning pianist and was once faced with the heartbreaking realization that she was too self-protective to reveal the passion necessary to move onto the concert stage.

It was not only a matter of the time she would have to spend practicing. Only in music did Josie let it all hang out. But that was not for other people to see.

I sipped my scotch, lulled by the music and the shifting play of light on the highly polished wood floors. The faint exquisite odor of her Joy perfume scented the room. A couple of hours later, Josie coaxed me from my chair and led me to the bedroom and turned down the white satin spread. A room fit for a queen. There were silk pajamas lying on the pillow. I barely had the energy to undress and put them on before I fell into the bed.

But our talk, I thought dully. *Our fun night.* This was supposed to be like a sleepover. Instead I had acted like Tosca and ducked my head and squeezed my eyes shut against images of tiny babies and little boys who couldn't walk right or talk right.

I slept like the dead.

Sunlight filtered into the room. I didn't want to wake up. I didn't want to go home. I didn't want to be a wife, or stepmother, or undersheriff, or regional director, or anything much. I just wanted to go back to bed. I wasn't groggy from drink but from the consequences of oversleeping. I headed for the bathroom, then called for my sister.

"Josie?" She didn't answer and I wrapped a terry robe around me, shoved my feet into slippers and padded on out to the kitchen. There was a note by the coffee pot.

"Have a class today. Make yourself at home. Tosca is at day care."

Finally, all coffeed up and fortified with a couple pieces of toast, I collected my toiletries and started a hot shower to see if I could get some blood flowing.

I was dimly aware of the phone vibrating as I shampooed my hair. I checked it after I toweled off.

There was a text from Keith:

Come home ASAP. All hell is breaking loose.

• ● ● ● •

I drove home with a minimum of stops. When I walked inside the house Keith, Sam, and Dorothy were sitting around the kitchen table. And in the great room, pacing in front of the fireplace, was Keith's oldest daughter, Elizabeth.

"Hello, Lottie," she said without a trace of warmth.

"Elizabeth," I acknowledged her and walked past the kitchen crew to put my purse in the closet and hang up my coat. I unwrapped my scarf, removed my heavy knitted cap, squared my shoulders and turned to face the group. I wanted to talk to Keith alone first, but obviously that was not going to be possible.

"What's going on?" That there was trouble I had understood from Keith's text. In fact, anytime Elizabeth was around there was trouble. If it wasn't there to begin with she simply brought it with her from Denver. She is a lawyer, "wicked smart" as Obama had once said of Hilary Clinton, and could outthink, outsmart, out-talk practically anyone I knew. Amazonian in height and posture, her blazing blue eyes could ferret out the truth before most people could get their wits together.

She did not like me and hadn't from the beginning. She was the one who found her mother, reported the death, and helped her siblings get their lives back together. She deeply resented her father's having married a woman younger than she. No matter what I did or said she would simply never get over me. What we had settled for was a superficially civil relationship that functioned without forcing others in the family to choose sides.

Elizabeth took it on herself to bring me up to date. "An asshole of a psychologist came blazing down here this morning like someone out of an old Western, all puffed up with authority, and stormed into Sam's office like he owned the place."

Ah, while I had been lolling around on Josie's silken sheets. Served me right. Ferguson had obviously made a beeline for Western Kansas and Sam's office. I recalled the way Ferguson had invaded the Regional Room a short time ago.

"I'm a complete stranger," Elizabeth raged, "but he didn't even stop to consider that he might not have any business talking about stuff in front of me. I mean really! Or question what I was doing there or anything else."

My eyes asked the unspoken question. *What was she doing there, anyway?*

"I had come home to see Aunt Dorothy," she said as though she had heard my thoughts. "When I talked to Dad the other day he said she was here. I have a couple of days off so I thought I would buzz down. Besides, I didn't like the way my father sounded."

"Oh, God." Keith gave a disparaging flap of his hand. But she continued talking about him as though he wasn't present. Naturally if there were something wrong with Keith I was to blame. She would get to that very quickly.

"Anyway, I got home last night. This morning Dad told me that Dorothy had rented a place in town. I called and she was at Sam's office. I hadn't been there thirty minutes when your colleague stormed in."

"He's not my colleague."

"Anyway, Commander Asshole started in on Sam right away. With me and Dorothy sitting right there." She paused. "Which was *rude.*"

"Rude was the least of my troubles," Sam mumbled.

"Anyway, he had reports on three members of the team and wanted them to submit to polygraph tests."

"He doesn't have the authority to demand that." I pulled up a chair and joined them at the table, stunned that Ferguson would go this far.

"That's not the only thing he doesn't have the authority to do," Sam said. "He demanded, *demanded* I tell you, to know what was put in the evidence room. Hell, all I had to do was tell him it was an old notebook that came to us from the historical society and that would probably have been the end of the whole thing. Would have done it, too, if he'd asked nice, but I didn't have a chance to think before Wonder Woman here," he gestured toward Elizabeth with his pipe, "jumped right into the fray like she had been involved right along."

"You're lucky I was there." Elizabeth's hands were on her hips, her legs splayed apart.

"That's debatable," Sam retorted. "Anyway, he said 'and just who in the fuck are you?' and she said she was Elizabeth Fiene, and that's when everything went to hell."

Elizabeth scoffed. "Went bad way before that. Anyway, Commander Asshole said this was unreal—having another Fiene to deal with…wasn't there 'anyone in this damn county that wasn't related?' He said he was going to hire a lawyer to check into the legitimacy of having one family involved in every level of law enforcement in an area."

Sam rolled his eyes.

"I told him that if he got a lawyer it had better be a damned good one, because I was the best lawyer this side of the Mississippi and that's when he stormed off."

Oh, boy.

"And you, Dorothy? Where were you in all this?"

"Just observing, as usual. Thinking. But I agree with Sam that it wouldn't have hurt to let him know it was an old notebook. But I wonder how someone as hotheaded as Ferguson got to be a psychologist?"

"My sister says a lot of her colleagues don't have any business treating people. That they are classic narcissists. But that's true of any profession. I don't care what. Teaching, medicine, politics. Ferguson is used to being at the top of a chain of command. Whatever he says gets done. He hasn't been out of the military that long. He hates being bested by women and, in case you haven't noticed, I'm way ahead of him at every turn. This has gone wrong for him. He didn't expect it."

"What I think has gone wrong is that he is a natural born asshole to begin with." Elizabeth's face flushed. She was a prosecutor and specialized in seeking justice for battered women. And she was capable of using other language. She talks real nice in a courtroom.

"Well, where is he now?"

"Don't know. Don't care."

"I think he went back to Topeka," Sam volunteered.

Then we all fell silent as though when we removed Ferguson from the conversation there was nothing to talk about. How are things going otherwise, Sam?" I said finally. "Anything else to talk about while we are all gathered here together?" It came out sarcastic. But honestly the peace I had hoped to bring with me from Josie's just vaporized. I had hoped to jump-start my normal routine. Finish my organizational chart for the regional center. Read some more about narcissistic disorders.

"Dorothy has a great idea."

So that's how she happened to be his office when Elizabeth came to town. Another great idea. But I couldn't help but notice that he had progressed from "Miss Mercer" to "Dorothy" and that she dropped by his office an awful lot.

"Dorothy has been thinking about Duck Boy. County business, I know, but I since you are still undersheriff, it's your business too."

But this was not Elizabeth's business. She's a quick study. "Whoops! I have stuff to do upstairs."

"No need to leave," Keith said. "It won't make any sense to you anyway without knowing the whole story."

"I need to go for a walk anyway." She went into the utility room and retrieved her coat and hat.

Sam took the lead. "Dorothy says our first step should be to figure out if he really saw something or is making up stories. Truth or fiction. Tales from a boy who desperately needed to be admired or the outpouring of someone in the midst of a tragic existence? She's come up with the ideal way."

I must have looked skeptical.

"No, really, Franklin Slocum obviously made it back to his special tree the next morning just like he said he was going to or we wouldn't have the book. He figured out a way to bury it even with his limitations, but what became of the handkerchief? Is it there too? Wrapped in plastic? According to his book he intended to bury it. If he managed to do that and it has bloodstains and semen on it, that will be proof of what Franklin claimed he saw."

Dorothy chimed in. "Not only will we have proof that Franklin is telling the truth, we will have the murderer's DNA contained in the semen and also blood from the little boy."

Sam nodded. "We would know his identify and together these would lead to the kind of solid evidence that's a lead-pipe cinch for a prosecutor to prove his case."

"Provided he's in the system."

"Yes, provided he's in the system."

"Won't the evidence have deteriorated after all these years?"

"In New York," Dorothy said, "we would put the handker-chief through all kinds of tests. And not assume in advance that the evidence was no longer any good. Tests. Base it all on tests."

I smiled. To her credit, this was the first time she had thrown New York at me. I rose and headed for the kitchen to get a drink of water while I mulled this over. It was a good idea, but with rotten timing. Winter, with the ground frozen solid, was no time to go digging around for a little piece of cloth. But we couldn't wait until spring thaw.

"Your call, Lottie," Keith said.

"No, this is county right now. It's up to Sam."

"Let's do it, then. But you're the best person to call Horn. He brought the book to you."

"Okay, I'll call Martin right now. He'll have to lead us to where he found the book."

"And I'll call Oscar Smith and make sure it's okay to go dig-ging around on his land," Sam said.

"Tomorrow morning. Bright and early. He'll meet us here," I reported when I hung up the phone. "He's happy to help.

"There's no need for us all to go." Keith glanced at his aunt. "Dorothy, why don't you stay inside here where it's warm?"

That got him as scornful a look as I had seen in a while.

Chapter Twenty-three

We took two snowmobiles. Keith's was a real workhorse. Built for utility, in addition to driver and passenger seats, it could carry another person on the cargo platform. Although it was originally designed to transport injured persons in ski areas, on our farm it was most often used to track down cattle. When there is heavy prolonged snowfall, cattle search for shelter and if an electric fence is down, hard telling where they will end up. Owners who don't have a snowmobile call Keith to help round them up. The worst-case scenario is when the animals stray onto a road and cause an accident.

Several times Keith had rushed to ponds to rescue kids or adults who had misjudged the thickness of ice and needed to get to the emergency room as fast as possible. He always carries coils of rope and solar blankets. Just in case.

Martin's was a hot little custom job, bright red and made for speed. It was a far cry from a racing snowmobile but he had tricked it out to look like one. He could probably run circles around Keith, although there was no thought of that today. In his early forties, Martin had a shiny broad face and a wide grin. He taught the 4-H woodworking class and, by the number of blue ribbons his students racked up at the county fair every year, I knew a fierce competitive streak lurked beneath his affable exterior. Besides, his Facebook posts indicated that he loved informal rural snowmobile races and went coyote hunting every chance he got.

Sam didn't like him. Once, when I suggested that Martin would be a good candidate for a reserve deputy, Sam vetoed the idea right away. I asked why. Sam shrugged. "Just don't like him, that's why." He shot me a look. "And I'm the high sheriff, Lottie." He puffed his pipe and blew a smoke ring. His way of telling me to shut up.

One of the first lessons I had learned out here was not to go too far in turning over rocks. Family, neighbor, political, township, county, animosities went so deep and were often so rancorous they were incomprehensible. I suspected some of them were holdovers from Kansas' county seat fights. Half the counties had been involved in them and some had ended in bloodshed. Quite a number of the good citizens in Carlton County could no longer remember why they didn't like a person. It was just sort of expected in their family.

But Martin was very eager to be included in "police business." When I called yesterday to ask him if he could lead us to the place where he had found the notebook, he agreed immediately.

"You bet."

"We are looking for a plastic sack in the same spot."

"I didn't think to look for anything else."

"No reason why you should have. I'm sorry we have to call you out to help us at such a sorry time of year."

"No problem."

He had come well prepared this morning and had even thought to throw in ice-melting salts. "After we dig down about a foot I think we should sprinkle a little bit on the dirt, layer by layer. Then work it with our fingers. Take our time. Since I didn't see the sack when I pulled out the book it was probably beneath it. I hope." He blew air on his mittens and stamped his feet. He had on tan cotton duck Carhartt coveralls. His matching hat had protective earflaps. A black balaclava would be pulled down when we took off.

"If the kid buried it someplace next to that binder instead of under it, we might have a problem. That would involve digging a circle around it and there's no telling how large it would have to be."

"I don't think Franklin Slocum was very strong. He wasn't even average height. So I can't see him having the strength to dig a large circle. If the sack is anywhere, logically, it would be underneath the notebook." My words pushed out in frosty bursts. "And remember, there might not be anything there. Which would be a blessed relief to all of us. We would know we are dealing with a little boy's imagination."

When I called Josie earlier I told her I would let her know right away if there was a handkerchief buried under the spot where Martin had found the commonplace book.

"Don't be disappointed, Lottie, if he's making it all up."

"Believe me, that would be the best way for all this to turn out. Simply a kid writing stories to liven up a pretty dismal existence."

Dorothy's nose was bright red. She was decked out in dark gray winter gear she had ordered from Cabela's. Lined pants, a double-layered parka, and waterproof boots. She had taken to online shopping immediately and boxes from Amazon were a familiar sight on her front porch.

She stood silent and unmovable like a grayed-out block of ice until Martin gave the word to load up. Then she gamely clomped toward Keith's snowmobile with the help of her formidable walking stick.

Most people were excited over their first snowmobile ride, but there wasn't a bit of emotion on Dorothy's face. She scrambled into her seat and stared straight ahead. Then I saw her lower lip quiver. Just a little. She had become bound up in Franklin Slocum's life.

Of all of us, Dorothy was the most certain that every word was true.

Josie believed we were dealing with a story written by a young adolescent making things up.

I was somewhere in between and dreading one outcome.

Sam stepped in after Dorothy and settled onto the utility platform. The engines sputtered then roared to life. Martin and

Keith turned a circle around the farmyard, then they headed out of our lane and down the county road leading away from our house. In about three miles we would reach the pasture that contained the large cottonwood where Franklin Slocum spent the happiest days of his life. And then the worst days. Days that were so terrible that most adults would not have been able to cope with them.

If they actually happened.

There was nothing wrong with making up stories, but I knew from criminology accounts that when adolescent boys started only reading porn that comprised violence and sadism it was bad news. A normal kid wanted to have sex with the women in the pictures. One that was developing the wrong way wanted to rape, torture, or kill them. If this was the kind of thing Franklin was making up it gave me a sick feeling. If it was for real, that didn't do a thing for my nerves either.

Snow covered all the dead vegetation in the pastures and the sun shimmered on the icy landscape. White as the snow queen's cape. Normally I would have been enchanted by the sparkling cloak of diamonds tossed on the slopes and gentles dips but when I looked down my hands were shaking. I honestly didn't know how I wanted this to turn out. If it were true, two sets of parents would finally have a chance to give their young sons a decent burial. If not, they would have to continue with the hell of wondering what had happened to their children.

In a very short time we would know whether Franklin Slocum was a highly inventive little boy or one who was terrified and abused and still determined to be a manly man like his Western heroes. At least in his imagination.

We ended up at a very large leafless tree next to a frozen creek. The view was an artist's dream. A celestial landscape with perfect composition. Martin stopped and parked his snowmobile about fifteen feet back from the tree and Keith pulled alongside him.

A flock of crows scattered from the leafless limbs of the huge cottonwood. Their harsh caws filled the air and I shuddered as though they were a bad omen.

There was a sudden gust of wind and the branches of the cottonwood rubbed together and made an eerie sound as if they were protesting our invasion. Our breath hovered in the freezing air as a cascade of crystals fell softly to the ground.

Keith and Martin got out of the vehicles and Dorothy and I followed. Sam's face looked like a death mask. He was certain he was dealing with a mother who should have been tried years ago for child abuse and neglect. No matter how things turned out here he had announced his intentions to investigate the father and see to it that the payments Biddy Slocum received for providing care for a disabled person went directly to Franklin.

Sam was the boss here. This had happened many years ago before Keith and I were married. However, as his undersheriff, I intended to assist him in any way I could.

The men all grabbed shovels and started walking toward the little drift against the tree that Martin singled out. Martin also carried a fine-tined digging fork in addition to the ice-melting salt and the kind of kitchen fork that could be found in every household. Sam carried official evidence-collection bags and plenty of labels. Dorothy brought her Nikon camera and was prepared to videotape every step of our work.

Martin did not have a bit of trouble finding the tree and the spot where he had found the binder. "It was a foot from this big root. I remember it well because it was going to be a real pain if I had to go under that root. Luckily, I didn't." Martin had a deep voice and seemed to relish bossing the older men around. "Okay. When you get any surface snow cleared, I'm going to see how far down the ground is frozen. This book was a good twenty inches deep. Anything you are looking for has to be more than that."

Ignoring the cold, I tried to think like a boy with a severe handicap. What would he have to figure out to do the job? "I'm guessing at least two inches deeper or you would have seen it. But it would be hard for him to go much further. I can't imagine how he was able to bury the book in the first place."

Dorothy looked at me. Her face was drawn and her eyes sorrowful. I knew she simply didn't believe that the plastic sack was the invention of a troubled child. She was convinced there was a handkerchief smeared with blood and semen. Solid evidence of a vicious killer's DNA.

"Ready?" Martin asked.

"Yes. Please be careful not to tear through any plastic."

"We already know we're safe to go down eighteen inches. I'll stop at fourteen just to be sure and then we'll switch to getting down an inch at a time with the digging fork and bagging the dirt as we go."

"Will the rock salt hurt the plastic? If there is plastic," Dorothy asked.

"No, ma'am. I tested it first. It's safe. I sprinkled the salts on a plastic sack and left it overnight to make sure the salt wouldn't eat a hole in it.

He briskly removed about twelve inches of soil. Keith held a gunny sack open and Martin emptied each load of dirt. Then he switched to the fine-tined fork and began scratching away layers. As he went, he sprinkled on salt and picked up dirt and rubbed it through his fingers like a housewife cutting lard through flour. He carefully worked the next five inches.

Nothing.

He worked another inch and then another. We looked at one another. I was simultaneously relieved and disappointed.

"Well," Sam said. "Well."

That was all.

The men picked up the equipment. My shoulders drooped. It was the very best outcome but it left us back at square one.

"There." Dorothy's voice rang out. "A corner. Just a tip. A little bit of plastic."

The men followed her gaze and switched back to the rock salt and smoothed the dirt away with their fingers and then a brush.

I turned to Dorothy and clutched her elbow. Just a tiny corner of plastic, and then a little more, and then a whole crushed dirt-stained sack. Toward one end was a clear space and we could see that it contained a yellowing piece of cloth. I felt a tremor sweep through her body.

"Don't open it," Sam hollered. And don't touch the plastic with your fingers. Wear gloves. I want it dropped directly into an evidence bag. Don't anybody move while I go get one. Don't even breathe on it." He rushed back to the snowmobile and returned carrying an envelope. "This might be the first time in the history of this county that we haven't fucked up retrieving evidence."

"The only prints on that bag should be those of Franklin Slocum and maybe his mother's when she brought it from the grocery store to begin with." Keith said.

"And the grocery-bagger." Dorothy added.

Keith grunted and glanced at Sam. They would be crazy to take off their gloves anyway. Unless they were looking forward to frostbite.

Martin brushed away dirt until the bag was completely exposed. Sam reached down with a twelve-inch pair of industrial tweezers and eased the bag out of its resting place. Then he sealed the packet, unzipped his coat to remove the felt-tipped pen that was warmed by his body heat and quickly filled out a chain of custody form.

No one said a word. But there was a gleam of triumph in Dorothy's eyes. The child was vindicated.

Then awareness dawned on all of us like we were watching the third act of a play. We all turned simultaneously like robotic puppets and stared at the clearing to the right of the tree. Buried under snow now. There was a stretch of trees on the far side. Proper cottonwoods of a decent size but no match for our tree.

And lying in front of the grove was a large log.

A sudden gust of wind blew off some of the snow and the crows returned and settled on the branches. Silently. Mocking our slow moving brains.

Still we just stood there. My stomach roiled. There were tears now in Dorothy's eyes. Keith bowed his head and I knew he was praying.

"I'll call the FBI and put in a request for cadaver dogs," Sam said.

● ● ● ● ● ●

Our snowmobiles flew back to the farm at jet-speed. We circled our driveway with the first stop being to let Sam out in front of his Suburban. Martin would drive home in his snowmobile.

"Come with me, Lottie. As soon as we put this sack in the evidence room I'm going to Slocum's and haul that bitch in for questioning."

"Don't do that," Dorothy said sharply. "Please."

"What?" Sam was incredulous. "If ever a woman was guilty…"

"I'm not talking about the woman. Yes. Without a doubt. Guilty of some sins piled to the sky. I'm talking about putting that sack in the evidence room."

We all stared at Dorothy. Uneasily, I realized Martin hadn't left yet and he was hanging on every word. With my back turned, I gestured with my head toward him and mouthed "later" to Keith.

With a slight nod, Keith approved my caution. He went to Martin and shook his hand. "Can't tell you enough how much we appreciate your helping us out today. Sorry the weather is such a bitch. And thanks, too, for coming up with the rock salt idea."

That's all it took. A bit of flattery and Martin revved up his vehicle and circled the drive again and waved like Santa Claus who had to be on his rounds.

We turned back to Dorothy whose face was twisted with urgency. "Don't notify everyone on the team that you are putting it in evidence. It's a mistake. I just know it."

"Maybe you're right," Sam said solemnly. "But it's the best place to put it. It wouldn't hurt none to just to keep a hand log, but everything is automatic when I put something inside. It's the way David set it up."

"Call him. Make him change it."

"He'll have to come here. There's some things he can only do from the server."

"Do that, then." Dorothy didn't seem to be a bit daunted by the fact that she did not have the authority to give orders to me—the regional director. Or to Sam, the high sheriff, or to Keith, our number one reserve deputy.

"Or, better yet, bypass him all together. Trust no one." She imperiously gave a sharp thump to her walking stick.

"We could keep it here, I guess. In the safe where I keep all my veterinary drugs." Keith pointed toward his animal hospital.

Dorothy unzipped her parka and stripped off the first layer of her headgear. "Sam, do you really think Biddy Slocum is withholding information about Franklin? He obviously went back to the tree the morning following the crime and buried the book and the handkerchief. But the trail ends there."

"For openers, I'm going to start quizzing that bitch about the welfare fraud. See what she volunteers." Sam held the package against his chest. "After the dogs get here tomorrow I'll go out to her house. She might not know much. Franklin didn't trust his mother. For good reason. And then I'm going to locate Franklin and his father if I have to personally go door to door myself to every house in Chicago."

"When we're done here, I'll take the commonplace book and the handkerchief to Dimon. And I think there will only be one dog. Not 'dogs.'"

"I want to go with you," Dorothy said. "I'll catch the bus from Topeka and go on to the airport at Kansas City and back to New York. My agent e-mailed this morning and there are some issues we need to straighten out with my publisher."

"Oh, you'll do no such thing. After I stop at the KBI and personally deliver this package to Dimon, I'll drive you to the airport myself. There's no need for you to take the bus."

"Well, thank you."

Sam and Keith headed toward the building where Keith kept his supplies. His safe was well protected with push pad encryption and top-of-the-line fire-proofing.

It was also bolted to the floor, in case anyone had ideas about raiding the local vet's drug supplies.

Chapter Twenty-four

Early the next morning a black van drew up in our driveway. A slight woman dressed in camouflage coveralls bounced out of the vehicle and went around to the back. She opened the doors for a German shepherd who bounded down and sniffed around before peeing in the grass. I didn't know much about cadaver dogs and had expected some exotic breed and a burly trainer, not a woman about five-foot two.

She walked over and introduced herself. "Barbara Abrams." She laughed at the difficulty of shaking hands through our winter gear. "The rest of the team is about two miles away. Normally, they wouldn't be along until Bertie finished his work, but you all sounded so sure we would find something that I thought it would save a lot of time if we arrived together."

"Good thinking." Sam glanced at the dog. "We'll start on the county road you came in on, but when we get to the pasture entrance we'll need snowmobiles to take you to the location we have in mind."

Barbara smiled and shook her head. "Bertie will be working off-leash and I want him to roam. The snow won't bother him. The land is so flat it'll be a piece of cake. As for me, I brought along snowshoes and cross-country skies. But I understand you are concerned about a very small area? Is that right?"

"Yes, ma'am."

"Even so, sometimes things are not as cut-and-dried as one

might think. Bertie will let us know if he finds anything before we get to your target area."

A dun-colored Humvee pulled up behind Barbara's van and a five-member forensic team got out. Barbara waved them over and after the usual handshakes and name exchanges, we made a plan for exploring the area.

She put Bertie back inside her van and we set off. We formed quite a caravan along our sparsely traveled country road, but thankfully there were no onlookers. Keith and Marvin had rounded up a couple of extra snowmobiles and the two men waited beside the pasture entrance.

By now, Marvin knew we were looking for bodies as did the owner of the pasture, Oscar Smith, but word hadn't gotten around to the general public. Sam had asked Oscar to sign a form giving us permission for the search so it wouldn't require a warrant. Only a short time ago, Sam would have skipped this step but he had learned from bitter experience to dot all the I's cross all the T's.

We all parked alongside the entrance to the pasture. The forensic team left their equipment in the vehicles and wouldn't transport it until Bertie sounded an alarm. We loaded onto the snowmobiles and headed toward the large cottonwood tree. The dog ranged from side to side but kept moving straight ahead at Barbara's commands. The snowmobiles slowed to accommodate the pace of the handler and the working dog.

When we got closer to the tree, Bertie's movements became animated. He lifted his head alertly and waded across the snow toward the clearing. His tail was curled into a tight kink. He dropped suddenly with a soft yelp and looked up at Barbara who immediately rewarded him with a treat from a bag she carried.

"Yes," she said softly. She pulled a small spiral notebook from her pocket and looked all around.

One of the men on the forensic team walked over to Sam. "We would like to drive the Humvee over here if that won't cause any legal complications. Tearing up the land, etcetera, etcetera. It will save us carrying a bunch of equipment."

"There won't be any legal complications, like trespassing, say, or tearing up his property. No warrant necessary because the owner has already given us signed permission. If the opening in the fence isn't wide enough, I have a pair of wire cutters in my Suburban. But mind the dips. Drifts are going to fill bone-jarring inclines and make it look like you are on flat ground. I'll lead the best way across the pasture with Keith's snowmobile." Sam's eyes were hard, his voice terse. He looked at me, then stared at the ground. Dreading to see for himself what the dog claimed was there.

We were silent. I looked around at all the people gathered around this place in a spot that couldn't by any stretch of the imagination be called woods. All of the trees and shrubs were along the edge of the creek. The land leading up to it was bare. I shivered. Digging for bodies on a dog's say-so. It suddenly seemed like a macabre fantasy.

But there was that handkerchief. That was real. Tangible.

I moved closer to Barbara. She showed me a checklist. "In case I have to testify in court. I've learned the hard way." There was a special emphasis on structural and technical details including wind speed and direction, soil composition, precipitation, and a detailed description of the surroundings. "Would you like me to mail you all the criteria involving cadaver dogs?"

Then the Humvee came roaring up—no trouble at all traversing the pasture. I could tell by the envious light in Keith's eyes that he would soon be adding a new piece of equipment to our already formidable collection.

The men piled out and began setting out stakes which they encircled with crime scene tape.

"They are that sure of the dog," I marveled. "That sure." There was a dream-like quality to all this. And here were rank strangers, outsiders, sure they would find dead people on the basis of a dog's ability to smell.

Once again I was swept with a sense of how little I knew and how much I had to learn. And even if we found two little boys buried here—the little boy in Franklin's commonplace book—and possibly the remains of another little boy killed earlier, that would not help us find the Ghost Baby Killer.

Dead babies as innocent as the driven snow. Babies with rosebud mouths and blue-white icy limbs.

The men pulled out battery-powered snow blowers and quickly cleared the area indicated by Bertie. Then came the shovels and rakes and long-handled brushes to keep from damaging bones. It didn't take more than twenty minutes of carefully removing the layers of soil before one of the men hollered "stop."

Bones. Small ones. A child's bones. I pressed my face against Keith's chest.

Then another site. The second contained the same kind of evidence, but the bones were smaller. Both boys were naked. Sam knelt to examine the bodies after they were brought up from their graves.

"Broken necks," he announced. Just like Franklin said in his book.

Keith and I watched gloomily, then turned to leave, but Bertie gave another of his odd-pitched whines and flopped down in a different spot about ten feet from the other two graves. Bewildered, my hands shook. We had found the two we were expecting.

The crows returned before the team started excavating the third site.

They flapped in and settled silently on a branch of the cottonwood tree that had been Franklin Slocum's home. His safe place. It was as though the crows wanted to bear witness to what we would find there. Secret messengers to the rest of Franklin's kingdom. Prepared to take the word to all the other animals.

An owl hooted and a squirrel sat upright on a tree opposite the site. I was aware of other animals who seemed to appear out of nowhere, unafraid of the gathered humans.

Dorothy was statue-still. She knew. It was there on her face.

The third little corpse was taller than the other two. Remnants of clothes clung to the bones. No stripping of this one, as though he had been too repulsive for sexual assault, or too old—in puberty.

At the end of both legs were acutely deformed club feet. Feet belonging to a child who had been jeered at and bullied all of this life before he met this tragic end.

He wore mismatched shoes—one a ratty sneaker and the other a heavy scuffed hunting boot. Scrounged up from somewhere by a mother who just didn't give a damn.

I moved closer to Sam. "Did Biddy do this? His own mother?"

"No. Whoever killed the other two killed Franklin but some things are different. He's clothed, for one thing. And his skull was smashed in. But Biddy Slocum is responsible for his death. She's the one who sent her child into the woods day after day and didn't give a damn how hard it was for him. She's the one who chased him out of his own home."

• • ● • •

We didn't wait for the forensic team to tag the bodies and collect all the other evidence. I climbed into Sam's Suburban. With his siren throbbing and the white snow throwing back reflections from his light bar he drove like a wild man toward the Slocums.

"Biddy Slocum, you are under arrest for fraud," Sam said furiously the moment she answered the door.

"You've got no right," She defiantly braced her wrist on her out-slung hip and lifted her chin. "No right at all."

"Fraud and accessory to murder." He whirled her around yanked her arms behind her but only managed to get the handcuffs on one wrist.

I moved toward her and kicked her legs out from under her and flipped her onto her stomach. She fought like a bobcat. She bucked and heaved and twisted but I dropped on top of her back and twisted her arm upward and anchored it with the second cuff.

"You have the right to remain silent," Sam's words were garbled and spoken through clenched teeth but he managed to get through the entire oath.

"Add resisting arrest to her charges."

He yanked her outside and shoved her into the backseat of the Suburban and slammed down the steel mesh partition separating the rear from the front. We sped toward the jail and Sam dragged her into what passed as our interrogation room. It was anything but private and we were already planning an addition to the Regional Room to update this aspect of our facilities. In the meantime, anyone who wanted to could hear all the questions and answers. Sam simply locked the outside door to the office.

"Do you want me to take over, Sam?"

"No."

We entered the room together. He switched on a recorder and told me to take a chair beside him.

"How long has this been going on?"

"What been going on?"

"You getting money for a kid you haven't seen for God only knows how long?"

She fell silent.

"How long?" He slammed his fist down on the table.

A tear trickled down her cheek.

"One year? Two? Twelve?" Sam leaned forward, his palms flat to control the faint trembling but the tone of his voice betrayed his fury.

"About ten, I guess."

"He's dead. Your son is dead. We found his bones this morning?

"You can't know it's Franklin," she said quickly.

"We know it was Franklin because the feet were deformed."

There wasn't a trace of surprise or shame on her face. No regret there either.

I stared, felt the color rise in my cheeks, then rose and walked out of the room. I stood with my back to the wall, my hands outstretched and braced against the wainscoting to steady my trembling knees. *The bitch. The evil bitch. She doesn't care.* I blew my nose and went back into the room.

Trapped, Biddy looked down, then around, then stared at the ceiling. She swallowed hard.

"Tell us what happened."

"Nothing happened." Her mouth trembled. "He went across the pasture one morning like he's done a hundred times before, only this time he never came back."

"Didn't it occur to you that something might be wrong?"

"No. I told you. He did it a hundred times before. Slipped in and out of the house. Usually when I was off at work. Pilfered through the food." Her voice lowered. "We never did get along. He was hard. Hard to get along with. Hard to raise." She suddenly sobbed with self-pity. "You don't know how hard it is to raise a kid like that. Retarded. Couldn't walk. Couldn't talk."

I thought of the passages in the commonplace book where he mentioned interaction with Biddy. "You didn't communicate at all?" I asked carefully.

"Oh, yeah, *I* did. But just me. No one else. He could make these noises. And write. Whole pages sometimes. Mostly demands. Wanting this or that. Better food. Clothes. Blankets. Like I was Madam Moneybags. It was always something. Longer pants. Larger socks. Bigger shoes. He was always after me about shoes." She caught herself. Looked stricken. Then looked away and around. "I guess he could sort of write but the pages were mostly scribbles."

Sam blinked. It was unlikely that "retarded" kids could write whole pages.

I recalled the calligraphy quality of the entries in his commonplace book. His lyrical poetry. His ideals. His love of nature. The soaring of his spirit every spring. His love of the moist earth. His sense of mystery. His affinity for the spiritual.

"Kids made fun of him. So did grownups. Especially ones who had normal kids. I'm telling you my life was a bitch. He never showed me an ounce of love. Not one bit."

Beneath the table, my hands were clamped together between my knees to keep them from flying around this woman's neck.

"The money," Sam said. "Why did you keep on taking the money?"

"I figured I had it coming. It was owed me for putting up with that kid and not putting him in some kind of institution. Wasn't all that much anyway."

"When did you realize he was never coming back?"

She fell silent again. Then said, "I want a lawyer. A good one. And then I'm going to sue your ass. You've got no right to come crashing into my home and abusing me. Police abuse. That's what this is."

Sam yanked her to her feet and shoved her into the jail cell.

Chapter Twenty-five

I left for Topeka early the next morning with the handkerchief locked in a portable biometric safe accessible only through the fingerprint of my right index finger. Keith used it to carry drugs he would be using for emergency treatment of large animals he couldn't bring back to hospital. It could store prints from other persons but even mine had been added only this morning. Either Dorothy or I would be in the car with the safe at all times. The commonplace book lay beside the safe in an evidence bag.

We were close to solving a crime that had haunted this county for years. Two little boys who had been raped and their necks broken. Another death that went unnoticed of a little crippled boy who had been abused and neglected all his life. If we hit a DNA match we could nail the killer. I wished there were some way to let the precious brave little boy know how much he was like his Western heroes. A manly man to the very end.

But his book was written before the Ghost Baby Killer terrorized the state. I had to shift my energy back to the crime that was under my jurisdiction. Find someone with a black soul.

I wasn't aware of any old documents that might hold a clue. Sometimes family stories hinted about a son or nephew who kept them awake at night. Children who didn't finish their education. Sudden withdrawals from bank accounts. Eight pound "premature" babies. Family members suddenly excluded from photos. Clues that were not included in law enforcement reports.

I picked up Dorothy at her house in town. She climbed into the car after stowing her carry-on bag in the hatch. She settled into the passenger seat. "Supposed to be getting a storm."

"It's not supposed to hit until afternoon. We'll beat it there."

"You have more faith in the weatherman than I do."

Neither of us felt like talking and after catching the top of the hour of NPR, I switched off the radio. Normally I had it on every mile, switching from music to news and occasionally listening to audiobooks. But it was cold and I didn't want to turn the volume up loud enough to compensate for the blast of the heater.

No noise. No weatherman constantly interrupting. No constant frantic announcement. No way of knowing I-70 was closing between Denver and Junction City. No warning of the cloud rolling toward us across the prairie.

We were on the east side of Hays when I saw a dark movement close to the ground coming toward us from the southwest. It was there before I could think.

"A ground blizzard," I hollered to Dorothy. "We won't be able to see our hands in front of our face. I've got to get off the road while I can still see."

A ground blizzard is the most terrifying weather hazard on the prairie. Ordinary blizzards were falling snow mixed with high wind. Ground blizzards were high winds that picked up dry snow already on the ground, mixed it with dirt and debris and created a lethal mud, coating anything in its path.

My windshield was plastered immediately. The wipers smeared the grayish paste. I steered toward what I thought was the ditch. Then I heard a sickening crunch.

"Oh, no. Oh, Jesus Christ. I've hit something." I switched off the engine. My stomach lurched.

"I just pray it wasn't another car." Dorothy's voice shook.

I splayed my fingers across my face. "Oh, no. Oh, no" I reached for my hooded parka and began bundling up. "Stay here. I'll check."

Dorothy eyes were filled with worry but she didn't argue.

"I have a rope in back. I'll fasten it on the glide under the backseat. It's easy to lose direction in this and then get hit by another car. You stay put. Under no circumstances are you to leave this car."

She nodded.

I unfastened my seat belt and climbed over the console to retrieve a coil of thin commercial grade paracord from the box of survival gear I stowed in the hatch. Although most drivers in Western Kansas packed an emergency car kit for winter travel, mine went far beyond the basic gear of a flashlight, batteries, blanket, snacks, water, gloves, boots, and a first-aid kit. I also carried jumper cables, tire chains, road flares, crime-scene equipment, and a substantial amount of medical supplies.

I secured the cord and then fastened the opposite end around my waist. I looped the excess over my shoulder and slid back into the driver's seat. The vicious southwest wind was against me. I pushed the door open just far enough for me to ease out. I didn't want to take a chance on the wind ripping it off its hinges. I felt around for the running board before I risked putting my full weight on my right foot. Sure of a solid connection I lowered my left foot to the ground and let go of the window post. It took all my strength to slam the door shut and anchor the narrow polypropylene rope.

I felt my way along the fender until I came to my front bumper, then I blindly reached for the large shape in front of my Tahoe. I eased along the side, knowing now it was another vehicle. A small one.

My heart pounded. *Oh, no. Oh, no.*

A smooth place. Glass. I pounded against it. I couldn't see inside. "Are you hurt?" I yelled.

A voice called out but I couldn't understand the words.

"Are you all right?" My eyes stung but goggles wouldn't have helped me see.

I made a blade of the side of my hand and squeegeed down the glass, clearing enough mud to make out a figure slumped over the steering wheel holding his head between the palm of his hands.

I rapped at the windshield and the man inside roused.

"Are you hurt?"

He mumbled. His words trailed off.

We had to get both vehicles off the highway. The risk of someone slamming into both of us was too great. With ground blizzards people had no choice but to stop. The problem was that all too often they stopped in the middle of their lane because they couldn't see to steer off to the side. I was worried about emergency vehicles who would try to drive anyway. Ambulances and firetrucks or even a tow truck sent to move a disabled police car off the road.

"My head," he repeated, more distinctly this time.

I froze at the familiar voice.

Dr. Ferguson. In his little green Volkswagen. I rapped at the window again. "Start your car," I commanded. "You have to get off the road."

He eased back from the steering wheel and straightened his neck as he twisted his head from side to side. He reached for a rag lying next to him and pressed it against the wound on his head.

Then he rolled down his window about a half inch so he could hear better. Through the murky interior I could see that he was not wearing a seat belt. Manufacturers hadn't required them in cars this old. There was a spiderweb crack in the windshield in front of the steering wheel and I knew it had come from him flying forward. I shuddered. I had to get help for him as soon as it was safe to drive.

"Start your car." The wind whipped my words away. I tried again. "Start your car," I yelled. "We have to get it off the road."

He nodded and twisted the key but all he got was a *r-r-r-r*. He leaned back and held his head between his hands again.

I hollered at him again and he twisted his head in my direction.

"Lottie? That you?" Before he recognized my voice, he had simply responded to loud orders.

"Yes. You need to get in my car where it's warm. You're bleeding. I need to tend to you."

"Just a head wound. Bleeding like a stuck hog. Not that serious."

"Maybe not. First, we need to get your car off the road so it won't cause another wreck."

"What?"

In despair I concentrated on the essentials. What he needed to hear. Bare minimum. "Yank your steering wheel to the right. Hard. Head into the ditch. Then put it in neutral."

He followed my instructions then grabbed his head again and gave a soft moan.

"Good job! I'm tied to a rope. I'm going to walk you back to my car. Can you do that?"

He nodded then groaned again.

"Don't fall. You need to hold onto me. Stay in back of me and put your hands on my shoulders. I can shield you from the wind." *A little. I hope*, I thought grimly. "But do not fall. Just concentrate on staying on your feet. I'm not strong enough to pick you up from the ground. I could drag you to my vehicle but I can't hold onto the rope at the same time. You've got to stay on your feet. Got that?"

I couldn't see his reaction but he was a soldier. Used to taking and giving orders. Blunt orders. He had to, by God, stay on his feet.

His door was a goner from the moment we opened it. It slammed against the fender but the hinges held. He jolted at the sound but stayed upright. I coiled the rope, taking up all the slack and looped it over my shoulder again.

I started back, pulling with both hands as I eased along the rope still held tightly in the door of the Tahoe. I shuffled with little duck steps like a baby. Carefully placing one foot in front of the other.

Ferguson's hands slipped off my shoulder and I stood paralyzed.

"You there?" I called. I twisted and slowly groped to the sides but stood in place. Then pulling against the rope I leaned back as far as I dared without losing my footing and bumped into him. Ferguson had stood totally motionless, no doubt as terrified as I was.

"Here," he said weakly. "Right here. Slipped. Sorry." He firmly gripped my shoulders again.

I tightened the rope and inched along until I reached the front fender. Gratefully, I laid across it for a moment before I felt my way along the right window. Then I located the handle of the back door.

When I had ordered my Tahoe, with napping grandchildren in mind, I had opted for a bench seat in back rather than captain chairs. Now the cushioned expanse was ideal for an injured psychologist.

Dorothy had managed to climb over the console into the back and gripped the door from the inside. I let go of the rope to steer the man past the opening and pulled at the handle. I braced the door and literally shoved Ferguson across the seat, and slammed the door shut. Then I opened the driver's door and squeezed through the narrow opening while retrieving the rope. We might need it again.

Exhausted, my hands encircled the steering wheel, and I laid my head against them.

"You okay?" Dorothy asked from the passenger's seat. "Here. Drink some water."

Amused by her sensible gesture I raised my head and reached for the bottle. I was scared shitless and she was as controlled as though this happened every day.

I dug a shop rag out of the console and wetted it. I dabbed at my eyes and swiped at the coating of dirt on my face. Then I started my engine and eased into a steady shove against the back of the little Volkswagen. It immediately began rolling gently down the ditch.

Now to get me off the road. I lowered my window a crack and listened for equipment coming my way. All I could hear was the wind.

Carefully I put the Tahoe in reverse and began backing. When I thought I was far enough away from the Volkswagen that I wouldn't land on top of it, I put the Tahoe in drive and slowly steered it into the ditch at a shallow angle where it was out of harm's way.

I switched off the ignition. Giddy over my success, I turned to Dorothy. "Mission accomplished." Relief flooded my body.

"Good job, Lottie. Seriously. Marvelous, in fact."

I looked down at my filthy clothing. I was covered with a coating of mud. My seats were all leather and it would not be a problem to clean up the car but I looked like I was auditioning to be a mummy.

Ferguson eased into a sitting position. "Glad you girls came along."

"We're the ones who caused this mess, remember."

Dorothy stiffened at the "girls." She couldn't stand the man. But part of my job was rescuing people. I couldn't pick and choose. "How are you doing?"

"Been better. What the hell is going on?"

I explained ground blizzards then fished around for my iPhone and activated the light. I swiveled and climbed over the console into the backseat. "Look up," I put him through an assortment of eye tests. "We're in luck. I don't see any signs of a concussion." I gently removed the cloth from his head and examined his cut. "Good news on that front, too. It isn't that deep."

"Just bloody. Hell of a headache, though."

"Dorothy, my medical kit is wedged beside the console on your side. Please get it for me."

She handed it over and I sponged off his wound with hydrogen peroxide then examined it closely. I closed it with a butterfly bandage. "Everything considered, you've come out really well, Doctor. This will leave a little scar but I don't really think you need stitches."

"Thank you. Good thing you came along," he said again.

"Actually, I was the one who plowed into you," I reminded him. "I caused all this." The repetition worried me. Maybe I should put him through a couple of memory tests. When we got to a town I wanted an emergency room crew to check him out. I scrambled back into the front seat, started the ignition and switched on the radio. Nothing but static.

"You had better call Keith and let him know we are okay," Dorothy instructed.

"Right." But all I got out of my cell was "no service." I had deactivated OnStar because the county had been paying for the service and we were looking for ways to reduce expenses since so much was now being financed through the regional center. Now I wished I had the service back because it was satellite-based and didn't depend on cell towers. Our police car radios were nearly prehistoric. I tried my radio anyway but only got a loud whine and no reception.

"Ground blizzards usually only last about three or four hours," I said after trying all of the systems again. "We won't be here forever. I have some Tylenol in my kit. Or aspirin, since your bleeding doesn't seem to be an issue. Take your pick."

"Aspirin."

He gulped down two and after we had sat for about five minutes in silence he dozed off. But it wasn't the deep sleep of a seriously injured person and in about fifteen minutes he jerked awake.

"Feel better?"

"Yes. Between the aspirin and the nap, I'm good to go."

"It won't be that simple. I still want you to go to the emergency room."

"Not necessary. Really. And anyway after Afghanistan I have a horror of emergency rooms."

"What are you doing out here, anyway?"

"I might ask the same of you."

"I'm….taking Dorothy to the airport." He didn't need to know I was going to see Dimon. He might decide it was some of his business. It wasn't.

"I was coming back from a drug store. Needed to pick up a prescription before I left on a trip."

"Afghanistan. Tell me about the people," Dorothy urged. She peppered him with questions. Basking in the attention, obviously cheered to be in the limelight again, he entertained us with details and anecdotes. Most of them were funny but I suspected he was withholding stories of another kind. At any rate I was seeing another, more humane side of this man. Who knew?

We offered food to Ferguson from the stash of sandwiches and cookies we had brought along. "There's coffee, too, in that thermos."

"Don't want to cut you ladies short."

"We have plenty," Dorothy insisted. "I don't like the food on planes. I always pack enough to do me through a flight. What we don't eat now I'll cache in my backpack. There's no problem getting through security as long as I don't take liquids."

He took a ham sandwich and an assortment of cookies. "So you have a flight ahead of you. Where are you headed?"

"Back to New York."

"Southwest?"

"Always." A discussion of airlines followed with United emerging as the clear loser. I smiled at our newfound camaraderie. Nothing like coming through danger together. It sure beat our previous mutual wariness that usually existed whenever Ferguson was around.

"Business?"

"Yes. A little row with my publisher. Shouldn't take too long to get things straightened out and then I'll be back."

"Hope this delay didn't mess up your flight plans."

"No, in fact my plans are already messed up. I've never seen Josie's apartment and hoped to go there first. But now we can't. I hear it's quite a place," Dorothy said.

I tensed. I didn't want Ferguson to flare up at any mention of Josie's affluence.

"And you, Dr. Ferguson? Where were you headed? Before the grand interruption?"

"Back east. To give a talk to a group of psychologists about the long-term effect on PTSD on neurological health. Very dry. Not that many interested, but I will get a nice speaking fee. And you, Lottie? Are you just taking Dorothy to the airport or are you going to visit your sister on the way back?

"My itinerary is a little more complicated and I can't spare the time to get in a decent visit with Josie, as much as I would love to."

"She's going straight back to Topeka after she drops me off. To take some evidence to Frank Dimon."

I winced. No way to shut her up without piquing Ferguson's curiosity.

"What kind of evidence?"

"It pertains to a local case. Not regional business," I said quickly. "An old, old case. Some new evidence came to light."

"Must be important if you are making a special trip to Topeka."

"It is." Dorothy twisted in her seat so he could look into her eyes. Proud. So proud of her role in this case. "About the most conclusive physical evidence we've come across in a long time."

"And speaking of plans, do you plan to stay in Kansas after we solve the Baby Ghost murders?" I asked, hoping to change the subject.

"Are you that sure you're going to close this case?" He laughed, scoffing as though I were a puffed-up little kid. "Seems like whoever is doing this is still holding all the cards."

Dorothy took umbrage. "Miracles do happen. We've just now had one in Carlton County. Sam Abbott says they have been looking for two missing boys for nearly eight years, but everyone assumed they had been abducted. It will be all over the papers today. For those lucky enough to get papers today, that is. A cadaver dog found their bodies yesterday. Right there in Carlton County. Right there under our noses all along."

"Wonderful. Good old Sam."

I looked at her sharply, but she had missed his sarcasm and just plunged right ahead.

"And there was another little boy who had never been reported missing. Terrible disabilities. Tragic, just tragic. But we can nail the killer now. We have a handkerchief containing some blood and semen."

Ferguson said nothing.

"Pervert. Totally sick. He deserves to be locked up for life. With prisoners who know how to punish rapists."

Ferguson said nothing.

"Dorothy, Sam wouldn't like for you to discuss an open case with anyone."

Wounded, she resumed looking at the front windshield. Ferguson had pushed her buttons by implying we didn't have a chance of finding the Ghost Baby Killer, but I had to shut her up because it was the truth. Sam would hate having this man know any of the details. He could barely stand working with Ferguson on the regional team.

I changed the subject. "Need more food, Dr. Ferguson? Coffee? More aspirin?"

"I'm doing okay. Everything considered."

Chapter Twenty-six

There was a sudden violent burst of static from the radio when I started the car to run the heater for a little while. I switched it off and stared morosely at the windshield. I didn't want to risk running down the battery.

Ferguson took several sips from the bottle of water he had used to chase down the aspirin.

"Still feeling all right?"

"A-okay." But storytime was over. Talking about killing little boys stifled Dorothy's talkative spell and apparently had a dampening effect on Ferguson too.

We all sat in silence for another half hour and then it began to lighten up outside. I risked cracking the front window again to peek out. The wind had lessened and the lifted swirling snow and dust was starting to settle back down on the ground where it belonged. I tried to get Keith again but something was still down somewhere.

In another fifteen minutes it was brighter inside the car and I opened the door to get a better look. A light coating of blasted-on dirt and snow pocked the highway. Deep in some places. Bare spots in others. But it was safe to drive now.

I glanced back at Ferguson who was staring at the opaque window at his side. He reached for the button and lowered it halfway but still did not speak.

I got out and went around to the hatch in back and got out a big roll of paper towels and the bottle of window cleaner I kept on hand to use when I went through the carwash. There was also a short squeegee. I went around the Tahoe squeegeeing first and wiping the blade on paper towels before I made the trip around again, this time using the spray bottle and cleaning in earnest. Nothing exactly sparkled, but we had good visibility. I would run through a commercial washer when we got to Junction City.

When I had finished I got back in the car and tried Keith again. This time the call went through.

"Honey? Just wanted you to know that we are safe and sound."

"Thank God. I've been worried sick."

"I was afraid you would be. There was a shallow ditch next to me. I took it to get off the road. But cell service has been blocked so I couldn't tell you how I was doing. And you'll never guess who I ran into."

Dorothy snorted.

"I hope to hell you don't mean that literally," Keith said.

"Actually, I do. Dr. Ferguson. I managed to total his Volkswagen. But he's okay." I gave him more details but sort of glossed over the rope rescue. Keith would know all too well how easy it would have been to end up facedown on the highway, exposed to the danger of some fool steering by a compass.

"The important thing is that you are all safe. Tell Ferguson that there is an excellent mechanic in Junction City. Body Peace. Why don't you drop him off there? They will send someone right out for his car and give him a loaner. Oh, and Josie has been trying to get ahold of you."

"Did she say what she wanted?"

"No, except that she had figured out what her dream meant. Said you would understand and it was the one where she was in the grocery store and she 'wasn't buying it.' She said it was important. But I doubt it."

"Keith," I chided, "honestly!" But he has no use for our "twin games" as he calls them. "I'll call you again from the motel and let you know where we are staying. Probably at Junction City. I've decided to wait and take this stuff to Dimon in the morning because I want to be rested when I talk to him. Needless to say

I'm filthy, and more than anything, I need to clean up." I didn't mention that I was also a bundle of nerves.

"Love you, honey. Take care. And be careful the rest of the way."

"Love you, too." I hung up and plugged my cell back into the lighter then asked Ferguson to hand me the thermos of coffee.

"I've been thinking," he said. "I can't leave my VW here while we go on. It's classified as an antique car and someone is sure to come along and strip it for parts. I need to get it to someplace safe until I can make arrangements."

"Our chances of getting a tow truck out here soon are slim to none," I said. "They'll be swamped with cars that are a danger to general traffic because they couldn't pull over. Hard telling how many collisions they will have to work today."

"I figured that. But I have another idea. Up the road a couple of miles there's a county road, then a dirt road that leads to an old farmhouse. I know the people who live there. Charlie and Louise Harrison. He's an old friend of mine and has plenty of equipment. Tractors and so on. I'm sure that he would be glad to come after my Volkswagen and store it in one of his outbuildings until I can arrange to get it repaired. That way I won't hold you up."

I glanced at my watch. The last thing I wanted was a detour. I wanted to find a carwash and then a motel. Fast. Hard telling how many other people had the same idea and were tying up facilities. But it was the least I could do for Ferguson considering I got him into this mess to begin with.

"Okay. Then after you make arrangements with your friends, shall we take you on to Junction City?"

"No need for that. I'll spend the night there. Have a good visit. Charlie will be glad to take me to the airport tomorrow. He'll welcome the money for storing my car and playing chauffeur. You ladies can just drop me off and be on your way."

"Are you sure you don't need to see a doctor?"

"Positive."

"Okay. Let's do it."

The ditch was shallow, and a couple of yards ahead there was a good spot for getting back on the highway. I engaged the four-wheel drive, maneuvered back and forth until I eased onto I-70, and then I gunned it. His "couple of miles" down the highway were more like six. Ferguson didn't have any trouble finding the rural road, which seemed to be well traveled, but then he guided us down a bush-laden back trail and then another.

The last turnoff was bumpy and irregular. I hoped it was clear of the kind of trash that would puncture tires. It zigged and zagged and there were a couple of ditches that gave us a good jolt. "It's over the hill," he said.

The farm had a couple of small outbuildings and a fair-sized barn. The white clapboard-sided house was closed in by a sagging wire fence. An old-fashioned storm cellar with an angular door stood far enough from the house that occupants wouldn't have to worry about falling debris if a tornado destroyed their home. No doubt canned fruit and vegetables were stored there during the winter. There was a wisp of smoke coming out the chimney, but no car in front and no dog to check us out.

Ferguson went up the walk and knocked on the door several times. He pushed on inside and then reappeared and called back to us. "He's in the barn. She's in the basement watching TV. Says if you ladies need to use the bathroom before you go on, come right on in."

Dorothy got out at once and I was close behind. I was suddenly exhausted from pent-up tension and wanted to get back on the road and check into a motel. I had a good book with me and Dorothy had her knitting. Good pasta, I decided. That's what I wanted for supper. And cheesecake. A sugar stupor.

I hoped the Holiday Inn Express in Junction City had a vacancy. In addition to all the standard stuff I carried in my car, there were a number of items in my pre-packed travel bag that I was never without. A swimsuit so I could loosen my tense muscles if a motel had an indoor pool. I imagined a hot tub with pulsing jets. Yet my top priority was a dependable in-room safe where I could store the commonplace book and the handkerchief.

We entered the galley kitchen directly from the porch. The linoleum had a painted-on design and in spots was bare, down to the black underlay. On the opposite wall was an all-in-one sink with built-in drains on either side. Below the sink was a red gingham curtain that closed off the area storing cleaning products and dish detergent. Renovators paid a hefty price for antique sinks and this one was in perfect shape.

"Are those sad irons? I've heard of them, but have never seen them." Dorothy gazed at a shelf above the burners of an old-fashioned stove.

"Yes, they are." Sad irons weighed a ton and were heated on top of a stove then used to iron starched laundry which had been dried on a clothesline. I knew the routine from oral histories I had collected from octogenarians. But even the ladies I interviewed had electric irons. They were talking about visiting their grandmother's soddy.

"The stove burns either wood or coal. Or cow patties."

"How very strange."

"Strange" didn't begin to cover it. A brand new microwave sat on a shelf adjacent to the sad irons. Bewildered, I peeked into the combination dining-living room. The areas were separated by identical narrow ceiling-high glassed-in cupboards on opposite walls. They contained a collection of depression glass and salt and pepper shakers. "I think she collects antiques."

I glanced at my watch. We needed to get going, but I was very curious about Louise Harrison. "Dr. Ferguson?" I called.

He stuck his head out of a door just off the kitchen. The TV volume could wake the dead. "Down here with Louise. Watching the news. You've got to see this. It's all about this godawful weather we just went through. It's a wonder we came out alive."

I used the bathroom while Dorothy waited in the hall. Then I started down the stairs. The steps were narrow and the basement smelled damp and musty. When I rounded the landing I could see an old black-and-white TV set sitting on a rickety cart. But the room was cold. Freezing cold. I pulled up the hood on my down parka.

There was a rush of air. A prick. No warning. Just that.

● ● ● ● ●

When I came to I was lying next to Dorothy, whose face was so waxen I was afraid she was dead. I edged toward her across the concrete floor and felt for the pulse in her neck. It was strong and even.

Dr. Ferguson. It didn't even make sense. Why?

I passed out again and when I roused for the second time I lay there with my eyes closed in case he was watching. I needed to collect my thoughts before I did anything.

Why? Why would he do this to Dorothy and me? And how could be possibly believe he could get away with it?

My head ached and my stomach churned but at least my brain was beginning to engage. I opened my eyes and looked at Dorothy again. She hadn't stirred. Still out to the world unless she was playing dead.

Dead. I was sure we would be if I didn't figure something out.

I replayed the whole trip in my mind from the moment we left Fiene's Folly. There was a series of unpredictable events. The ground blizzard. My being on the road. Running into him. It was all random. Every bit of it.

He could possibly have planned in advance to waylay Dorothy and me? Was his head injury causing this behavior? Some sort of brain trauma? Yet this place. How did he know about this place? But why? Why would he do this?

I ran through the conversation in the car. Had we said anything? Done anything while in the car? But even so, this was crazy.

Think, damn it. I started from the moment I hit his Volkswagen. That was an accident. Unplanned and unavoidable. What had set this man off? During our wait for the blizzard to subside he had been chatty. He'd even joked. Shared a few war stories.

And when I got to Dorothy telling him about the handkerchief, I knew. Knew in my gut. That's when he stopped talking.

He was the man who killed those little boys. The monster who destroyed the little Duck Boy. *Of course.* He had to stop us from getting that handkerchief to Topeka. He was in the Army. Reserve status, but his blood type and DNA would be on file.

He was the one who had killed those little boys.

Dr. Ferguson. Of course he couldn't let us get to Topeka. Had he even been around here ten years ago when Duck Boy made the last entry in the commonplace book? I couldn't remember. Damn the shot.

Those little boys. Those terrified tragic little boys. My tongue felt like cotton. I tried to swallow. I recalled Dorothy's words that did us in. *Sick. Pervert. Deserves a lifetime prison sentence.*

There was a soft moan. I edged closer to Dorothy. I wanted her to continue lying immobile although I couldn't see any way he could be watching. It was still daylight and although visibility was faint there was light leaking around the edges of the steel door leading into our room. The walls and the floor were solid concrete.

High up on one wall toward the ceiling was a small iron door which I estimated to be no more than two-foot square. It swung open from the bottom and rotated from a rod at the top. *The door to a coal chute.* I recognized it from illustrations in old Sears Roebuck catalogs. We were in a coal room, where years ago homeowners shoveled in the winter supply of fuel.

There was a way to get outside.

Cautiously I rose to my feet, then realizing that staying quiet would not do us a bit of good, I rattled the door leading to the basement room where he claimed Louis Harrison had been watching TV. Only now I knew there was no Louise. No Charlie, either.

Dorothy rose up on her elbows. She still had on her long Chesterfield coat but our purses were missing. No gun, I thought bitterly. And no iPhone.

"Ferguson. You can't possibly get away with this." I pounded and hollered.

At first there was no sound at all. Then on the other side of the coal room I heard a weak voice cry out. I turned away from the door to the TV room and walked to the wall opposite. I felt for hinges and found another padlocked opening.

"Lottie?"

My blood turned to ice. I knew that voice.

"Merilee?"

"Yes. Oh, yes. Thank God you've come for me."

I drew a deep breath and told her. Fast and brutal. "He has us too."

"Oh, no. Oh, no. Us? Why did you say 'us'? Is someone there with you?"

I closed my eyes and struggled with the words. "Dorothy. Dorothy Mercer. We were going to Kansas City." I told her the bare bones of how Ferguson had abducted us. "But you've got reinforcements now, Merilee." I faked assurance. "Other people to help you think. How are you, physically?"

"Cold. Just freezing. There's no heat down here, but he brought a lot of blankets. And I got to keep my coat."

"We have ours too. Kind of the bastard. But we don't have any blankets."

"You won't need them. He's going to kill us," she wailed.

"Merilee, I can't get in. Your room is padlocked. Ours is too. He has to walk through this one to get to yours. How does he get food to you? And water? You've been here over a week now."

Then all I heard were ragged sobs. Then, "Blood. Blood all over. The mattress is covered with blood. Joyce Latimer's blood. She died having a baby. She was dead when I got here. Stinking. I saw her face." Minutes passed before she could control her hysterical weeping. "Two nights ago he came and took her away."

Blood. All the blood. No doubt postpartum hemorrhage. No way to control it outside of a hospital. I took a deep breath but had forgotten how to exhale. Reeling from shock I tried to construct a timeline but I couldn't focus. Joyce abducted a year ago. Died ten days ago. Baby put in arms of *Reaching Woman*. Brent murdered. Marilyn abducted. Then Dorothy. And me too. None of the "when" mattered, so I quit thinking.

"We know where he took her baby," Merilee said. "But I don't know where he put Joyce's body. Buried her here on this farm, maybe." Her voice caught again. "He lured Brent to the Garden of Eden by telling him that Joyce was alive and he could see her."

"How did he know Brent would answer the phone?" Dorothy asked.

"He told me when he saw my parents' car in town he was sure my brother would answer."

Sick at heart I was speechless. He had killed his own baby. His own daughter. Left her to freeze in the arms of *Reaching Woman*. Ferguson wasn't only the rapist and killer of little boys. He was the Ghost Baby Killer. He had done it all. All of it.

Dorothy struggled onto her feet with the help of her walking stick.

A weapon. We had a weapon. Dorothy's walking stick. Obviously he should have taken it away but no doubt was focused on forcing us both into the coal room. All it would have taken was for him to say "Lottie is through that door" and Dorothy would have checked, out of curiosity. He probably even held the door open for her, I thought bitterly. "Come join her." And then he stabbed her with the same needle that had done me in.

Tears stung my eyes. Like lambs to the slaughter all of us.

Her walking stick. A lot of good that would do us with a combat soldier. Right, Lottie. Just whack him a good one.

He would be back.

Merilee fell silent. I sank to the floor and wrapped my arms around my knees and rested my head. We had to get a plan together before he got back. My eyes had adapted to the faint light in the room. I looked around.

"Do you have a flashlight stowed on you somewhere?" I asked Dorothy, hoping for one of her subtle concealed devices.

"No. There's one in my purse. On my key ring."

"I use the one on my iPhone. But he's the one who has it all. Purse, key rings, phones. Everything." What was in that shot? I couldn't think straight. Couldn't plan. I think better when there is more light.

"You're wearing yourself out, Lottie. Rest until the shot wears off."

"This room isn't set up right," I mumbled. "He didn't plan for us. Merilee says she has blankets. And he has to get food to her somehow. Provide a pot for body waste. He has to come here to this farm. Every other day, at least."

"He comes here, Lottie," Dorothy said gently.

I was slow. Blame it on the cold. Blame on fright. Blame it on my tendency to whitewash ugly situations. You can sure as hell blame it on the shot. I stared at her. "Oh, no. Oh no, oh no." I buried my head in my hands and slid against the concrete wall until I was resting on my thighs.

"Oh, Merilee."

Chapter Twenty-seven

At some point during the night, I startled awake. There was an eerie voice coming from Marilee's room. "Merilee, Merilee. I'm coming for you." Haunting, low-pitched, straight from a Halloween horror movie.

I wobbled to my feet and felt around the wall until I was next to her door. Terrified, I stood there listening. In a minute the words were repeated.

"Merilee?" I whispered.

She moved close enough to the door for me to hear her ragged voice. "It's another recorder, Lottie. He said he figured I would miss my little friend. He wanted me to have some company."

"How? When did he get in your house?"

"The same way he got me here. He walked in the front door. He told me he was on the regional team and asked to see my room. I suppose he put it under my pillow then. And when he wanted me to go into town with him, I said 'Let me get my coat.' Worked slicker than hell."

"Merilee. I'm so very, very sorry."

"I'm cold. I'm going back to bed."

Stunned, still thick-tongued and woozy, I slid down the wall again. I thought of David Hayes telling Sam and me about the torment he had endured as a student. He'd sworn there were persons who lived to ruin people. Who enjoyed torture. Raised it to an art form. Yes, David had been right. It's what that recorder was all about from the beginning.

I dozed again. Sometime toward morning, I think, the door to the coal chute opened at the bottom and I heard a thump on the floor, the door clanged shut.

"Don't touch anything," Dorothy ordered. "Wait until daylight so we can see what we are doing."

Neither one of us could get back to sleep but when the sun came up we opened the plastic sack lying on the floor and found apples and high protein candy bars and crackers. There were bottles of water and the kind of female urination device used by campers and an empty gallon jug for our waste.

● ● ● ● ●

He came back two days later.

"Honey, I'm home," he called cheerfully. His footsteps thudded down the stairs. "Miss me?" he called through the door.

Fully recovered from the medication now, I gasped and then tore into him. "You'll never, never get away with this. Never."

He laughed. "Actually, I've gotten away with quite a bit for a very long time. In fact, I'm quite certain I can do just about anything that comes to mind. Wouldn't you say?"

"They'll find us. Fast. Do you think for one minute that Sam and my husband won't track us down in a flash?"

"They'll try. Just like they tried to find poor little old Merilee. A lot of good that did them. But let's face it, neither of them are too terribly bright. People just think they are."

"Are you nuts? They'll track my Tahoe right away. Your Volkswagen. You might as well have left a trail of breadcrumbs like Hansel and Gretel."

"They'll track it, all right. And here's what they will find. The tracks on the county road will be covered over by the school bus tomorrow. And that's just one of the vehicles that travels that road regularly. There are many, many more."

"The tracks on this little side road leading up to the house. No one else goes here. They'll identify the tires in an instant."

"Well let me enlighten you. After I eat, that is. Upstairs, where it's warm."

He was teasing us. Enjoying tormenting us. I could hear it in his voice. Jeering. Taunting us with his cleverness. Twisting us like puppets in his control. My stomach roiled with hatred and I shivered from the cold.

In a half hour he came back downstairs. I decided not to give him the satisfaction of explaining how he would deal with the Tahoe tracks. I wouldn't ask. But he couldn't resist flaunting his brilliance.

"Like I was saying…as to the Tahoe problem. There's no reason for them to look for tracks out here. I simply drove it on to Junction City the other night. As planned. As you told your sorry-ass husband you intended to do. I used my credit card to get two rooms at the Holiday Inn motel. The clerk will remember me because I made it a point to ask for one with a king-sized bed and the other with two double beds 'for the two women,' I said. 'They're in even worse shape than me,' and joked about my clothes."

"You bastard."

"Then I drove to the mechanic shop Keith recommended and made arrangements for them to tow my Volkswagen and repair it while I was at the conference. So, as far as everyone is concerned, we all made it to Junction City just fine. No problems at all. Pretty clever, don't you think?"

I was torn between wanting him to keep talking on the chance I could spot a hole in his plans and wanting him to shut up and stop tormenting me. I clenched my fists. My iPhone. They would be able to use the Find My Phone function on my iPhone. I'd told Keith I would call him when I arrived. He would have been worried when I didn't.

"No comment? Don't you have something so say?"

I gritted my teeth. There was more light in the room today. No sounds from Merilee's room, but no doubt she could hear me.

"Oh, and by the way. I sent your husband a text when I got there. Letting him know you had arrived safely. Kind of me, don't you think?"

"You won't get away with this," Dorothy said. "You're underestimating Sam Abbott."

"That old dried-up pile of shit? He couldn't think his way out of a paper bag."

"You're forgetting Find My Phone," I blurted. "They will trace my iPhone."

"So? It will be on the front seat of your car. Which is in the parking lot of the Holiday Inn, by the way. Did you think I would be stupid enough to bring it back here?"

I said nothing and neither did Dorothy.

"But you and the great mystery writer will be nowhere to be found. They will have proof you checked into the motel. But, doggone it, boys, we seem to have lost them."

Cocky, derisive. My muscles tensed. Was this a game to him? A matter of beating the best minds in law enforcement. But I suspected it ran deeper. His words were rage-driven.

"The next morning, I took the Super Shuttle on to the airport and even made my flight. As planned of course."

"How did you get back here?" I couldn't stop myself from asking even knowing he was eager to show off.

"In my own little Volkswagen. By the way, I owe Keith a word of thanks for recommending that shop. It's terrific. I paid them extra to have everything done by the time I got back from the conference and, what do you know? They got 'er done. Great job too. A nearby salvage yard even had a replacement door for the one that was ruined. Imagine that! New paint. She looks brand new."

More than anything this man wanted admiration for his ability to think.

"People will report seeing your car out on I-70."

"So? People see it all the time anyway. I treat vets with PTSD all over Kansas. It's my specialty. That and tracking down serial killers." He guffawed. "And as for this little detour. Had to deliver groceries to my houseguest. And get gas. There's a 7-11 back down the road a bit. Of course when I'm here I park in one of the outbuildings. To get it out of the weather. So if you were thinking Google Earth, forget it."

"This house. Is it yours?"

"Sort of. My grandmother left it to me. Oh, you're worried about the taxes, aren't you? Bless your heart. They are paid. Every year. By her nephew. Who no one has ever met. He's just a name on a check."

"You couldn't have planned that accident. I don't see how."

"Oh, you dumb bitch. You incredibly dumb bitch. You're almost as dumb as your sister. Even dumber than Frank Dimon, if that's possible. No, I didn't arrange it, but that's why I'm a genius and you're not. I know how to take advantage of circumstances and spin them on their head. I see opportunity in every crisis. You have to plan the shit out of everything. All I have to do is hold my hand out while it rains gold."

If he was expecting admiration he wasn't going to hear it from me.

"As an example, when that little fiasco at the Regional Room played out, I hadn't planned to go back to Topeka empty-handed. You and your Tarzan of a husband stormed into Dimon's office and got nowhere, whereas I turned dross into gold. Again. If life hands you a lemon…"

He stopped then and made ape calls. He laughed when I did not respond.

"Anyhoo. I left another little offering for the baby gods and stepped forward—smartly, I might add—and got to be the main man in the investigation, by default. The press thought I was Jesus Christ Almighty. See? That's how to take advantage of circumstances. You might be the leader on paper. But goodness, gracious, I think CNN knows better."

I froze in place.

"Now about that houseguest…"

I lost it. "Stop, stop, stop…" I covered my ears and backed away from the door. I huddled against the far wall. Dorothy walked over and put her arms around my shoulders.

"Keep him talking, Lottie," she whispered. "As long as he's talking, he's not doing anything to us. Or to that poor child. And we might learn something that will help us. We already know he flies into a rage when anyone underestimates his abilities. He might be easy to goad into doing something foolish. Keep going."

"What do you get out of tormenting someone as fragile as Merilee?"

"It's fun. Try it, you'll like it."

"The Suters. Why did you keep on persecuting this family?"

"The perfect 4-H family? The icon of American wholesomeness? To see what it would take to break them. Not much, by the way."

"You're insane," I blurted.

He walked away and I heard his footsteps going up the basement stairs. He was gone a couple of hours. When he came back down I walked back over to the door. "My sister. And Harold Sider. You are up against the A-team. Way out of your league."

He jeered. "Oh yeah, your sister. The great Josie Albright. Everyone genuflect now. Or just fall on your knees."

I was taken back by his venom. "What do you have against Josie?"

"Other than the fact that she's full of shit? And a fraud? And other than the fact that she ruined me? Caused the whole psychiatric community to turn on me?"

Revenge? But Josie hadn't even met the man until the organizational meeting. It didn't make sense. This was all about revenge?

Speechless, I walked back over to Dorothy. I didn't have the slightest idea what he meant. She pressed a finger to her lips. "S-h-h-h. Don't say another word. I was mistaken. Getting him to talk is fueling his anger."

I shook my head and angrily spun around. Staying quiet wasn't working either. No one would be looking for us out here and we were running out of time. I didn't care what kind of label psychologists would pin on him. He was pure-D crazy. I wanted to goad him into making a mistake. He had covered his tracks so well that I couldn't imagine how anything could be used to our advantage. But Dorothy was right. His greatest weakness was his need for constant admiration. Unwavering praise. He couldn't resist letting people know how smart he was.

I thought about the Unabomber and the BTK killer. And the Zodiac Killer. They all taunted law enforcement: "See how dumb you are and how brilliant I am?" All three wrote letters to newspapers teasing the police. Childish games risking exposure: "See how smart I am? See, see?" But they had taken years to reveal themselves and we didn't have that kind of time.

Josie had once said that in addition to CEOs and politicians and serial killers, some of the biggest narcissists and sociopaths were psychologists. She'd then come up with examples of intra-professional warfare that left me gasping with laughter.

I would go for his weak spots. He would never, never admit he was inferior in any way. Never admit that he was a pedophile. Or that there was much wrong with assaulting children. He would come up with some elaborate rationale to account for raping little boys. Or perhaps deny it altogether or wipe it from his mind.

I hugged my coat tighter around me and marched back to the door. I stopped cold. Just what was my goal here? What did I want to make happen? Certainly not for him to rush in and kill us. No doubt he owned plenty of guns, big ones, more on the lines of assault rifles. But I doubted they were stored in this house. An outbuilding maybe. He was too flagrant to be the conceal-and-carry type.

"Yoo-hoo. Cat got your tongue?"

My head throbbed. But I hit a dead end. He surely would have taken my gun from my purse.

If I could just get him to call Josie. Just call. Call to torment her. Everyone already had to be going crazy. Worried sick over our disappearance. They would know by now that I hadn't made it to Topeka with the evidence for Dimon and that Dorothy hadn't made her flight.

No matter how he tried to disguise his voice, a call to Josie would give her and Harold a chance to do some whiz-bang thing. Something with electronics. *Something.*

Keith, Dimon, Sam, Harold Sider, David—they would all pounce on a phone call. I decided to skip the pedophile accusations—although it was true, it was too risky. I needed to find out what had happened between him and Josie so I would know how to proceed.

"My sister would never deliberately hurt anyone."

"Your sister is a sadist bitch and a pathetic excuse of a psychologist."

"That's not true. You know her reputation. She's brilliant." I wished I could see his face. I depend on facial expressions when I take oral histories and that stood me well when I moved into law enforcement. I could tell when to take a softer approach and when to press harder. Right now I wanted him angry. Angry enough to let someone know that he was the unrecognized genius behind the murder of those little boys. Angry enough to call my sister. But not mad enough to kill us.

"Your sister. Your sister. She doubted my Madonna theory, which was one of the finest psychological works I'll ever produce. In it I proved a connection between serial killers and cradling mothers that is in direct conflict with the classic theory of the cold unfeeling mother. I built on Jung's theory of the Whore/Madonna complex and it was received with a great deal of acclaim."

"But the Whore/Madonna theory is Freudian," I jeered. "It wasn't Jung's work at all."

There was an ominous silence. Then his voice changed. Low and deranged now. "Your sister ruined me. With a single review. She said she 'wasn't buying it.' Not any of it."

"But that's basic psychology. Freud, not Jung. She had to be honest. Peer reviews are taken seriously." What he was proposing was so wrong that I doubted if his paper had ever received "great critical acclaim" from anyone. He was simply nuts. And as for Josie not buying it. Of course not. A college freshman taking Psychology 101 would have been skeptical.

Josie wasn't buying it.

Her dream. The dream that had haunted her. Her subconscious was trying to tell her that the killer was right in front of us.

"You sick, depraved pervert. You're a sadist." Dorothy spoke slowly and her accusation sounded like the final judgment of God.

"What fun! The great mystery writer has decided to join in."

Dorothy was right, I realized suddenly. That's why the sex of his victims was not an issue. He needed to torture and maim. Boys and girls, men and women. I grasped the bridge of my nose between my fingers and bowed my head. Not just a narcissist but also a sadistic sociopath. I tried to remember everything I had read, but none of the cases analyzed were bad enough.

The babies. That was pure evil. There was no motive behind that other than to commit a crime too shocking and depraved for law enforcement to get its head around. He wanted to prove how inept my sister was. No deep subconscious compulsion. Just revenge. The universal motive since the beginning of time.

My head exploded with hatred. "She'll figure this out. Josie will connect all this with you."

His laughter echoed. "Ya think? She's not doing a very good job so far."

Tears rolled down my cheeks. "You bastard."

"Can't hear you. Louder."

"They'll trace phone records. Link this place to you. Your landline. Your cell. It's all there."

"Nope. No landline here and I've never used my cell from this location. In fact, I always leave it in Topeka when I'm here."

Paralyzed with despair, my mouth worked like a guppy gasping for air. He really was smarter than all the rest of us. And more powerful. Shocked into submission I walked away vowing not to say another word.

Chapter Twenty-eight

Dorothy had heard everything and was no longer able to stand. Using her walking stick for support she lowered herself to the floor. Once there, she slumped against the wall and tried to wave me away. Her color wasn't good.

I whirled around and walked back to the door. "Water. Dorothy needs water. She's not well."

"Not very tough, is she?"

"You'll have everyone in the country after you if you let this woman die. There will be no place you can take her that cadaver dogs won't sniff out. Nowhere."

"Wanna bet? I just found a place that was ideal the other day."

"For who? Who?"

"A mother. A very recent mother. A precious little mother that everyone has looked high and low for. Guess who? It would be a good spot for our great literary genius too."

A recent mother. "Joyce Latimer, of course." Making me guess was part of his sadism, this obscene teasing. Presenting everything as though it were a riddle. My stomach knotted. "Why did you pick Joyce?"

"Because she was there. I've already 'splained that to you. I know how to make the most of opportunities. Mediocre minds can't grasp that. She was just strolling along. Picking daisies, if you will."

"I don't care where you buried her. They will find her."

"Nope. The place I put her has already been scrutinized inch by inch. The spot where they found the little boys. I buried her after the forensic team finished. No reason for anyone to look there again."

Stunned, I braced my elbows on the door and rested my head against them. He was right. No one would ever think to look there. Not a second time. Was it true that he was simply too smart for the rest of us?

Dorothy called to me and I went back to her corner and sat down beside her. "You're wearing yourself out," she said softly. "It doesn't work to try to reason with a madman. We need to think. We're both going to die. And soon. He can never let us out of here. As for Merilee, he's going to keep her for a long time We know why she is here. She is destined to be the next 'little mother.'"

Merilee hadn't made a sound now for over twenty-four hours. No doubt weak from lack of food. Cold. Drained of hope. Barely clinging to whatever sanity she had left.

"Merilee…" My throat was dry. "Merilee can't help."

"We've got to get Ferguson in here. He has to pass through here to get to Merilee. He wants to keep Merilee alive."

I nodded. "But after we get him in here? Then what?"

"Just get him in here. Now help me get to my feet."

She hoisted herself up. "When he comes through the door. Get in front of him. If you've had self-defense training, I doubt it will do you a bit of good. I'll be behind him. You can try to get through the door, but I doubt if you will make it."

I scoffed. "You're going to whack him, Dorothy? He'll brush me off like I'm a gnat and then go for you."

"Just do it."

"He won't come in for us. Not even if one of us is dying because that's what he wants to happen in the first place."

"If he thinks something is happening to Merilee, he will come. She's important. He doesn't want anything to happen to her."

"He'll take your walking stick away from you first and then use it on me."

"Yes, I know. That's what I think he will do, too. But we've got to try. He'll disarm me and then go for you. He'll kill you and then me. He'll disable the biggest threat immediately. That's you."

She blinked like a wise old owl and reminded me of Sam Abbot in her willingness to face the inevitable, no matter how harsh.

She was right, of course. We were going to die anyway. Might as well go down fighting.

I walked back to the door. "Ferguson. Something is wrong with Merilee. I think she's trying to hurt herself."

Sadly, I looked at Dorothy. There was something majestic about the stoicism with which she was preparing for her death. She stood perfectly straight with heroic bearing. Regal in her long chesterfield coat, dry-eyed with her head held high. "I've never done anything like this before," she murmured. "Never. Just written about it. I would like you to know this isn't coming naturally to me."

"Oh, Dorothy," I groaned.

"Proceed please. And remember, keep in front of him."

"Ferguson!" I yelled. "Better hurry if you want to save her."

The lock clicked and the dead bolt snapped back. He crashed through the door and anticipating that one of us would be hiding behind it, he smashed Dorothy violently against the wall. Then he slammed the door shut with his foot before I could escape and whirled and yanked the walking stick from her hands.

Windless and body-shocked, Dorothy leaned against the wall, swayed, and struggled to maintain her uneasy footing. She could topple at any moment. We might as well have handed Ferguson a script, so accurately did our worries play out.

Then he turned to me and tossed the stick from hand to hand. "Fast? Or give you a taste of what Merilee has been enjoying? I just can't decide." He made a quick feint toward me.

Just for fun.

I tensed. Ready to kick out if he came any closer. Dorothy was right and as Keith had warned me, my experiments with martial arts weren't going to do me one bit of good. There was too much distance between me and him. But he loved the verbal sparring and would keep me alive as long as I could come up with retorts. He admired my quick mind.

His movement was so fast it hardly registered before the walking stick cracked my collarbone. My hands flew toward the injury. Then he danced backward and spun the stick like a baton twirler.

Nauseated, I knew he intended to bludgeon me death. One blow at a time, with a lot of time between blows.

"Is revenge this important to you? After all these years? All this is about a paper you wrote."

"Oh, gosh, no, sweet pea."

Flash. Thump. He swirled to his side and hit me in the side of my right thigh. Sharp, quick. Like before, but leaving the bone intact this time.

"Your sister makes it more interesting, that's all. Guess again."

I bent and grasped my leg. If I was going to die, I wanted some answers. I wanted to know if he had raped Franklin before he killed him, but I couldn't get the words out right. All I could manage was "the little crippled boy. Franklin."

"Ah, yes. I remember him well. He tried to run. It was most amusing. He squealed like a rabbit and went from side to side. This way and that. He kept tripping over himself. But at the end he turned and faced me. And stood as straight as he could."

A manly man at the last. "He's the one that got you, you know. The one who buried the handkerchief."

Ferguson's eye's widened with anger. "Now, there's irony for you."

The next blow was a glancing one to my head. Not hard enough to knock me out. I suspected he knew all about torture. How much a victim can take. I reeled. His skills would have been honed in Afghanistan.

"If it's not revenge against my sister, what?"

"Money, honey. There's this man who wants to build private prisons here in Kansas." He smirked. "All that space going to waste. They are looking for a top-notch psychologist to oversee it. And naturally, they couldn't do any better than me."

Another movement so fast that I barely saw it. The pain in my elbow was so intense I thought I would pass out.

"And all we had to do was to knock the hell out of your little half-assed regional center. Just a nudge or two more and the press will be asking for your head. Inept, stupid bitch."

My finger this time. His movements were as skilled as a dancer. I stood us straight as I could manage. *Do it for Franklin. Do it for Franklin. He stood at the end. Like a manly man.*

"Did Dimon know? Is Frank in on this?"

"That wimp? He's not worth dealing with. Stubborn starch-shirted fraud."

My face would be next, I guessed. I stood full square.

The air quickened. Dorothy. Came up behind Ferguson.

Suddenly his eyes widened and a metallic tip emerged from his stomach. Ferguson's mouth flew open and his face froze in disbelief.

He stared at the blade. His arms flailed toward his back in a useless flapping motion. Rage tightened his throat and choked off his words. Words that strained toward me. Words that yearned to destroy me. Steal my soul. Then he slowly sank to the floor like the air escaping from a balloon.

Incredulous I looked at Keith's aunt—then down at the walking stick Ferguson still clung to. Carved with the murder of crows.

It was missing the very top.

Blood gushed from Ferguson's middle. Dorothy had hit the aorta. Then without removing the weapon, she braced one foot on his body, levered it upward and sideways to nick the heart.

"A sword cane," I gasped. "Your walking stick is a sword cane!"

"Yes." Dorothy viewed Ferguson with curiosity and not a trace of remorse. "He was evil through and through." She wiped the blade on his shirt and returned it to the shaft, carefully lining up the murder of crows.

"But where? Where was it?"

"Up the sleeve of my coat." She was matter-of-fact—neither victorious or regretful. "Historically, that's why people greet by shaking their right hands. To make sure they don't have a weapon up their sleeve."

"Call," I mumbled. "His body. We've got to call. Keith, Sam. Everyone." My voice shook. I couldn't think straight because of the pain.

"There is no landline out here and he made it a point to leave his cell in Topeka, remember?" She was eerily calm as though Ferguson was a character in her book.

"Merilee. We've got to get her out of here."

"Get his keys," Dorothy ordered.

They were on the floor about three feet from Ferguson. I scooped them up and went to the door leading to the room where Merilee was confined. When I opened it she was huddled in a corner wrapped in a blanket. Her eyes were vacant and there was no movement. I pulled her to her feet and forced her to walk.

"It's over, Merilee. You're safe now. Come with us. We'll get you help. Decent food. Your parents. A hospital."

God only knew how long it would take to restore this child's soul if it could be done at all. I threw one of Merilee's arms around my uninjured shoulder and Dorothy supported the other arm. I shuddered when I passed Ferguson's body. I had a sick vision of him rising from the dead. I hobbled to the door and bolted it behind us.

Just in case.

We struggled upstairs. Our purses lay on a kitchen cabinet. My gun was still inside. No doubt he had left it there because he knew he wouldn't need it. No doubt he thought he could easily outwit two women. Besides, he preferred slower methods.

We made it to the fence and then closed the gate. Dorothy stayed in front of it with Merilee and I went to the outbuilding where Ferguson had housed his Volkswagen. There was no way to call from his car but at least I knew how to use a stick shift.

Throbbing with pain, I drove over to the two women. It didn't take long to reach I-70 and the nearest filling station.

Once inside, I asked the startled clerk for the use of his landline.

I choked back tears and called home.

Chapter Twenty-nine

Three days later, I felt ridiculously pampered lying on the sofa in front of the fire. Keith wouldn't let me out of his sight. He brought me food and books and lugged a TV set down to the great room so I could binge-watch. I had a concussion, a broken collar bone, a chipped elbow, and massive bruising on my thigh from where Ferguson had bludgeoned me with the walking stick. I couldn't stop sleeping, which was supposed to be a good thing.

Dorothy was receiving the same treatment but she wanted to sit in a recliner so she could knit when she was awake. Her fingers still worked. Badly bruised from being slammed against the wall, she was in agony and on pain pills for the first time in her life. She had been ordered to move as little as possible and give her body a chance to heal. Keith brought her fresh ice compresses and fetched anything she desired. It would be a while before either of us regained our energy.

Despite Dorothy's black-and-blue appearance, an occasional smile crept across her usually impassive face because there had been a breathless call from her agent yesterday. Her latest mystery had shot to the top of the *New York Times* best-seller list. Our ordeal had made the national news. Talk shows came courting.

Sam was at our house from early in the morning until late at night. Yesterday he had shyly presented Dorothy with three skeins of cashmere yarn. "Know you like to keep your hands busy. The shopkeeper told me this is enough for a shawl. You can exchange it for a different color if you want to. It's sort of a crème color," he needlessly pointed out. "Knew you wouldn't want anything too gaudy."

"It's perfect. Absolutely perfect. What a wonderful gift. Thank you so very much, you dear thoughtful man."

Touched, I looked away.

• • ● • •

Today when we were finally alone together I asked Dorothy the question that had been bugging me.

"Why didn't you tell me?"

She understood immediately. She laid her knitting on her lap. Her chair was positioned so she could see my face. Her gaze was stern, but kindly. "Because you would have taken it away from me. Insisted on it. You're younger, far stronger. And God only knows more agile. Quick. Smart. But you couldn't handle it."

I started to protest, then said nothing.

"The blade is razor sharp. Damascus steel. I was trained in its use. To kill someone with a single thrust—especially from the back—requires a specific motion. We could never have managed to do this from the front. He would have disarmed us immediately. You saw how easily he took away the walking stick shaft and used it against us."

I drew in a sharp breath and struggled to take all this in. All the time I'd been yelling, pleading, trying to outwit Ferguson, she obviously had been planning, plotting, trying out different scenarios in her mind.

"And this depended on surprise, Lottie. Surprise is a mystery writer's specialty. What we are never quite sure about in the beginning becomes clear in the ending."

She wasn't finished. I could tell by the hardening of her features that I was going to receive one of her little lectures.

"I could not count on you to keep a sword cane a surprise. I've watched you. Studied you. No. It would not be a surprise. It would be written on your face. Too often what you are thinking is there in your eyes. I couldn't risk it."

"You were trained, Dorothy? Actually trained to use a sword cane?"

"Of course. Do you think mystery authors just make up all the interesting research in their books? I visit locales, take courses, contact experts. I owe it to my readers to make all the details as accurate as possible." She picked up her knitting and gave me a haughty gaze.

"That's why I'm on the best-seller list."

• • ● ● •

Josie came that afternoon. Tosca preceded her into the room and jumped onto Dorothy's lap. I struggled into a sitting position. My sister and I hugged and I started crying as she stroked my hair.

"I'm so sorry," she said. "Sorry I didn't realize in time. Even after I realized why I was haunted by that dream and the meaning of 'not buying it.' I knew he had a narcissistic disorder and clung to whacko theories, but that describes every other psychologist I know. We hate to give up our pet ideas. It took far too long for me to realize he was dangerous."

"He was evil," I said flatly. "Pure evil."

"Yes. I could throw a lot of names at you. Malignant narcissist, sadistic sociopath, anti-social personality disorder, and cite study after study. Blaming genetics, blaming the environment, blaming this or that, but 'evil' covers it. Ferguson was in a class all by himself."

"Dimon is the one who dropped the ball. He told me that Ferguson had been thoroughly vetted and he couldn't have been. He lied on his application and said he was."

"He *was* vetted," Josie said. "Harold checked. But he said sociopaths can beat a lot of tests and someone like Ferguson, who is brilliant and trained, knows all the answers. Since they don't feel guilt and remorse, they breeze right through lie detector tests."

She headed for the closet with her coat and hat. Earlier, Keith had thrown cedar logs on the fire and the odor wafted through the room. After Josie settled into a recliner, I passed her a bowl of popcorn.

"No thanks. I ate a late lunch."

A music channel on the TV played arias from old musicals. Soft. Pleasant. Sunshine spotlighted a patch on the floor. The room was warm. Everything as comfortable as could be.

But my soul was chilled. "Tell me about Merilee."

"Not good, Lottie. Too much damage for her to be restored by simply going home. In fact, I don't know if home will ever be the same for her. Or her parents. Right now I want her to skip the rest of her school year and maybe it won't be a good idea for her ever to go back to her class."

I cringed at the thought of the lewd questions she would be subjected to under the guise of compassion.

"So where?"

"Right now she is at my house. Wrapped in satin and given every luxury I can dream up. Perfume and bubble baths. Which she takes three times a day, I might add."

"Splendid!" Startled, Tosca looked up when Dorothy boomed her approval.

"There is no hospital, no place, no group that I am aware of that could possibly help her at this time. And her parents are in only slightly better shape. But they are relieved that their daughter is in an absolutely safe environment. They can e-mail and phone Merilee every day."

I had been with Merilee when she was reunited with her family. They all hugged and cried and wept but when it was time for them all to go home, Merilee screamed in protest and pulled away. "No," she wailed. "No."

Joyce Latimer had been picked at random. Because she was there. Walking alone on a gorgeous fall day under a cloudless sky. In love. Full of hope. She was the victim of a "crime of opportunity" committed by a sociopath who used the baby to taunt the law. Despite seeing Ferguson's dead body, Merilee was still terrified of suffering the same fate. She dreaded being alone. Dreamed of empty stretches of road. Barren landscapes. Pursued by monsters.

"Patricia and Ernie may have to leave Western Kansas too. But for right now their biggest challenge will be to pull themselves together. And I'm going to do everything I can to help them. Even if I have to pay for a place for them to stay in a tranquil setting for a month or so. On the other hand, they are church-going people and members of a loving congregation. Being around people who have been their friends all their lives may be the best route to go."

"And their farm is homestead land. Ernie might never get over leaving it."

"Yes, and spring isn't too far off. Ernie will be out in the sunshine working the land. Blue sky overhead. The smell of dirt. Growth. I suspect that will do more good than any advice from a psychologist."

Especially from a psychologist. Right at this moment I hated psychologists. Sisters excepted, of course.

"A friend of mine has agreed to see Merilee. Dr. Shore's the best at treating this type of trauma, although I doubt she's seen anything to equal this. Merilee has lost her brother. She associates her home with ghosts and voices. She did tell me she had asked Ferguson why her family had been singled out. He told her searching for Brent was the only way to draw people to the Garden of Eden. And of course, the only way he got Brent there was to tell him Joyce was alive and waiting for him."

"But he couldn't have planned on Dorothy and me going there."

"No. You two were there by blind chance and worked into his plans perfectly."

Suddenly she lost her professional tone and shook with fury "Goddamn that bastard. Now I understand revenge killers who take the law into their own hands." Tears streamed down Josie's face. "Sorry." She whistled to Tosca who jumped off of Dorothy's lap. "We're going for a walk."

By the time Josie returned, Keith had finished choring. She had regained her composure and was ready to question him.

"Joyce Latimer? Did you find her body?"

"Yes. We didn't need the cadaver dog this time. Since we knew what we were looking for from the very beginning, it was easy to spot the most recent dig. Ferguson didn't even require special tools because the forensic team had turned over so much soil."

Josie nodded sadly, knowing the stages of decomposition and the likely state of Joyce's body.

Keith stared at the fire. "People always talk about 'closure' but I don't think there is any. The Latimers were glad to get her remains and will have a real burial and that's some comfort. I guess they can sort of move on."

"Doesn't happen," Josie said. "Not really. It's a myth."

"And the first baby? The one found ten years ago in the Elizabeth Polly Park? Who was the mother?" Dorothy asked.

"We may never know." I readjusted my quilt. "We have the baby's DNA. And the DNA of thousands of missing girls are in the national databases, but most are not. There may never be a match."

"I'm going to back to New York," Dorothy said abruptly. "I want to go home, where's there's a lower crime rate per capita. But I've decided to buy my little house here in Gateway City and come back from time to time. A small town will add an extra dimension to my research."

We all applauded. *And to see a certain sheriff,* I thought.

• ● ● ● •

Dimon leaped his feet when I entered the room. His face blanched when he saw the extent of my injuries. Keith had volunteered to come in with me but I wanted to face Dimon alone.

"Lottie, I can't begin to tell you how sorry I am. I had no idea."

"There's an old saying out our way…'He who would sup with the Devil should use a long spoon.'"

He looked away. "Not quite sure I follow," he mumbled.

"Oh, I think you do. It means if you mess with lying hypocrites for the sake of money, you aren't going to be able to keep enough of a distance. Not money—funding, as you call it. Sounds a little better, but not much."

"I swear I didn't know, Lottie."

"I believe you didn't have a clue that injecting Ferguson into our investigation was a ploy to sabotage the regional center, but you're dining with Devil when you mess with the PAC in back of Timothy Williams. He's a dolt. A tool. A play toy."

He splayed his fingers across his face and then dragged them down over his features and revealed bloodshot eyes, deeper lines in his face.

"They are letting me take the fall."

I didn't have to ask who. The press was roasting him alive.

I looked at him for a few more minutes. He had been used. And he was fundamentally a good man. I intended to set the record straight. Lift the pillars like a female Samson and bring the temple down.

• ● ● ● •

The morning was winter bright. The sky overhead was an intense blue. I looked out from our podium at a sea of people, not only from Topeka but from all over the state. I turned to the line of dignitaries on the platform with me. I still looked like hell but took a perverse pleasure in showing the good people of this state how close I had come to getting killed.

I nodded my head and an honor guard proceeded up the steps to the stage. Following was the entire Northwest Kansas Regional Team. The crowd rose to its feet and the crescendo of voices exploded when Dorothy appeared. She held her head high and gave a queenly nod of acknowledgment. She had helped me research the details that would form the foundation of my acceptance speech.

The governor gave a touching introduction and officially launched the Northwest Kansas Regional Crime Center. His praise reached to heaven. Then he acknowledged the various members of the team. One after another they came forward and received their medals. There hadn't been this enthusiastic a reception since the Royals won the pennant.

It was my turn. I stepped up to the microphone and gazed at my notes although it was unlikely that I needed them for what I was going to say. Cheers rose. I choked back tears and held up my hand for them to stop.

"Thank you, thank you," I began. There were a few more pleasantries, then: "Ladies and gentleman, a political action committee aided by Congressman Williams attempted to destroy the Northwest Regional Crime Center before it achieved official designation. The motivation was money. As usual. When is it not? These men wanted to install private prison systems in the western part of the state and, to speed things along, they injected a psychopath into the most inflammatory investigations in the state." I turned and gestured toward the committee.

Cameras clicked, reporters jostled one another to get the best angles.

"Think of that, ladies and gentlemen. A juvenile detention center run by a sadistic sociopath who murdered and raped at will."

The crowd gasped. I knew they would. Williams was on the platform along with three members of the political action committee. The press had a heyday.

In the rest of the speech I made it clear that Frank Dimon had been duped. An "innocent bystander." Bystander was hardly a good label for the agent in charge, but it was certainly better than the "thief," "corrupt manipulator," and "depraved rapist" that the press was gleefully typing into their iPads. Dimon looked like he wanted to sink through the Earth's crust, but it was the best I could do for him.

I ended on a positive note, pointing out the exemplary work done by my team and my recommendation that the whole western half of the state be partitioned into regional crime centers, using ours as an example.

"The political action committee did not intentionally inject a psychopath into our structure, but they had no business telling us who to hire. They are not qualified to judge the merits of proposed personnel." Originally the line had read "they don't know shit." But I had softened it.

I looked out over the shocked silent crowd. "Money corrupts. Politicians will stop at nothing. Vote. Make your voice heard." Before I sat down, I turned to the governor and asked him to form a committee to investigate the involvement of the men advocating the prison systems.

Mics were thrust under our noses and I answered the same question over and over. "What are you going to do next?"

"Heal. Then finish planning the structure of our regional system and help launch others."

Dorothy was surrounded by fans waving books for her to autograph.

It was a very good day.

Author's Notes

The Garden of Eden really exists. Although I've tried, words cannot describe the peculiarity of this place. It's matchless Grassroots Art. The term refers to art created by people with no formal training. The creator, Samuel Perry Dinsmoor, was a Civil War soldier (Union side). The soaring structures which embodied his religious and political outlook are breathtaking. It was a huge undertaking and an engineering marvel. The balance achieved at great heights in sculpture after sculpture is testimony to his genius and persistence. Kansas ranks third in the States in the number of grassroots art sites, after Wisconsin and California.

My mysteries have varied from one sub-genre to another. That is probably not a good idea. It wasn't planned. It's just the way the stories have worked out.

Deadly Descent is more of a traditional mystery with a healthy dollop of suspense. *Lethal Lineage* is a locked-room mystery. It was more than a little scary from a construction viewpoint, as locked-room mysteries are fiendishly difficult to write and the readers are a savage lot. They pounce on any inconsistency. *Hidden Heritage* contained a secret, but I had returned to a traditional mystery again, with a strong mix of history. It dealt with water rights which will soon be the most lethal worldwide fight in this century.

The impetus to write each book has involved a powerful image. In the case of *Deadly Descent*, it was a line from my favorite book of poetry, *The Spoon River Anthology*. A woman was standing in the crowd murmuring, "my son, my son," while a politician was giving a speech. With *Lethal Lineage* the image was that of a female priest dropping the chalice during communion. The image in *Hidden Heritage* was that of a man drowned in a livestock truckline's washout pit.

And for this one, *Fractured Families*...well, let's just say a totally soulless serial killer was essential.

The words psychopaths and sociopaths are often used interchangeably. Usually. Mostly. My editor asked for the proper word for describing my villain and I chose psychopath rather than sociopath because of the work done by some psychiatrists who describe psychopaths as being the more organized and intelligent of the two. And scarily enough, quite a number of psychopaths had loving families. In fact, most psychopaths and sociopaths are not killers. But they can sure play thunder in the workplace and in people's lives.

I'm a rather peaceful soul by nature. I hope the image for my next book will be something less scary.

As for prisons for profit—it's one of the fastest-growing industries in America. Challenge, investigate, and do a little bit of sleuthing on your own before you go to the polls. As always, follow the money!

Acknowledgments

I especially want to thank my dear friend, Mary Alice McComb, clinical and forensic psychologist, for referring me to books about psychopaths and sociopaths that were based on sound scholarship. *Fractured Families* evolved into a much more frightening book than I had intended when I began.

The suggestions of Annette Rogers made this a much stronger book. I deeply appreciation her editorial insight. I thank John Crockett for his eagle-eyed ability to catch errors.

Multiple award-winners Barbara Peters, editor-in-chief, and Robert Rosenwald, publisher, have built Poisoned Pen Press into a literary powerhouse that has garnered worldwide acclaim. I am deeply grateful to be one of their authors. Their support is legendary and all of us lucky enough to publish with Poisoned Pen praise them to high heaven.

And again, I want to thank my wonderful agent, Phyllis Westberg, at Harold Ober Associates. She keeps all my literary shenanigans sorted.

To see more Poisoned Pen Press titles:

Visit our website: poisonedpenpress.com/
Request a digital catalog: info@poisonedpenpress.com

RECEIVED MAR – – 2017